The Prism Society

GABI SALAS

ISBN: 979-8-9889056-0-8
ISBN: 979-8-9889056-1-5 (ebook)

Dad and Grandma, *please* don't keep reading

To the girlies who have made smut your entire identity...I hope you enjoy

TROPES, TAGS, AND TRIGGER WARNINGS

Tropes:

Best friends to lovers, he loved her first, small town to big city

Tags:

MF, good girl, sex club, chosen family, coming of age, sex positivity, exhibitionism, voyeurism, boys club politics, small business, horoscopes, romantic comedy, friendships, consent-focused

Trigger Warnings:

This book uses explicit language and very descriptive sex scenes. Sex happens both privately and in spaces where other people are in attendance.

PROLOGUE

"Emma, will you please explain why you decided on a college that requires such a lengthy flight?" Liam's voice echoed in the hallway outside my bedroom, cutting through the busy atmosphere of last-minute packing. I turned to face him as he leaned against the frame of my bedroom door, the fabric of my packed-to-the-brim suitcase straining under my hands as I wrestled with the zipper.

I looked up at him, my teeth gritting as I tried to put my weight on the suitcase. "You know I didn't choose it because of the distance, Liam. I picked it for the design program, as I've told you eight-*hundred* times." Liam stepped into the room and put his weight on top of the suitcase. Finally, the zipper caught, and I let out a huff of air, blowing a stray strand of hair out of my face.

My chest felt tight anxiety, the rhythm of my heart beating in anticipation of the independence that my move from California to New York would bring. Eighteen years of small-town California living—the comfort of my mom, our cat

Hashbrown, and the constant, comfortable presence of Liam, my best friend of over a decade. We first met when he took it upon himself to walk me to my mom's work after school. One day we were just classmates who sometimes saw each other in the lunchroom, and the next, he was waiting for me outside our school steps.

Situated in the quaint heart of our town, just a stone's throw from the ever-vibrant Main Street, was the medical clinic where my mom worked as a receptionist. The clinic, which was an intrinsic part of the small-town fabric, had a tucked-away cozy break room at its rear. It was a serene sanctuary, a welcome respite from the hubbub of unending daily appointments, incessant phone calls, and the overall bustle of the clinic.

This break room, with its worn-out furniture and perpetually brewing pot of coffee, was initially intended to be my after-school refuge. The idea seemed straightforward: once the final school bell rang, I'd make my way to the clinic, ensconcing myself in the break room. There, under the warm glow of the single overhead light, I'd chip away at my homework, waiting for my mom's shift to end while the hushed sounds of the clinic's operations served as background noise.

It didn't take long for Liam to weave himself into this routine of mine. In the beginning, his role was solely protective —a self-appointed guardian angel ensuring my safe passage to the clinic. But as days turned into weeks and weeks into months, the flavor of our walks changed. They became less about reaching a destination and more about the journey itself, replete with infectious laughter, shared secrets, and inside jokes only we understood.

In time, the small break room ceased to be just a makeshift

study spot. Instead, it transformed into a private haven—a place where we could be ourselves without fear of judgment. Its pastel-colored walls, adorned with chipped paint and an out-of-date community events calendar, bore silent witness to our evolving friendship. They absorbed our muffled giggles, echoed our whispered dreams, and bore witness to our passionate debates about everything from the abstract to the profoundly mundane.

It was within these walls we had talked about everything. The latest bands we liked, the intricacies of Liam's ongoing experiment with teaching himself how to play the guitar, and my constant recap of the stack of books I was going through at the time.

Even the air in the break room seemed to carry our shared history, imbued with the faint scent of coffee and our mutual aspiration. Each speck of dust floating in the afternoon sun, each stain on the old, lumpy sofa, and each frayed page of our discarded textbooks had a story to tell—a tale of an unlikely friendship that was born from typical childhood angst but sustained by the effortless ease of being together. And so, amidst the everyday chaos of the clinic, we found a sanctuary, a place where we felt seen and heard—a space that was uniquely ours.

"I was hoping to share UCLA with you, you know. Show you the ropes," Liam stated, a playful wink in his eye that contradicted the solemn undercurrent in his voice. His words pulsed through my veins, each syllable stirring up a whirlwind of emotions within me—nostalgia, anticipation, and an uncharacteristic pang of regret.

I lifted my gaze to meet his, catching the sun as it filtered through Liam's unruly, ever-untrimmed hair—his personal symbol of rebellion. His eyes held mine in a silent conversation, filled with unsaid words and hushed confessions that had yet to cross our lips. It was as if his stare was whispering secrets his voice couldn't articulate.

With each return visit from UCLA, I saw a transformed Liam, subtly different from the last. He seemed older, not just in age but in spirit, each new wrinkle in his college experiences etched lightly on his expressive face. Yet, beneath this confident exterior, I also sensed a layer of secrecy, a shield that protected parts of his life he chose not to share. It was as if his newfound freedom had also bred a certain reserve, a protective barrier separating his UCLA life from our shared past. And that secretive edge, while mystifying, was a poignant reminder of how our paths were diverging, hinting at the many unexplored facets of Liam I had yet to discover.

He'd already been living his UCLA story for the past two years, yet here he was, back in our shared childhood setting, sacrificing his time to help me pack. The action was such a quintessential Liam thing to do, selfless and thoughtful. Yet, in the wake of his wink and his knowing smile, a strange, unfamiliar sensation fluttered in my stomach. It was a mix of gratitude, apprehension, and a touch of something else I couldn't quite place. It was a feeling that seemed to color our friendship in a hue I hadn't recognized before. And it was a feeling that, whether I admitted it or not, would hitch a ride with me all the way to New York.

Getting into the New York School of Interior Design was no small task, and even Liam had a huge help in making it happen. I'd worked tirelessly to make that dream a reality, pouring countless hours into my application and portfolio and hunting for scholarships and grants. Every single night was a balancing act of school assignments, part-time jobs, and never-ending scholarship applications. The breath I was finally able to release when my acceptance letter had come was a relief.

New York wasn't just about the design program, though. I had plans, big plans. I had my sights set on some of the top design firms in the city for my internships. I had a roadmap to my dream job, and I was ready to do whatever it took to get there.

"Liam," I started, a wry smile playing on my lips as I raised an eyebrow at him. "You must be some kind of miracle worker, being able to fit me into your bustling social calendar." I couldn't help but chuckle, slinging my backpack over my shoulder with a lightness that contradicted the heaviness of my heart. Something flickered across his face that I couldn't quite decipher—was it surprise, annoyance, or perhaps a hint of embarrassment?

"And tell me, who was the unfortunate girl you had to ditch tonight for your best friend's departure? Was it Lucy or Sierra?" I was pushing the boundaries, but that was our dynamic—we'd always been open and playful about these things.

I'd watched over the years, a silent observer of Liam's evolving love life, from our high school days, when his parents' strict rules forbade him from dating, to his newfound freedom at UCLA. With the leash of restriction removed, it was like Liam was making up for lost time, his room acting more like a busy hotel suite than a personal space.

"You know," I continued, trying to keep the atmosphere light despite the swirling emotions inside me, "with your revolving door of romantic interests, I'm genuinely surprised you remembered that today was my big move."

Underneath my teasing, a part of me wondered about Liam's feelings amidst all this. Did he ever feel hollow inside, moving from one fleeting relationship to another? Or was he merely relishing the freedom he'd long been denied? I couldn't help but hope that one day, he'd figure out what he was searching for in these women, find someone who made him want to stop his revolving door and invite them in to stay.

He chuckled, running a hand through his hair. "Yeah, well, some things are more important."

His response left me in an unusual silence, my mind momentarily caught up in the physical transformation before me. I watched him as he lifted my overpacked suitcase with an easy strength that seemed new yet familiar. The afternoon sun filtered through the windows, casting a spotlight on his defined arms, the rippling muscles a stark contrast to the lanky boy I'd grown up with. He had indeed grown taller, but it was more than just physical height—there was a raw masculinity about him that I'd never really noticed before.

I found myself studying his face as he carried my suitcase down the hall, taking in the subtle shifts of his features, the sharp jawline, and the unruly curls that framed his face. It was strange, unnerving even, to acknowledge this change in him, this unfamiliar yet undeniably attractive man walking through my childhood home. I shook the thought away, focusing instead on his consistent friendship.

Liam—always the charmer, the protector, the consistent presence in my life. He was my rock throughout the tumultuous journey of adolescence, a safe haven amidst the storms of high school drama. But now, as I prepared to leave for New

York, and he planned to return to his life in California, I couldn't help but realize how much our lives were about to diverge. I felt a sense of apprehension, laced with a twinge of sadness, at the inevitable changes that were looming on our horizons. Would our friendship withstand the test of distance and time? I hoped so, but the reality of our separate paths was becoming more apparent with each passing minute.

"Are you seriously thinking you can haul this onto a plane, Em?" He grunted slightly as he heaved the bulging suitcase off the floor, a teasing glint in his eyes. "You clearly need me to fly out with you. I can help get you settled."

"I absolutely do not," I retorted, half-serious, half-joking. "You'd just act like my overprotective brother, scaring off every guy in my dorm with your death glares. I'll end up being the loner."

I leaned into the car, ready to sling my backpack onto the backseat when a strong grip on my forearm yanked me back. Before I could react, Liam spun me around, the world blurring for a second before I found myself standing inches from him.

He was so close that I could see the small freckles scattered across his nose and could smell the faint scent of his cologne. It was a momentary intimacy that hitched my breath. "Emma," he said, his voice suddenly serious, "I am not your brother. Remember that."

And then, just like that, the moment was gone. He released my arm, a playful wink replacing the intense gaze of seconds before as my mom descended the steps toward us. He turned away from me to walk toward her, his infectious charm spreading a smile on her face. His charm worked on almost everyone, but he wouldn't be able to charm me into staying. I wouldn't be swayed from my path.

As he laughed with my mom, I realized that my journey of self-discovery was truly my own, and it would have to be without him. As bittersweet as the thought was, I knew it was necessary. I was ready to embark on my own, to carve my path in this world, and it would start with this flight to New York.

ONE

FOUR YEARS LATER

"I swear, there isn't a single thing in existence more unflattering than this absolute abomination of a gown," I groaned, my hands gliding over the itchy, coarse polyester of my somber, pitch-black graduation gown. I turned a full circle in front of my mirror, wincing at my reflection, then sent a distressed glance at my roommate, Jessie, who sat comfortably sprawled in her desk chair.

Jessie, perpetually calm, didn't even look up from her tarot deck. "That's why what you wear underneath matters even more, Em. It's a statement of your own style," she declared, her fingers casually shuffling her worn-out tarot cards. She offered a playful smirk. "We need to get you something absolutely smashing, girl."

Jessie and I had been roommates since the very first day of college. We were a peculiar mix, both of us starkly different from each other yet somehow perfectly compatible. I had been a small-town girl from sunny California, stepping into the intimidating frenzy of New York, while Jessie was a born-and-bred New Yorker, her spirit as vibrant and fast-paced as the city itself.

Despite our differences, our bond had only deepened over the years.

My first impression of our dorm room had been one of fascination mixed with a healthy dose of skepticism. Jessie had, with a dedicated artist's touch, transformed every available surface into a delightful hodgepodge of dream catchers, crystals, scented candles, and the odd array of handwritten tarot interpretations. I remember questioning how our personalities would jive amidst her mystical eccentricities.

But each morning, without fail, Jessie would bound over to my side of the room, cradling her smartphone lit with the day's horoscope predictions in one hand and a steaming cup of herbal tea that tasted like wildflower meadows in the other. She'd squeal with excitement, eyes gleaming, "You've already met your soulmate, Em!" she would yell, her eyes lighting up like a kid in a candy store, "But don't worry, the universe will bring you two back together when the timing is right." I would roll my eyes, not yet a firm believer in all her witchy ways.

There was something undeniably captivating about Jessie. One of those souls you can't help but feel you've encountered in a past life. She was a bundle of energy, her quirky ways strangely endearing. Long twisted locks of hair cascaded down to her waist, her tiny tattoos peeping out from the edges of her clothes like secret stories etched in ink. The silver nose ring that she wore glinted under the New York sun, catching the light at just the right angle to make her seem ethereal.

Jessie was the anchor I needed when I found myself adrift in a sea of change, far away from my familiar Californian shores. She had not only filled the void of a new city but also the absence of a best friend. With a sigh that carried more weight than I intended, I tore my gaze away from the mirror, letting it settle on a faded photograph pinned haphazardly on my corkboard.

The picture was of me and Liam, caught in a moment of carefree laughter on a California beach. The sun had been shining brilliantly, casting our shadows long and our smiles bright. I felt a bittersweet pang of regret and nostalgia—a longing for an old friend I had left behind in my quest for self-discovery.

It wasn't as if I hadn't tried. The frosty winters in New York were a harsh contrast to the warm California sunshine I was used to. During one particularly bitter winter break of my freshman year, the piercing cold and pangs of homesickness drove me to fly back to California.

I remembered the anticipation in my chest as I neared Liam's apartment near the UCLA campus, the idea of surprising him with our favorite Chinese takeout and indulging in a *Law & Order* marathon like old times. But as I climbed the steps, my heart full of familiar comfort, I stopped dead in my tracks. There was Liam, stumbling drunkenly towards his door, a petite brunette clinging to his side.

A knot tightened in my stomach. I found myself frozen in place, feeling oddly intrusive. I didn't want to interrupt, didn't want Liam to stumble over an explanation. So, I stayed hidden in the shadows, an unintentional voyeur. The sight before me was surreal: Liam, his cheeks flushed from alcohol, his hand securing the girl at her waist, his mouth brushing her neck. This was a side of him that I'd never witnessed before.

The girls in Liam's life had always been abstract, nameless figures that came and went—I'd heard stories and had seen glimpses of them on social media but never saw the reality. But seeing him now, so intimate, so evidently couple-like, ignited an unsettling emotion within me. Was this . . . jealousy? It was a foreign feeling, like a sharp jab to my heart, and I was utterly lost on how to deal with it.

That night, I retreated silently, leaving behind a piece of my innocence. The taste of unintentional betrayal lingered in my mouth, and a gnawing discomfort twisted in my gut. Our frequent text exchanges gradually grew sparse, the lines of communication fraying until there was nothing but silence.

Liam reached out once, confused and possibly hurt, questioning if he had done something wrong. I struggled to articulate the turmoil within me, so I fell back on the excuse of a busy schedule, and he let the lie ring true.

I could feel Jessie's quiet stare at my back as I unzipped the graduation gown and slid it back on the hanger. She knew all about my conflicting thoughts about my old best friend. She had suggested that perhaps there was more to our friendship than I was willing to admit, a suggestion that I had shrugged off, preferring to stay in my comfort zone of denial.

"Okay, it's time for your daily horoscope." Jessie cleared her throat dramatically before she read from her phone. This was a routine we got into shortly after we met, where Jessie would read our horoscopes and hypothesize about everything they could mean. I never really gave them much weight, but sometimes they were eerily accurate.

She continued, "Beloved, the Universe has long paved a path to true love for you, a journey you've yet to fully embark on." Jessie raised her eyebrows and looked over at me. "But brace for a cosmic shift; an unexpected comet, an old friend, is poised to re-enter your orbit. This arrival will alter your life in unimaginable ways. Be open to the transformation and the new roles old companions might assume, for it is within these age-old bonds that new love may bloom, forever changing your destiny. Embrace this, for love often sprouts from the most unexpected soil."

I looked over at Jessie with skepticism, "Okay, yes, that was creepily on the nose, but come on, Jess. We hear what we want to hear from those things."

"So you *do* want to rekindle with Liam, then?" Jessie teased as she unfolded herself from her chair to change for class. We were in the final weeks of our program and still needed to pitch our capstone projects to the council soon. We hoped to both land internships at our dream design firm once we graduate.

"That's not what I said, and that's not what's going to happen. Besides, why are you so hung up on *me* finding love when *you* are so against it yourself?" I started gathering my computer and some snacks in my tote bag.

"I'm not against finding love; I'm against the *labels* of traditional love," Jessie hollered from the bathroom we share with two other suitemates. New York is so damn expensive that we both opted to stay on campus for all four years of school and over those years, I've seen plenty of guys (and girls) sneak in and out of our room for Jessie.

Throughout my college years, I dabbled in the dating scene, entering and exiting fleeting relationships like a passenger hopping on and off a train. Men with charming smiles and intriguing conversations crossed my path, and while there were moments of thrill and anticipation, they were often followed by a sense of emptiness. The laughter was hollow, the connection superficial, and the intimate moments felt like a choreographed dance with a stranger rather than a soulful intertwining of two hearts.

I was searching for an unspoken understanding, a familiarity, and an ease that always seemed to elude me. Every "good night" text left me unsatisfied; every shared secret felt like a performance. Despite the promising starts, these relationships turned into disappointing ends. The spark would fade, the conversations would become monotonous, and before I knew it, I was back to being single and reflecting on what went wrong.

Perhaps my standards were too high or my expectations unrealistic. But I couldn't settle for less. I craved a depth that seemed to exist only in my mind, an intimacy that was far more than physical. Love, for me, was more than holding hands under the city lights or sharing a dinner across a candlelit table. It was about shared dreams, enduring support, and a bond that transcended time and space.

These failed attempts, however, did not deter me from my primary objective. My eyes were firmly set on the horizon: graduation, my thriving internship, and the full-time job opportunity at Spectra Creations, one of the city's top design firms. The dream I had held since my high school days was on the verge of becoming a reality. I was too close to the finish line to let anything—least of all a romantic entanglement—pull me away from the path I had carved out for myself.

As Jessie and I made our walk to class, I allowed my brain to think about what Liam could be doing right now. I would find myself, after having one too many glasses of wine, thumbing through his profiles, indulging in the digital remnants of his life, seeking fragments of the past four years to weave together an idea of his present. The photographs and captions were cryptic, painting an incomplete portrait of his life that my imagination eagerly filled in.

Still, the mystery of Liam's life intrigued and frustrated me in equal measure. It was a constant reminder of our drifting lives, once so entwined, now floating in different directions. I felt a twinge of sadness as I realized his daily routine, his laughter, his playful banter—they weren't part of my everyday life anymore. And despite the craving, I had to come to terms with the fact that my past with Liam had given way to a present without him.

After sharing a casual wave and a promise to meet for coffee tomorrow, Jessie and I separated at the crossroads near Central Park. She disappeared into the thrumming crowd of New York, making her way uptown towards the city's most popular vegan bar, where she held her evening shifts. In the embrace of New York's brilliant symphony of blaring horns, bustling people, and towering skyscrapers, I ventured into the city's labyrinth alone.

Drawn into the heart of SoHo, I wove in and out of high-end boutiques and vintage thrift stores alike. I found myself lost in a sea of dresses—billowing chiffon, sleek satin, embroidered silks—their colors painting a kaleidoscope on the shop racks.

As I shuffled between the two dresses in the dressing room, my reflection bounced back at me from the mirror. The journey from the small-town girl I once was to the woman I had become seemed to flit before my eyes. The dresses symbolized more than just a garment to wear under my graduation gown; they represented my past and the future I was yet to embrace.

Balancing my collection of bags and my lukewarm coffee, I trekked back to the dorms. As I approached the building, my thoughts tangled with everything that I still needed to finish over the next couple of weeks; I almost missed the figure standing on the steps. A familiar silhouette, tall and strong against the backdrop of the setting sun, rooted me to the spot. I squinted, the figure gradually solidifying into a face I hadn't seen in years.

There, leaning against the stone facade of the dormitory, was Liam.

Here.

In New York.

My past and present collided in this moment.

The weight of my shopping bags slipped from my grasp, coffee pooling at my feet.

TWO

"It's good to know you haven't lost your clumsy streak, Em." Liam grinned and bent down to scoop up my bags before the coffee seeped into them.

A surge of familiarity washed over me, his words a reminder of our past playful banter. But my mind seemed to freeze, overwhelmed by the shock of his unexpected presence. My heart thumped against my chest in a rapid beat, and my words seemed to be caught in my throat, unable to voice the whirlwind of questions spinning in my mind.

"Uh, oh—let me just," I stammered, kneeling beside him in a clumsy attempt to help clean up the mess. But by the time I'd collected my thoughts, Liam was already discarding the empty coffee cup in a nearby trash bin; my bags hung over his muscular forearm. The tattoo peeking out from under his shirt sleeve caught my eye—a new addition since our last encounter.

I forced my eyes to blink a few times to get myself together, but it only made me feel dizzy. It had been over three years since I'd seen him in the flesh, and it was clear that the pixels of him I'd been given over the years from my snooping hadn't done him justice. And it wasn't just the way his body seemed to take up more space or how his tan skin flexed as he shifted his weight on his feet, but the way he carried himself with newfound confidence. It made me wonder what else had changed.

Breaking the silence, he said, "Sorry for the surprise. Thought it'd be nice to catch up over dinner. You free tonight?"

I felt a tug-of-war inside me; a part of me yearned to embrace him like old times and another part wanted to flee. However, one thing was crystal clear: I needed to regain my composure. "I mean, I don't have any plans," I conceded, attempting to sound nonchalant, "but, Liam, what brings you here? And how did you track me down?"

"Amazing what you can find out with a little social media digging," he replied, a spark lighting up his eyes. A wave of embarrassment washed over me, making my cheeks warm. Did he have any idea how often I had scrolled through his online profiles? "I'm here to discuss something with a friend from UCLA who lives in the city. We're considering . . . collaborating on something." The ambiguity in his voice suggested there was more to this story, yet it seemed we were both treading lightly, uncertain if our once effortless trust could be resurrected.

"Working together?" I repeated, an eyebrow raised in disbelief. "What kind of work?"

Liam offered a noncommittal shrug, his gaze pinned on me as though unsure of how I'd react. "We're still piecing that together," he confessed, lips curving into that familiar half-smile that made my heart flutter in ways it shouldn't. "I would love to take you out to dinner, maybe share a bit more about it. If that's something you're comfortable with." His voice hung in the air, creating a window for me to voice any reservations.

A part of me was itching to do just that. The sight of Liam's hands lingering on another woman's waist years ago had been a wake-up call; our friendship couldn't endure in the way it had been. We'd established boundaries then, and pushing beyond them felt like venturing into treacherous waters, uncharted territory save for the occasional fantasies I allowed myself.

He had never seen me in a romantic light; his parade of women was evidence enough. Yet, his social media feed had ceased featuring other women a couple of years back. I'd deliberately not let myself ponder the reasons for this, attributing it to a probable serious relationship, maybe with someone who valued her privacy.

Yet, despite my best attempts at denial, curiosity gnawed at me persistently. Not having seen Liam for three years, I was intensely curious about the man he'd evolved into. Now that he had reentered my life, the desire to uncover his journey over the years was more tempting than ever. Besides, it was only dinner, right? Nothing more than a chance to reconnect with a long-lost friend.

"I'd love to," I finally said, a small smile tugged at my lips. "Um, let me go upstairs and put these away. And—" I looked down at my yoga pants and tennis shoes, "I think I might have coffee stains to deal with, so I'm going to change." I reached for my shopping bags, and I felt Liam's warm fingers graze mine as he slipped the bags into my palm.

His voice was deeper when he said, "I wouldn't be mad if you picked one of these dresses to wear." His eyes were locked on my face as I glanced up at him.

"You could only be so lucky." I didn't miss the way his face lit up with a playful, flirtatious grin that I remembered so well as I pivoted and made my way inside.

I ended up choosing something simpler than what was

waiting for me in those shopping bags. I didn't know where we would be eating, and the longer I overthought about what to wear, the more it felt like a date, and that's definitely *not* what this was.

I walked out of the building doors, half expecting Liam not to be there. Perhaps my overstressed mind had conjured him up like a mirage. But there he was, hands in his pockets, pacing the sidewalk, the reality of him quelling my doubts.

He looked different now. The angsty teenage boy I used to know was replaced by a man who held a new kind of confidence. He was tall, taller than I remembered, with dark, unruly hair that begged to be tamed. A layer of stubble framed his jaw and neck—a new feature that stirred something within me. His frame was sturdy, not the lanky boy who used to joke around to get people looking anywhere but at his own insecurities.

Now, he wore his maturity like a well-tailored suit, his stance sure and unyielding. I wondered how it got there. A crease was etched deep between his brows, a silent testament to worries and experiences that I hadn't been a part of. My fingers itched to smooth it out, to ask him what thoughts kept him awake at night.

There was a familiar comfort to him, a pull towards him that made me believe we could easily find ourselves sitting side by side in the park at night like we used to, stepping back into the ease of what we used to have. But that was impossible. The Liam I once knew was replaced with this man before me, and a pinch of nervousness fluttered in my belly.

Would we fall easily back into our banter, or would we stumble over our words? Would the lighthearted jokes come like they did when we were kids? Would it be awkward, full of silence, and talking over each other? Would I be who he remembered? Had I taken up real estate in the back of his mind these last few years like he had in mine?

The heavy door clicked shut behind me, and Liam stopped his pacing and spun to face me as I walked down the steps. I had chosen a floral summer dress; the hem blew a bit in the evening breeze. I didn't have a large shoe collection here, so I had rummaged through Jessie's closet and found some lavender pumps to borrow. I'd thrown a little dry shampoo in my hair and made a two-minute attempt at some makeup.

Liam's eyes widened as I descended the steps, and I could see him taking in my appearance from head to toe. I felt the heat rise to my cheeks as I got closer, and I wondered if I'd made a mistake in wearing the dress.

"You look amazing," he breathed out, his eyes locked on mine. "I mean, you always look amazing, but . . ." he trailed off, his hand coming up to brush a stray hair from my face, "you look especially beautiful tonight."

"Um, thank you." I nervously ran my hand through my hair and met him on the sidewalk. I don't know why it felt like we were meeting for the first time. If the last few years hadn't happened, he would've welcomed me with teasing comments and a nudge to my side.

We walked side by side a couple of blocks before settling on a tiny Italian restaurant that looked like we could get a table right away. We were ushered to a corner booth with red-checkered tablecloths and twinkle lights strung up above us. I took in the cozy atmosphere, feeling grateful that Liam didn't take us to some stuffy fine dining place where I'd feel out of place.

The soft hum of conversation from the surrounding tables and the clatter of utensils broke the silence. I watched as Liam quickly scanned the menu, and we ordered a carafe of sangria.

Opting for directness, I initiated a casual conversation, "I noticed you graduated recently. Congratulations." I held up my glass in a toast.

"You caught that, did you? So you've been keeping tabs on me as well?" He gave me a knowing wink and took a sip of his drink. I found my gaze drawn to the face that was once so familiar to me, so comfortable.

I ignored his question, "How are your parents?" I knew I was deliberately opening a can of worms with that question, but I wasn't ready for him to ask me about us yet. There was no "us," I reminded myself; I couldn't mourn the loss of a childhood friendship forever. We were just friends, nothing more.

Liam groaned and took a deep swig of his drink before saying, "I don't really know. I haven't spoken to them in," he glanced at his watch, "nearly two years."

I couldn't hide the shock that colored my face. "Seriously? What happened?" I knew that Liam had never had a great relationship with his parents. He was the baby (and a surprise) of six. His parents were the kind of deeply religious that made you wonder if they moonlighted as cult leaders. All of his siblings had fallen in line with his parents' expectations and gone on to marry young and given them countless grandchildren.

He shrugged like it wasn't a big deal, even though his parents' opinion of him had always affected him, "Oh, you know, they got even nuttier in their old age if you can imagine that. They disapproved of nearly every decision I made and let me know every chance they got." He tore off a piece of warm bread and popped it in his mouth, "Even when they had every right to be concerned about what I was doing," he said between bites, "I knew I couldn't ever really be myself with them in my life."

"Like what? Did they finally disown you for not getting married at eighteen and becoming a pastor?" I asked the question, hoping I'd get the answer to the question I didn't outwardly ask.

He grinned, pointing his breadstick at me, "Something like that, yeah. They actually sent me a strongly worded letter when they found out I was working in real estate. Filled with all the fire and brimstone you'd expect." He chuckled, shaking his head. "They said I was 'wasting my God-given talents on worldly pursuits.'"

"Wasting? God-given talents?" I gasped dramatically, clutching my chest in mock horror. "You heathen!"

Liam smiled at me, and for a second, it felt like we were right back to sitting in the park after the sun went down, complaining about his parents and their ridiculous rules.

"So, real estate, huh? That's new." I refilled both of our glasses of sangria and dug into the bread.

Liam chuckled a bit before answering, "Yeah, real estate. A friend of mine, Dominic, that I met back in UCLA, he's who I'm here to see actually, introduced me to the world, and it's kind of addicting."

He was here to see his friend. Right. The clarification hurt more than it should have, but it had me sitting up straight and reminding myself of the line I drew all those years ago.

"What just happened?" Liam's face was masked with concern. "What just went through your head?"

I forced neutrality onto my face, "Nothing. I'm just getting comfortable."

"By sitting like you're in a job interview? Something just went on in your brain that made you shut off just now." Liam pressed, but I had no explanation that would make sense. Not to him. Not after all this time.

"I'm fine. I promise." The waiter came by and dissipated the awkwardness, and by the time we rattled off our orders, the air between us had calmed.

My curiosity was still high, so I asked, "So, Dominic. Real estate. What's that about? Are you buying property here in the city?"

Liam's face lit up, and I could tell that this was his happy place. It felt good to see it spread through his pores. His parents had really done a number on him when we were growing up. There were constant comparisons to him and his siblings and not-so-quiet demands for how he should behave and what he shouldn't be doing.

He walked me through project ideas that he and Dominic had thought about, but he was vague in the details, telling me that it was still in the very early stages. He was here to tour some commercial property spaces for a place they hope to open up next year, but the only description I got is that it's some kind of private event space of sorts.

"So this is where you come in, Em. I heard the best designer in the country lives in the city. And I'd love to hire her." He nodded his head toward me as I stared blankly at him.

"Oh. Me? You don't mean me, do you? I haven't even graduated yet, and after graduation, I'll have to do a residency of sorts at a firm and then hope that they—" He cut me off as my anxiety rattled off all the reasons he must not mean me.

"I most definitely mean you. And I'll wait until you're licensed, but yes, you. I only want you." I swallowed at his statement, trying not to read more into what he said. But it all makes sense now. He didn't come back to New York to rekindle our friendship. He wanted to hire me for something I wasn't even qualified for and nothing else. The small talk had just been a formality.

"I'll need to know more details before I can give you a definitive answer." I took a gulp of my drink to ease the anxiety in my belly.

"I can definitely let you know more as things . . . progress." I couldn't pinpoint why he was being so elusive, but everything out of his mouth felt like it had a double meaning.

Our food arrived, and we dug in, needing carbs to fill the space in our bellies where the alcohol was making its home. He asked about my mom and checked in on Hashbrown. I told him about Jessie and the job I hoped to transition into once my internship wrapped at graduation.

When the conversation shifted to reminiscing about our shared past, a warm ease settled between us, and we exchanged memories and laughter, fueled by the fruity sweetness of sangria that tinted our cheeks with merriment.

After paying the bill, we opted to take a scenic route back to my dorm. We walked side by side under the mellow glow of the streetlamps, the sounds of the night enveloping us. The soft murmur of the city around us, the distant laughter, the hum of passing cars—it all felt strangely intimate. The cool night air felt refreshing against my skin, carrying the hint of an upcoming summer. I could feel the heat emanating from Liam as he walked close, a warmth that made my heart flutter and my thoughts race—the night had shifted from a casual meet-up into something teetering on the edge of the known and the unknown.

Our shoulders bumped as we walked block after block, the wine serving as the warmth I needed in the not-quite-summer nighttime air. Liam took a deep breath, and I knew that we were about to talk about what happened.

"I'm sorry I wasn't there for you over the last couple of years." He surprised me by starting off with an apology. One that I didn't feel like I deserved. "I guess you being so far away was harder for me to juggle than I thought."

"I never expected you to juggle a long-distance friendship. You don't need to apologize for that," I whispered in the dark, glad he couldn't see every thought on my face.

"Why did you ignore me that night? I didn't even know you were coming, but I called for you, and you didn't turn around." I stopped walking and turned to him.

"What do you mean? What night?" My face showed my confusion because there was no way he meant *that* night.

"You were in town and outside my apartment. I was just coming home . . . with a friend . . . but you walked away. I called for you, but you didn't turn around," he repeated himself.

"You didn't call for me. Yes, I was there; I—I didn't want to interrupt, but you didn't call for me." My face heated with embarrassment that he saw me that night.

"Yes, I did. I let my friend inside, and then I came back out and called your name. I saw you turning the corner, so I yelled louder, but you kept walking. I convinced myself for a while that it wasn't you, but I finally got the nerve to ask your mom if you had been in town, and she told me that you had, but only for a couple of days. You'd already gone back at that point. I just thought—that you were mad at me for something."

I shook my head, trying to clear my thoughts. That night was one of the most painful nights of my life. Liam had no idea what he was dredging up. But if I was going to keep the peace between us, I had to be honest.

"You were with someone, Liam." I gave my head a swift shake and resumed my walk, not wanting him to see the hurt expression etched on my face. "You were with someone and didn't need me disrupting your peace just because I missed home."

"Homesick . . . and you came to see me?" He began walking backward, maintaining eye contact with me, and I watched as his eyes darted as he struggled to put the pieces together. "Emma, I would've gladly sent her home in an Uber so we could hang out. You should've just—"

"That's not fair. You busied yourself *a lot* with all sorts of women; how was I supposed to know how you felt about this one? You kept treating me like your kid sister when you went off to college, so I didn't know where we stood back then. Hell, I don't even know where we stand now, so don't just assume that I would've known what to do." My tone was more heated than I intended, but I couldn't take it back now.

"You're right." I opened my mouth to argue before my brain comprehended what he just said, so I let him continue. "I —I wasn't making the best choices back then. That's actually right around the time I met Dom—I really want you to meet him. He—I don't know, he helped get me right."

He continued, "I think I got my first taste of freedom when I left to go to UCLA, and I abused it. He really helped me when I couldn't even see how I was ruining everything I cared about. And I would've reached out sooner to you, but I didn't know if you'd throw your coffee in my face as soon as you saw me." He chuckled and bumped into my shoulder on purpose, trying to lighten the mood. "Luckily, it slipped out of your hand before you could make that decision."

"Well, I'm glad you found me. I'm really happy we got to do

this tonight." I stopped walking and turned to face my building. "I really did miss you, you know."

Liam reached out and grabbed my hand, rubbing the rough pad of his thumb against the inside of my palm. Shivers went down my spine, and we both just stood there like that for a moment.

"I missed you too. I missed this, us." His voice was deep and quiet.

My brain was swirling with thoughts, and there were a thousand things I could say, but instead, I asked, "Do you want to come upstairs?"

THREE

I swiped my key card against the access reader, and the door emitted a sharp beep allowing us to yank open the door. I led Liam into my dorm building, keeping an eye out for any nosy RAs or security guards. There's a strict "no visitor after 10 p.m." policy, and there's something that felt extra scandalous about bringing in Liam, who's older than all of us by a couple of years.

The halls were quiet since it was a Tuesday night. My hand gripped Liam's, and our palms were sweaty. I felt like the second we crossed the threshold, whatever had been waiting to shift would finally be in place.

Each door we passed was a countdown, and the silence of the hallway felt like a heavy weight threatening to crush us both. The second the door to my dorm room shut behind us, I felt the shift; a strange yet familiar energy wrapped around us. The space was small, made smaller by Liam's imposing figure filling up the room. The few guys I'd brought back were college boys, their youthful exuberance seeping into every corner. But Liam was different.

I clicked on a lamp, casting a soft glow around the room. The pale light danced off his features, highlighting his sharper jawline, the slight scruff on his cheeks, and how his eyes seemed to darken in the dim light. It was a face that held traces of the boy I grew up with, but it had matured, much like the man who wore it.

I knew Jessie wouldn't be home from her shift for a while, but we still whispered and tiptoed as we got settled. "You are, uh, bigger than you were last time I saw you, but I think you can fit," I said as I shut the door behind us.

"Bigger? You think I'm bigger, huh? And fit where exactly, Emma? Where would you like me?" Liam whispered in my ear, sending shivers down my spine. His eyes found mine, and the look he gave me was intense, full of questions and emotions we'd yet to voice out loud. The air in the room felt charged, the vibe between us shifting. Suddenly it wasn't just two old friends catching up; it was him and me leaning on the edge of a cliff waiting for whatever was about to unfold—and hoping that it would catch us.

I rolled my eyes at his comment. Liam had always found a way to bring flirting into every conversation and I guess I missed how it made me feel. "Fit there," I said, pointing to my twin-size mattress on the other side of the room. "You don't mind snuggling with me, right?"

He swallowed, and I thought he might actually mind. "I didn't imagine this is how it would be when we first slept together, Emma, but I can make it work," he said, winking at me as he slipped his shirt off over his head, and my eyes stole a glance at the body that's no longer defined by boyhood.

"You've always been such a charmer, Liam—no wonder the ladies couldn't resist. I'll be right back," I said, grabbing an oversized t-shirt from my drawer before heading into the bathroom and shutting the door behind me.

Somewhere between the restaurant and here, something shifted between us. There were enough truths voiced that must have us both feeling vulnerable. Liam had always been flirtatious and teasing, so I didn't know what was for show and what was meant for me. I've watched him turn those skills on countless other women and watched as they melted right before him. He had a way of making you feel seen and truly understood. I'd gotten that from him before too, but it made me sad to realize how much I'd missed it over the last few years.

I didn't want to do anything either of us regretted, but it was nice to have someone look at me like he had tonight. I splashed water on my face and brushed my teeth, changing into my t-shirt before opening the door. I realized I had grabbed one of Liam's old t-shirts that I must have stolen from him years ago.

My eyes took some time to adjust from the bright light of the bathroom, and they squinted as they focused on Liam sitting up in the middle of my bed, leaning against the wall. His long legs dangled from the edge of the bed, and I smiled to myself at *him* being *here*.

"Is this my shirt?" Liam's voice cut through my cloudy thinking.

"I don't know what you're talking about; I've always had this shirt." I held my chin high in my lie and scooted up on the bed next to him, our shoulders sank into each other as the mattress dipped.

"I'm really glad you said yes to dinner tonight." Light from the lamp created shadows over Liam's face and as he spoke, he tapped his knee against mine. "Can I admit that I was nervous when I first saw you come up the steps?"

I chuckled, "Well, count on me to squash any nerves with that coffee fiasco. But what was there to be nervous about?" I turned to look at him and folded my leg underneath me, "It's just me."

Liam's gaze held mine, his brown eyes shone through the dim room, "Exactly."

I laughed a little to fill the silence in between us, "Okay, so you've filled me in on what's going on with your parents, your job, why you're here in the city . . . what else?" I didn't let myself overthink when I asked, "Are you seeing anyone?"

Now it was Liam's turn to chuckle awkwardly, "No, I'm not seeing anyone."

"Oh my god, are you a virgin?" I asked.

"No." Liam's brows furrowed as he turned toward me. "I literally just told you at dinner how—" He cut himself off when he noticed the laughter threatening to spill out of me. "Oh, okay, I see. Are *you*?"

I shook my head, still stifling the laughter in my throat, but looked up at him when I asked, "A virgin? Or seeing someone?"

Liam shrugged like he wouldn't mind the answer to either of those questions.

"No. And no." My eyes hadn't left his face and there was a stillness in that pause that made me wonder if he was going to say anything else.

We fell into an easy silence, the sounds of the city shutting down for the evening filled the gaps. I yawned and sank down a little further into the mattress. Liam stood and tugged back the edge of my blankets, so I slid off the bed.

"Dominic isn't expecting me until tomorrow," Liam

pointed out. "I didn't really think through where I could stay tonight so . . ."

"Wow, what magical words you weave to get into my bed, Liam," I teased him as I pulled my hair up into a silk scrunchie. It was my only hope for it to not be a tangled mess tomorrow morning. He slid in between the sheets and scooted himself up against the wall to give me as much space as I could expect with sharing an extra-long twin-size bed with this *man*.

I didn't know whether to face him or not; there were pros and cons to both positions. I decided to give him my back, but the second I scooted back into him and felt *him* against me, I thought I'd made the wrong choice. But it was too late now; Liam threw his arm over me since there was nowhere else for it to go. I reached over to the edge of my desk and flicked off the lamp.

His voice cut through the quiet, "I had fun tonight." I almost thought we were both just going to sleep; it had been quiet for so long.

I whispered back, "I did too."

"We should do it again, you know. Go on another date." It felt like he was holding his breath, waiting for my response.

"*Another* date? Was tonight a date?" He pulled me in closer with his arm and squeezed.

"I'm offended you question the date validity. I guess I'll have to try harder next time." I couldn't believe Liam had just showed up earlier this evening, and now here we were *spooning* in my freaking dorm room. How did we get here?

"I can hear you thinking." His breath was hot above my ear. I rolled over to face him; the moonlight coming in through the window shone on his face.

"That's impossible. You can't *hear* someone thinking," I

said as he wrapped one arm around my waist and tugged me closer to keep me from falling off the edge—at least that's what I told myself. His arm felt firm against my waist, and I wanted to reach out and squeeze his shoulder.

"It is possible," Liam said, "because I know that you make these little huffs in your breathing when there's something you can't figure out when you're confused or frustrated. And you were just doing it." I dropped my gaze at his admission, confused about how he noticed something about me that I didn't even know myself.

"You know," I said, "some people might find it annoying how perceptive you are."

"Oh, *some people*, huh? Are 'some people' in the room with us right now?" Liam chuckled against my forehead as he placed a kiss on my hairline.

I tilted my chin up to look at his face. I tried to decipher his intentions behind his eyes, through the crease on his forehead. There were so many things I wanted to ask, but I couldn't figure out how to voice them. So instead, I pushed myself into his body and lightly pressed my lips to his mouth.

There was only one way to figure out if whatever this was would light us both on fire and burn us or let us shine. I heard the gasp in his throat as our lips met, my minty breath fogging against his teeth. His hand moved to behind my head, his fingers intertwined in my hair as our kiss moved from tentative to exploratory.

I could taste the orange from our sangria coating his tongue as he slowly invaded my mouth, testing the waters. My hands rubbed against the stubble on his face as they found their home in the back of his hair, behind his neck.

Our breath came out heavy as I bravely pressed myself into

his frame, feeling the proof of his excitement pressed into my belly. A small groan escaped him, and I put a hand on his chest, where I could feel his heart beating rapidly. Even if he didn't come here for this, even if this was the opposite of what he had in mind, I didn't regret it.

My bottom lip was in between his teeth, and my brain was jumping ahead to where this might be headed when I heard Jessie drop her purse loudly on her desk. I froze, and she hummed loudly to herself as she gathered her things to take to the bathroom.

She talked to herself, but clearly for our benefit, "I'm just going to take a *very* long shower, but I will be back and am a very sleepy girl." She cleared her throat as she passed by my bed and shut the bathroom door behind her.

I pulled away from Liam and ran my hands down my face, lingering a bit on my swollen lip. He caught his breath and chuckled, "That's not how I imagined meeting your roommate."

"Oh, she'll be fine; I've walked in on her *plenty* of times; she owes me." My breathing started to even out, and I bravely looked at Liam.

His hair was disheveled, and his lips were swollen; I reached over to smooth down his hair, but he grabbed my hand and laid my palm on his cheek. We laid in the quiet; the only sound was the running water of Jessie's shower.

"Well," I said awkwardly, "*that* just happened."

Liam groaned before saying, "Kissing you has been on my bucket list for a *very* long time, and that did not disappoint." He placed a kiss on my forehead as if he needed to prove his point further.

"I don't know what this means now; I'm sorry if I messed

things up," I whispered the confession hoping he wouldn't hear it.

"First," he started, "do not apologize for that. Second, you don't have to let it mean anything if you don't want it to." He snuggled into the bed a bit more, and I could tell he was fading. I looked up, and his eyes were closed, so I let it be.

Of course, it didn't mean anything. Not to him, so I couldn't let it mean anything to me. It was normal for us, especially after all these years, to try out kissing, but we didn't have to let it go to our heads.

FOUR

Waking up to Liam in my twin-size bed, with my roommate still asleep across from us, wouldn't have been awkward except that sometime in the night, my shirt must have crept up to above my waist. And Liam's large arm had found its home thrown over my hip, and his hand was dangerously close to cupping the underside of my boob.

And *that* probably would've been less awkward if I couldn't feel a rock-hard Liam pressing against my ass.

But here we were. And *shit, fuck,* Jessie's alarm was going off. I quickly made sure the blankets were covering us and shut my eyes.

"Oh well, hello there, friends," I heard Jessie's groggy voice from across the room. I kept my eyes shut but lifted up my hand and flipped her the bird. She chuckled and shuffled off to the bathroom. I heard the toilet flush and the sink water trickle as she brushed her teeth and held my breath, afraid to even move against Liam.

But I felt his warm hand squeeze against my thighs. "Oh,

you are *so* warm; come here." And he dragged me even tighter into his chest. And into *him*.

I froze as I felt him twitch behind me.

"Sorry." He paused the small circles he had been making on my legs. "It's, uh, the morning."

I swung my legs out from under the comforter and tugged the t-shirt down over my underwear, "Uh huh, yeah, no, I get it." I turned and tried to find my sweats, "I mean, I don't *get it, get it*, but you know, it's fine."

"Hey." Liam sat up in my bed, and even with (what I have to assume would be) morning breath and rumpled hair, he was freaking gorgeous. "Emma. Take a breath."

"You want to just go grab some coffee? Or something?" I didn't turn to watch as he slid out of my bed and slipped his pants on. I heard the bathroom door open, and Jessie joined our awkward standoff. I rolled my eyes as hers darted back and forth between us like she was watching a tennis match.

"Hey, I'm Liam; you must be Jessie." Liam shook her hand as he slipped his arms through his shirt, and it was only then that I turned around, still pant-less.

Jessie grinned like a goddamn Cheshire cat. "Ah, *Liam*. It's so great to finally meet you." I scowled at her use of the word "finally," but it's too late. Liam noted it and grinned widely as he turned to me.

"As much as I would love to continue to watch you blush all morning," my cheeks reddened more at his callout, "I promised Dom I would meet him this morning so we can go over details for the project." Liam walked over to me and placed a kiss on the top of my head. "Can I take you to dinner tomorrow night?"

"We just had dinner last night. I'm sure you have other

things you need to—" Was Jessie literally just going to keep standing there watching me fumble this with Liam? Apparently.

"And what, you don't eat other nights of the week? That's a travesty. I like feeding you, so let me take you to dinner." Why did everything he say sound so sexy all of a sudden? Was I becoming one of those girls who fell over everything Liam did? I thought I was the one girl in the country immune to him, and now look at me—an idiotic fool.

"Sure, okay. Dinner tomorrow night." He grinned; his dimples peeked out and completed his already perfect face.

Jessie snorted. I glared at her, already feeling the heat returning to my face.

"Sounds like a plan." He reached for the door handle. "I'll call you later."

He waved his hand in goodbye as he walked out the door, and I watched him go, slightly dazed.

"What was that?" Jessie asked, her eyes boggling with curiosity.

I shook my head, still in shock. "I have no idea."

"Well, *I* will take you to coffee because you, girl, have some explaining to do." Jessie tossed me my sweats that were hanging on the back of my chair, and I gave her a look that just said, "Don't."

We walked to our favorite spot, Urban Brews, and luckily our favorite spot that faces the bustling sidewalk (perfect for people-watching) was open. Jessie carried over both of our drinks, a Chai for her and a honey cinnamon oat milk latte for me.

"So remind me again why my horoscope app is always

wrong, and we just hear what we want to hear," Jessie said as she slid into the stool next to me.

"Ha. Ha." I slid my latte over in front of me, wrapped my hands around the warm mug, and took a deep inhale, hoping the caffeine could get absorbed in my system through smell.

Once I had my first sip, I started from the beginning. At my absolute shock that Liam was *here* and that he had found *me*. At the ease in which we fell back into old habits of storytelling and joking with each other. About how being around him felt the same and so different all the same.

After I caught Jessie up, she said, "Okay, so I won't read you your entire horoscope for today because it just might be the thing that sends you over the edge. But I will read you this one line because I think it's important. Do with it what you will."

She cleared her throat and read from her phone, "An old acquaintance resurfaces, pushing you to the precipice of self-discovery—leap and find yourself anew in the dance of the familiar and unknown."

I went to speak, but she raised her hands, "Hey, don't shoot the messenger; that's what it says right here." She spun her phone around to me and pointed to the highlighted text on her screen.

Sure enough, she's right. And before she turned her phone back around, my eyes glanced at words like "fate" and "partner" and "life-changing." I groaned, "Ugh, I don't know what this *means*, Jessie."

I spun on my stool to face her. "We were *best friends*. Best. Friends. And then it got awkward for us, and we literally both just ghosted each other. What if that's our move?"

Jessie waved a dismissive hand. "Maybe it's about time you have a heart-to-heart. Discuss your fears, your thoughts, and your feelings. Let's not repeat the romantic comedy trope of missed opportunities just because you two can't open up to each other."

I inwardly groaned, not really wanting the weight of figuring out this new development, at least right now. Jessie and I both had *way* too much on our to-do list. We were weeks away from getting to present our projects to the capstone committee, which meant I was weeks away from graduating with my degree in interior design from the New York School of Interior Design.

I was that much closer to getting to check the metaphorical box on a lifelong dream, and I had to use all of my time and energy to make sure I crossed the finish line. I had lived and breathed design, both as a coping strategy and creative outlet, for as long as I could remember. With rent spikes and greedy landlords, my mom and I had found ourselves moving nearly every eighteen months until things finally settled down when I was in middle school, and Mom married Glen.

I had learned how to pick up on the telltale signs of an impending move. It began with my mom sitting at the dining table with a pencil between her teeth and a calculator in front of her. If the numbers didn't look good, I would see boxes start to line the hall of our tiny apartment, and I knew we would be in a new place by the next month. After our third move, she realized that if she made it fun for me, I would be a lot more cheerful about the whole ordeal.

So she made unpacking and rearranging a game and a challenge. We weren't just moving to a different apartment; we were reinventing ourselves and finding a new style. We would flex our creative muscles within the confines of our new space and figure out how to best show up there. She would let me try out my ridiculous ideas, like swapping the living room and dining space or storing our small appliances in the linen closet.

But what I'd learned in all those moves is that the space you're in, the furniture you sit on, the things you collect and style, could find ways to breathe new life into you if you let it. I had learned to see the potential in every space, the beauty in every object, and the power of design in transforming our lives.

Ever since our freshman year, Jessie and I had been united by a shared ambition: to work for Spectra Creations, the company renowned as the crowning jewel of the design industry. Jessie, with her innovative architectural prowess, and me, with a passion for interior design that was as deep as it was personal. The allure of Spectra was powerful and intoxicating, as it only selected eight out of the sea of hopeful graduates every spring for its coveted internship program. Of those chosen few, only a fraction would be offered full-time positions. It was a crucible of talent and ambition, as demanding as it was rewarding.

The competition was intense, and the stakes were high. Jessie and I had celebrated with a tearful, joy-filled embrace when we both secured a spot on the internship team, our shared dream taking its first steps towards becoming a reality.

This internship was a grueling rite of passage. Despite the glamour associated with Spectra, we weren't immune to the grunt work that came with being interns. We filed documents, ran errands, and made countless cups of coffee for the team. These mundane tasks, though necessary, felt far removed from the actual design work we longed to immerse ourselves in.

But the promise of a full-time position was our beacon of hope. Out of the chosen few, only a fraction would be offered the golden ticket to a permanent role. Jessie and I knew the score and understood the harsh reality of the game. But we had come this far, fueled by our shared dream and tenacity, and we were more than ready to step up and prove our worth.

My mother and I had made countless sacrifices to get me here. Long nights of studying while she picked up extra shifts, scrimping and saving to afford tuition fees and materials. All for this dream, this goal that was now within my reach. This was not just a job; it was a testament to our resilience and determination, a validation of every sacrifice made along the way.

The prospect of working for Spectra meant more than just prestige; it was the opportunity to be a part of something truly influential. It was the chance to contribute to the design of remarkable structures like libraries that fostered knowledge or hospitals that facilitated healing. I would be collaborating with globally celebrated designers, imprinting my name on projects that would stand tall and proud across cities.

The imminent prospect of such an opportunity felt almost surreal, a thrilling mix of exhilaration and anxiety. My years of relentless work, and my persistent chase of this dream, was nearing a monumental juncture. In just a few weeks, we'd see if the countless hours, the sleepless nights, and the relentless pursuit had borne fruit. The anticipation of it all had me on edge, a cocktail of excitement and fear. This dream of mine was no longer just a dream; it was a reality unfolding right before my eyes.

FIVE

I'd been locked in hours of capstone prep with Jessie and Noah, another one of our program partners who would be competing for those coveted four spots at Spectra. Noah was like a firecracker in a button-up shirt, his slender frame pulsating with a fervor that was hard to overlook. He may have been small in stature, but his charismatic demeanor packed a punch. It was a cocktail of charm and wit that, when directed your way, was hard not to appreciate.

"Hark, peasants!" Noah's sharp voice would occasionally slice through the air, shattering the peace in our commandeered classroom. Every now and then, an unsuspecting lowerclassman would wander in, hoping to utilize the room for their own work. Noah, however, was quick to assert our dominance, his voice booming out like a disgruntled monarch dismissing his underlings.

"Noah, chill," Jessie chided him, rolling her eyes. "They're just as stressed as we are." But Noah just shrugged and leaned back in his chair with an unapologetic grin.

"Survival of the fittest, Jess," he said, turning back to his work with a determination that was hard to fault.

I used the disruption as an excuse to pull out my phone and see that Liam had messaged me on Instagram. I tap the message, a little flutter in my belly coming to life at the sight of his profile picture popping up in my DMs.

@liamnotlima: After texting your old number all morning, I'm going to cross my fingers that you, in fact, have a new number...

@heyitsemma: Hi! Yes, lol. I do.

I sent over my number and waited for his text to come through. Within seconds, my phone buzzed in my hand.

MAYBE LIAM BENNETT: testing, testing, is this thing on?

Emma: hi again

Liam: hi

Liam: how's your day going?

Emma: my brain is turning to mush after staring at my capstone project for the last three hours straight, you?

Liam: my brain is also mush after talking work all morning with Dom

Liam: shall we let our mushy brains hang out together? Could I possibly steal you before dinner?

> Emma: I think we could make that happen.
> Meet me outside my building in an hour?

> Liam: Deal. Wear comfy clothes.

> Emma: 😜😜😜

Liam didn't respond to my emoji-spoken question. I wrapped up with Jessie and Noah, promising to meet at the same place, same time tomorrow. Back in my dorm room, I stared at my options for comfy clothes (but *cute,* comfy, cause . . . come on).

I settled on black yoga pants with a white stripe down the side and a white cropped tank. I threw my shoulder-length hair up in a bun, out of my face, before slipping on my tennis shoes and heading downstairs.

I spotted Liam pacing the sidewalk in front of my building, hands in his pockets, giving what must be a classic stance of New Liam. My brain had been cataloging the shiny new details of my oldest friend. It's like a game of "Can you spot the difference?" in these two images, except it's a real-life human standing in front of me.

He'd always been a pacer, but the hand in the pockets was a new move. So was the rocking back and forth on his heels as he stared out into the city. So was the look of what felt like constant calculation on his face, trying to figure out his next move.

I could see the anxiety ease from his face as he turned and spotted me, and the lopsided grin of old Liam was back; it made me feel sixteen again.

"I have *the best* surprise for you," Liam exclaimed with his arms spread open at the base of the steps. I made it down to the sidewalk, and he placed a kiss on the top of my head. I didn't know what, if any, move to make after last night, but the casual friend-level kiss on the head set the tone for me.

"You know I don't *love* surprises." I set my face in a cringe but started walking in the direction Liam led us.

"Yeah, but this is just us." He bumped my shoulder as he spoke, "No crowd of strangers for you to worry about, my dear."

We walked for a couple of blocks as I bored Liam with details of my upcoming capstone presentation. We strolled leisurely through the streets, my words creating an eager rhythm as I shared about my impending capstone presentation with him. I told Liam about the intricate, exhaustive research and the meticulous design that had culminated into my final project, my hands gesturing animatedly as I tried to capture the scale of it all. I painted a picture of the anticipatory thrill that coursed through me every time I thought about my designs being seen by the Spectra selection panel.

As I shared, sweat formed little droplets on my forehead, the sun piercing the once-cloudy sky with a brilliant array of light. The heat was an ever-present, lazy blanket that threatened to suffocate us, but we moved at our own pace, unhurried and content.

"So, what's the surprise?" I asked, unable to wait any longer.

"You'll see." Liam winked at me, a mischievous glint in his eye.

We walked for a few more blocks until we reached a park that I'd never been to before. It's lush and green, with a large pond in the center. Liam took my hand and led me over to a small booth a bored teenager was managing.

"Wait here," he whispered in my ear before walking up to the window.

I was left standing there, my heart racing with anticipation. A few moments later, Liam headed over, holding two pairs of roller blades with a look of complete elation on his face.

"From what I remember," he said, bending down to set our blades in the grass, "is that you kicked my butt last time we were on these. So I would like a rematch."

"Oh really? Calling in a rematch, what, a decade later?" I kicked off my tennis shoes, thankful I decided to put socks on today, and plopped down in the grass to lace up the skates.

"Better late than never, right?" Liam held on to my gaze, sending a shiver down my spine.

I broke away, looking down at my laces, "Well, as long as you don't go crying home like you did last time." As we strapped on our rollerblades, a flood of memories washed over me. The last time we'd done this, we were teenagers. Now, we were worlds away from the naive kids we'd once been. My hands twitched, struggling to fasten the straps. Each click echoed my nerves, growing louder with each passing second.

"Talking smack already? We'll see Sinclair, we'll see." Liam pushed himself up into a wobbly stance and reached down to help me stand. My hands slid into his, our clammy palms meeting midair. My ankles seemed to have momentarily forgotten their purpose, feeling shaky and unsteady, as if the ground beneath them had turned to a bed of wobbly jelly.

We struggled to find our footing, our movements clumsy and unsure. We began to move, our feet uncoordinated, reminding our bodies of the forgotten rhythm of rollerblading. The wheels beneath us felt strange, foreign.

We both seemed to hold our breath for the first few minutes, afraid even the slightest movement would have us ass-down on the pavement. My thighs tightened as I held myself up, so I released a breath, trying to remember the movements that would force a breeze through my hair.

I was cruising down the sidewalk within a couple of minutes, surprised by how much I missed this feeling. Liam and I used to blade through our neighborhoods, gossiping about people at school, complaining about our own rules at home, and dreaming about the type of people we'd be once we finally left our small town.

I slowed my descent as the sidewalk turned down slightly and shifted a bit to see how far behind Liam was. I couldn't stop the loud cackle that escaped me as I watched his arms flail, and his legs turn into each other, his skates touching.

Liam seemed to be mimicking a flustered flamingo, his limbs twisting and contorting in the most hilariously awkward ways. He was off-balance, his arms waving wildly through the air like a windmill, his eyes wide with a mixture of fear and determination.

Unable to stifle a giggle, I turned back and started to glide toward him, feeling a bit more in control now. The muscles in my thighs tensed, my body moving in a more coordinated fashion than before, and I was just about to congratulate myself on getting the hang of it when suddenly, I felt a strong tug on my arm.

I looked back to find Liam clutching onto my arm, his knuckles white from the intensity of his grip. His skates had crossed, and he was leaning dangerously to one side. A laugh threatened to bubble to the surface, but there was a sense of urgency in his eyes that made me hold back.

I felt a jolt of adrenaline as I threw my free arm around his waist to keep him upright. Our bodies were pressed together, his heartbeat drumming erratically against my side. His grip on my arm lessened slightly, his breaths coming in short, ragged gasps.

A rush of warmth spread through me. Liam was heavier than he looked, and supporting his weight required an unexpected amount of strength. Yet, as I held him, feeling the solid weight of him against me, I couldn't help but feel a surge of satisfaction. We were here, in the moment, thrown off-balance and holding onto each other, just like the old times. And for the first time that day, my nerves settled, replaced by a comfortable familiarity, an echo from the past that felt like coming home.

"I don't think you're made for this anymore, bud," I teased Liam as he finally decided to plop down on the grass off the sidewalk. I stomped my skate-covered feet over to Liam, sat down next to him, and started unbuckling the blades.

"My body just isn't made for this anymore, Em." His breath was still coming out heavy like he was genuinely afraid to fall a minute ago.

"I'm not sure if your body was *ever* made for skates," I teased.

"*You* still look great, though. As usual." He looked down as he untangled the knots on his laces. "Maybe skating wasn't the best idea," he added.

"Why did you pick skating? We could have done . . . literally anything else." I nudged his shoulder and picked at the grass under my legs.

"I don't know. I just—I guess I get nostalgic when I'm

around you. There's some comfort in that with how much has changed over the years," he said.

His words hung in the air, the unspoken memories and what-ifs eerily present. I wanted to say something, say everything, but fear gripped my tongue, tying it down. I played it off with a smile and tightened the elastic around my bun. "Well, I'm glad I could make your nostalgic dreams come true." My voice sounded too high-pitched, betraying my lack of confidence.

Liam's eyes were insistent on mine, but he said nothing. The weight of his gaze was too much, so I redirected my attention to the blades in my hands. I needed to look busy, put together, not like someone distracted by the sound of their own heartbeat.

The atmosphere remained quiet and heavy as if the mere act of movement could break the spell.

Liam's voice broke the silence, "Hey, how's your mom? I haven't seen her in forever."

I shook my head to clear the shadows of daydreaming lurking around my mind, "She's good. Still works at the same clinic off Main." I looked out into the park at the people milling about. "I think she's surprised I actually like the city. I think a part of her was crossing her fingers that I would make the move back home."

"When it had been just the two of you for so long, I can only imagine how hard it was to watch you leave," Liam said. "My parents, on the other hand," he chuckled in the way that I knew he was about to use humor to mask how much something actually hurts him. "They couldn't wait to get me out of their house. I was 'tainting the family image.'" He used quotes around the phrase, so I was confident it's something his parents, most likely his mother, actually said to him.

I never understood his parents. To me, it always felt like they used their religion and beliefs as a way to control their kids rather than support them. If you dared step out of line, you would face the wrath of their judgment. And Liam, with his disdain for authority, the temptation to break the rules, and a strong desire to live life on his own terms, wasn't the easiest to mold into what they wanted.

There were plenty of times growing up when my mom let Liam sleep on our couch simply because he didn't want to have to sit through hours of lectures that would welcome him once he stepped foot in his front door.

"I'm sorry, Liam," I said, reaching out to touch his arm. "I'm sorry you had to deal with that."

"It's not your fault, Em," he murmured. His eyes darted away to focus on a small group of children feeding the ducks by the pond. There was a hard set to his jaw as he continued, "I just—I don't understand how they could be so . . . restrictive."

"They just didn't understand you," I said, my hand still resting on his arm. "You always wanted something more than what they wanted for you, something different. It's truly their loss."

His eyes met mine again, and there was an intensity in them that made me feel like I was the only thing he'd ever truly seen. The world seemed to narrow down to just the two of us.

"Thank you, Em," he whispered, his hand reaching up to cover mine. "You have no idea what seeing you again has done for me."

Suddenly, the tension became palpable, the air around us thick with unsaid words. My heart hammered against my ribcage. He was so close, his face inches from mine. I could see the flecks of gold in his eyes and could almost taste the mint on his breath.

Then he pulled away as if snapping himself out of a trance. He cleared his throat and said, "But enough about my depressing family drama. Let's focus on the now."

I was annoyed he took the easy way out by trying to change the subject, so I asked the question I'd been wanting to ask since we first had dinner the other night.

"Okay, so what did you mean the other day when you said you abused your freedom? What does that look like now?" My question was simple, but my face was begging him to let me in. Let me *see* him. I'd been playing the conversation over and over in my head, trying to figure out what he meant.

"Well, I was always the one who couldn't be tied down, who wanted to experience everything, who . . . didn't want to be 'domesticated' as my parents have lovingly put it," he started, picking his words carefully. "So when I left for college, that's what I tried to do. Live free, experience everything life offers, sleep with whoever I wanted . . ."

He took a deep breath and continued, "But, not to try and be *such* a cliche, but those things didn't actually make me feel good." He turned to face me. "Would you believe me if I told you I've changed?"

I scoffed, unable to hold back a small smile. "I'd say that sounds like a lot of crap."

"Why?" he asked, genuinely curious. "Is it so hard to believe that I could change? That maybe I've grown up?"

I shrugged, "It's not that, Liam. It's just . . . you've always been a chaser, going after the next bright thing that caught your eye. It's hard to envision you as someone more grounded and committed."

Liam sat back; his eyebrows furrowed in thought. He ran a hand through his hair and said, "Maybe I'm not that different. Maybe I've just . . . evolved."

"And what does evolved Liam look like?" I asked, teasing him with a smirk.

"Evolved Liam," he began, pausing for effect, "has discovered that constantly chasing the new and shiny was a mere distraction. That just maybe everything I've been looking for has been here the whole time."

His words hung in the air between us, and for a moment, I couldn't focus. It felt like there was still more to be explained, more to the story of evolved Liam. As his gaze held mine, I found myself analyzing the etchings of his sun-kissed face under the glare of daylight, my brows furrowing in an effort to decipher the hidden meanings etched into his words and expressions.

Liam shook his head, a slight smile tugging at his lips, shattering the heavy silence that had settled around us. "Anyway, just some food for thought. So, about that dinner? Are we still on for that?"

His words yanked me back from my introspection, and I found myself blinking at him, the potential implications of his "evolved" state just beginning to sink in.

It was a strange feeling holding Liam's hand as we walked back to my dorm, chatting about our plans for the evening. It felt comfortable and familiar but also exciting and new. It was as if we were picking up right where we left off, but this time, we weren't just teenagers dreaming about what our lives could be.

This time, we were adults living our own separate lives, hoping they somehow intersected.

Back in my dorm room, I picked out a simple outfit for dinner—a soft, pale blue sundress that settled over my hips, paired with strappy sandals. I glanced at the mirror, the butterflies in my stomach fluttering at the thought of the evening ahead. This wasn't just dinner with a childhood friend; this was dinner with Liam. And something told me it was the start of something new. Something different.

The low hum of a late evening crowd enveloped us as we stepped inside a hole-in-the-wall sushi spot recommended to Liam by Dominic. Nestled in a lesser-known corner of the city, Umi Sushi was a hidden treasure of a place, with warm, hardwood floors and strings of soft lights casting an inviting glow over the small, intimate tables.

Our shoes clacked on the polished floor as we followed the hostess to a quiet corner booth. As we settled into the plush seats, my eyes glanced over at Liam, tallying up all the ways he felt new to me.

I reached over and slid my fingertips up past the sleeve of his shirt that was pushed up past his elbows, "When did you get this?" I asked, tracing the outline of his tattoo with a curious gaze. It was an intricate design of the Earth, as seen from space, a patchwork of blues, greens, and swirling whites. The level of detail was stunning, the continents clearly outlined, surrounded by the vast, seemingly endless blue of the oceans.

He grinned down at my hand on his arm, "I got this my freshman year. When I realized there was a whole heck of lot more out in the world than what had been preached to me at home."

"It's beautiful," I said softly. "I'm not sure I could ever pull off a tattoo. Having something that broadcasted what I loved for everyone to comment on feels . . ." I glanced around the restaurant, ". . . overwhelming."

"But that's the beauty of it," Liam said, his eyes locking with mine. "It's a part of you. You choose what it represents, not the other way around."

His words hung in the air between us as we placed our orders. Soon enough, our table was brimming with dishes: steaming edamame, spicy crab salad, and countless sushi rolls, their vibrant colors vying for attention.

As we began to pick at our food, the conversation shifted from the tattoo to my first year here in the city, to school, and my dream of Spectra. I filled him in on all the details of my life I'd held in the last three years.

"And then," I said, between a mouthful of a Philly roll, "once the internship wraps after graduation, I can officially apply for a full-time position as a junior designer. It's *really* hard to land so I'm crossing my fingers."

"How's the internship going? Is it everything you thought it would be?" Liam asked, picking up a piece of sushi with his chopsticks.

I hesitated, the truth simmering just below the surface. "It's . . . I mean it's an internship, right? All grunt work and coffee runs. But that will change once I'm full time. I'll finally be able to actually get to design, get to work on projects in the city."

"But you," I steered the conversation toward Liam, unwilling to dive deeper into the negative aspects of my internship. Yet, the gnawing dissatisfaction I felt towards Spectra's boys' club culture lingered in the back of my mind.

Jessie and I had squealed when we got our letters from Spectra, inviting us to be a part of their internship team. We knew the experience would be invaluable, and even having their name on our resume would set us up for major opportunities in the future. The excitement and anticipation of learning from the best in the industry had been nearly intoxicating.

But, as weeks turned into months, we hadn't expected it to feel so much like a boys' club. The internship team was made up of mostly women, with the exception of Noah. And yet, despite our hard work and dedication, it felt like Noah was the only one getting significant opportunities to prove himself and work on substantial projects.

It was frustrating to feel overlooked, especially when we were pouring our hearts into every task we were given, no matter how small. But Jessie and I were determined, vowing to work twice as hard to prove our worth. I tried to push those thoughts aside, not wanting to dampen the mood of our night. After all, tonight was about reconnecting, not complaining about work.

I switched gears, looking back at Liam, "But what about you? You're the one with a big-kid job and starting businesses."

Liam's face brightened as he began to talk about his own experiences, a softness creeping into his eyes as he mentioned his friend Dominic. "Yeah, it's strange being out of the college bubble," he admitted, reaching for another piece of sushi. "But it's been invigorating, you know? There's so much more freedom and potential for creativity out here."

He gestured loosely with his chopsticks, as if trying to encompass the breadth and depth of the real world outside of academia. "And starting a new business . . . it's scary but exciting. I'm not just following a curriculum anymore, I'm having to figure it out myself."

He took a bite of his sushi and chewed thoughtfully before continuing. "And Dominic, he's been a huge part of that. I want you to meet him soon. He might come off as quiet, but don't let that fool you. He's one of the most supportive and loyal people I've ever met. He's got my back, and I've got his."

I nodded, my gaze dropping to the spread of sushi between us. That might have been how Liam and I would've described each other just a few years ago. And it seemed like he still would've used those words if I hadn't severed our connection back then.

The thought hung heavy between us, an unspoken acknowledgement that prickled at the edges of our conversation. We shared a long look before our attention drifted back to the food on our table.

"So," Liam began, his voice cutting through the silence. His lips quirked up into a grin, the familiar playful light sparking in his eyes. "Last I knew about you was that you preferred reading three books at the same time." He paused to take a sip of his water, his gaze never leaving mine. "So, what are you reading these days?"

My lips parted in surprise, his question bringing back memories of lazy afternoons spent curled up with a book in hand. He had always teased me about my reading habits, how I could manage to keep track of three different storylines at once. But he had also been fascinated by it, would often ask for updates on each of the books I was engrossed in.

I'd happily recap everything I was reading, weaving in my own opinions about the storylines as they progressed, sharing my guesses for what would happen next. He had joked that I was his very own Audible subscription just without the ability to pause and rewind.

"Well," I started, tucking a loose strand of hair behind my ear, "my TBR is a little drier these days. I've been reading *Design as Art* by Bruno Munari, a fantastic book on the role of design in our everyday lives. I've also got *The Secret Lives of Color* by Kassia St. Clair on the go, which delves into the history and cultural significance of various colors. And then there's *The Goldfinch* by Donna Tartt, a novel I've been meaning to read for ages."

My explanation was met with an approving nod from Liam. "Sounds like you're still the same bookworm I remember. I bet you have plenty of annotations and sticky notes throughout those books," he teased, a soft chuckle punctuating his words.

I rolled my eyes, an involuntary grin spreading across my face. "You know me well," I admitted, our shared history momentarily blurring the lines between our past and our present.

Our conversation ebbed and flowed with a comfortable rhythm, punctuated by laughter and moments of nostalgic silence. We delved into our reservoir of shared memories, resurrecting stories that hadn't been told in years.

"Do you remember that time in middle school when we put soap in my parents' pool?" Liam began, a mischievous twinkle in his eyes.

I snorted, a giggle escaping me as the memory flooded back. "Oh my god, yes! It was a tsunami of bubbles, and your dad was so pissed!"

He chuckled heartily, nodding in agreement. "I think that's when he turned up his cursing to the Heavens. He kept finding soap suds in the weirdest places. Good times," he reminisced, a smile gracing his face.

As our laughter died down, I found myself ensnared in the warmth of the moment, the years of separation between us momentarily forgotten. Liam's company felt as familiar as the worn pages of a beloved book. Despite the turns life had taken, we still knew each other. Perhaps not as intimately as before, but enough to resurrect a shared past that seemed distant yet palpably near.

As the night wore on, the lively chatter around us slowly faded away. The staff were tidying up for the night, the soft lights overhead casting long shadows over the warm wooden tables. Liam glanced at his watch, his eyebrows furrowing slightly.

"Looks like it's getting late," he said, finishing off the last piece of edamame. "I should probably head back. Dominic was kind enough to offer me his guest room."

I felt a bittersweet pang as our evening drew to a close. The night had sped by, colored with shared smiles and nostalgic stories, reminding me of the friendship we once cherished. Pushing those feelings aside, I nudged him playfully.

"Sounds like you're in for a fun evening of settling in," I teased, my smile soft in the low light.

He chuckled, the sound resonating in the quiet night. "You know it. Although, I bet his guest bed isn't as comfortable as yours."

My face warmed, remembering how tight the squeeze was his first night in town, but I couldn't help the grin that threatened to spread out over my face.

As we stepped out of the cozy warmth of the restaurant into the cool night air, the city night came alive around us. The distant hum of traffic, the occasional shout, and laughter all blended into a familiar urban symphony that felt as comfortable as our shared silence.

We started the walk back to my dorm, our steps falling in sync with each other. The city's nightlights cast a soft glow on the sidewalks, lending an ethereal quality to our surroundings. As we meandered through the streets, I started pointing out my favorite spots to Liam.

"That café over there has the best croissants," I said, gesturing to a quaint little establishment tucked away in the corner. Its windows, although closed, glowed warmly, casting inviting shadows onto the quiet street.

"And that bookstore," I continued, pointing out a narrow building crammed between two larger structures. The books displayed in the window were backlit, their covers glowing softly in the dim light. "I've spent hours lost in there."

Liam listened with rapt attention, his gaze following my pointing fingers, his smile softening with every revelation. The city had seen me grow in ways our hometown hadn't, and sharing this part of my life with him felt strangely intimate.

As we reached my dorm building, the vibrant buzz of the city mellowed to a comforting hum. Liam looked at the imposing structure, a small smile playing on his lips.

The night had felt so familiar, yet new at the same time. "Thank you for the date, Liam," I said, my voice soft in the quiet evening.

His eyebrows shot up in mock surprise. "Oh, so it's a date now?" he teased, a grin spreading across his face. "It's about time you recognized."

SEVEN

"Okay, how about this?" I shuffled my papers, cleared my throat, and started again, "Hi, my name is Emma Sinclair. As an upcoming graduate from the New York School of Interior Design, I am honored to present this project." I crossed out a few lines and jotted down a new sentence.

Jessie was listening to my introduction for what felt like the millionth time, waiting patiently as I tried to get it just right. Liam said he would head over to help me practice—I had to get confident enough with it so the shakiness stopped lining my voice.

I cleared my throat before rereading, "Hi, my name is Emma Sinclair. As—" A knock on our door cut me off, and Jessie hopped up, probably happy for the reprieve from my neurotic practicing.

The door swung open, and I was surprised to see Liam on the other side, "I snuck in behind someone after they swiped their card." He winked and stepped into our room, his height making itself known in our cramped quarters. Every time Liam was around, I felt an odd jolt of nerves that was hard to place.

The familiar Liam I knew was there, hidden beneath this new grown-up version of him, but reconciling the two left me unnerved and off balance.

"I'm gonna go grab us some coffee, okay?" Jessie was halfway out the door before I could even register that she was leaving. "I think it's gonna be a long night!"

I glanced over at Liam. I was sure there was panic behind my eyes thinking about this presentation because his expression went soft. "Hey, Em," his voice was low and kind, "you're gonna crush this. Let me hear what you have so far."

"I have nothing so far!" My voice was high-pitched and frenzied. "I have 'Hi, my name is Emma Sinclair'—that's it!"

Liam chuckled and settled onto my bed, his back against the wall. "Okay, that's a great start, Emma Sinclair." I threw my pencil at him and rolled my eyes.

"I'm supposed to lead with what I believe design does, like for the greater good, and I don't know what to say." Tears threatened to spill over the edge of my eyelids, and I looked away, embarrassed.

Liam reached out and took my hand; his thumb rubbed soothing circles over the back of my hand. "Hey, it's okay. Take a deep breath," he said, his voice calm and steady.

I closed my eyes and took a few deep breaths, trying to shake off the nerves that had been building up inside of me—Liam's touch was grounding, his presence a comforting weight by my side.

"Okay, let's start again," he said, still holding my hand. "What do you believe design can do for the greater good?"

I took a moment to think, feeling the weight of Liam's

words. "I believe that design can create spaces that inspire people, that make them feel safe, and that bring them joy. It's not just about aesthetics; it's about creating an experience for people." I kept going even though I felt like I was rambling. "I believe that design can break down barriers and foster community. I think, when done right, design can bring people together."

Liam was grinning when I dared a glance at his face; my breath caught in my throat. "What?" I said, momentarily concerned at the wicked look on his face, the unfettered emotion behind his sharp eyes.

"There it is. That's the magic," he said definitively.

The charge of the moment froze in time as the door opened, and Jessie popped in with a beverage tray of three iced coffees. "Have we made any progress? Do we feel ready to take on the design world now?" she asked as she handed out the lattes.

"I don't know about taking on the design world, but I do think I have my artist statement written." Liam handed me the pencil I threw at him, and I jotted a couple of notes down in the margins.

"Well, that's incredible progress! Now for the rest of the entire presentation . . ." Jessie held up her cup in a mock cheer as she sat down at her desk and started writing her own presentation.

Jessie and I were able to present together, but we both had to come up with our own artist's statement. I'd allowed myself to get hung up on this for months, but talking it out with Liam brought the much-needed clarity to put pencil to paper finally.

We spent the following few hours writing sections, swapping papers, and reading out loud to Liam as our audience of one. He would critique here and clap there until Jessie and I had a solid draft of our presentation.

We'd be giving our talk in just a week in front of the design council that judged capstone projects. Our ability to even *apply* for our full-time positions at Spectra relied on us crushing these presentations. Everything I wanted for my future was riding on this.

As the evening rolled on, Liam and I decided to take a break from the project. In truth, I decided it was time to give Liam a reprieve from hearing me rehearse the same lines time and time again.

We sat together on my bed, sipping the remnants of our coffees, talking about everything and nothing. It felt undeniably normal and comfortable, being with him in this setting. We effortlessly shifted from one topic to another, like a well-worn trail that we navigated without thought. It was as if no time had passed since we were teenagers, when we used to hole up in the back room at my mom's office, poring over plans and dreaming up our futures.

But now, something had shifted in our dynamics. A wordless desire loomed in the space between us, sending electric jolts through our shared glances and brushed touches. I saw it in the way his eyes clung to mine a beat longer than necessary, the way his fingers grazed mine with a touch that seemed heavy with implication, the way his voice softened to a husky murmur that sent shivers down my spine. Despite my efforts to sideline these feelings and focus on our conversation, my heartbeat pulsed in my ears, defying my attempts to remain composed.

I didn't want to be some stand-in for what Liam thought he was supposed to want. I knew there was a level of novelty that comes from going back to your childhood crush and didn't want to be someone's trinket.

My heart was guarded in this new, evolved phase with Liam. I knew how easily we ghosted each other back when it got awkward, and I didn't think I could go through that again.

As Liam started to nod off next to me, I found myself wide-awake, my thoughts spinning in my head like a broken carousel. I could feel a different energy with him, an energy I wasn't sure I was ready to confront.

I stole a glance at his sleeping form, trying to make sense of my tangled emotions. Why did his presence feel so different now? Why was there this heat between us that hadn't been there before?

It scared me. The shift in dynamics. The unknown. What did it mean for our friendship? Will things go back to how they were if we cross a line?

In the quietness of my room, I finally allowed myself to confront the truth I'd been evading: my feelings for Liam were deepening. It had transcended the realm of a mere teenage infatuation into a profound, adult affection. This revelation was terrifying, sending a chill of apprehension down my spine. A part of me wished to flee from these intense emotions, to hide behind the safety of denial. But the tides of my feelings were too strong to be stemmed, too real to be dismissed any longer.

As dawn tiptoed into the room, spilling golden sunlight onto our slumbering forms, I knew it was time to face my apprehension. The question of how to broach this conversation, whether to wait for Liam or to take the first step, whirled inside my head.

Jessie walked in from the bathroom just as Liam started to stir beside me. She looked at us, sleep crinkled in her eyes, then at the stacks of papers strewn about the room, and chuckled, "Looks like you guys pulled an all-nighter. How's the presentation going?"

It was a welcome distraction, and I eagerly jumped at the chance to talk about something other than my confusing emotions for Liam. We delved into the presentation, and for a while, I managed to push my feelings aside. But as the morning progressed, I knew I couldn't avoid it forever.

I needed to talk to Liam, lay my cards on the table, and face whatever came next. Because our friendship meant too much to me to risk it over unspoken feelings and assumptions. And maybe, he felt the same way too.

But before that, I had a presentation to prepare for. It was time to focus, time to show the world what Emma Sinclair was made of. So, with a renewed sense of determination, I dove back into the work, preparing to face one of the biggest challenges of my academic career.

EIGHT

"God, presenting our capstone felt like stepping off a cliff." My hand subconsciously reached for my stomach as if to quell the nerves that were suddenly resurfacing. Jessie and I both sat on the edge of my bed, laptops perched precariously on our knees as we refreshed our emails. I couldn't help but go back over every tiny detail from our presentation.

The moment I stood at the front of that room, everything went blank. I tried to remember our carefully rehearsed speech, each word we'd agonized over, but it all seemed to slip away. It wasn't until I caught sight of Jessie, her steady gaze rooting me to the spot, that I found my voice again. I dove straight into my artist's mission statement, and everything else seemed to flow out of me like I was on autopilot.

Jessie interrupted my train of thought, her voice as cool and composed as the green aventurine she was absently turning over in her hand. This gemstone, known for bringing good luck, seemed to be her silent talisman in this moment of suspense. "They said we'd hear back by the end of today," she stated. Her calmness, combined with the soothing motion of the gemstone rotating in her hand, somewhat eased my anxiety. The prospect of a definitive verdict, whether in our favor or not, promised a certain degree of relief.

The wait, however, felt like a marathon, with each passing second a tormenting reminder of our capstone presentation. I recalled how my voice trembled slightly as I mentioned the importance of inclusivity and community. I couldn't help but ruminate over whether that small hesitation cost us our dream. Jessie, on the other hand, seems to be growing more anxious by the minute, her fingers twitching every few moments as she refreshes her inbox.

When the email finally came, it felt like time itself had stopped. Fear clutched at my heart, and I found myself unable to click on it. I cast a quick glance toward Jessie, and I was met with the same apprehensive look. She clutched her laptop, her hands trembling slightly as she finally opened her email.

"We'll read them at the same time, okay?" I suggested, trying to keep my voice steady. We locked eyes as we opened our own computer screens, scanning the email for any sign of our fate. A moment of silence passed before we both let out a collective squeal, the words of congratulations registering simultaneously. The relief that flooded through me was indescribable; the tension in my chest finally dissipated.

Jessie leapt up to dance around our room in joy, and we threw our arms around each other, our hands clasped tightly in a celebratory embrace. All the sleepless nights, the stress, the uncertainty—it all felt worth it. The email was the validation of our hard work, the confirmation that we'd made it through the rigorous process.

But as we parted, the weight of our next challenge hit me.

We had to finish our application for Spectra Creations and hope that we both get approved. I let out a shaky breath; my fingers automatically moved to share the news with the two most important people in my life: my mom and Liam.

I couldn't help but feel a twinge of happiness and nostalgia as I typed out the message to him. Our relationship had changed and evolved from childhood friends to . . . whatever we were now. It felt natural, easy, like the missing piece to my puzzle.

And I was surprised by the pang of longing that shot through me. I had missed this. I had missed having him as my confidant, the one person who understood me like no other. As kids, he was always my first choice, the person I would run to with my successes, my failures, and my fears. But somewhere along the way, we had drifted apart, built walls around ourselves, and I had lost my person.

But now, sitting here with my heart racing, a warm glow of achievement surrounding me, I realized that this new version of friendship, of togetherness, was something I didn't even know I needed. It was something I didn't realize I was missing until I had it again. The thought of losing it again made my stomach churn with dread.

Shaking off the negative thoughts, I sent them each a text, my heart pounding in my chest. My phone started buzzing immediately as if both of them were waiting by their phones for my news.

Mom: Congratulations, honey. I am so proud of you! Don't forget to celebrate :)

Liam: Yesssssssssss, Em!!!!! You fucking
DID THE THING. Drinks at The Smith? I'm
with Dom, you should bring Jessie!

I smiled at Liam's message. He was always so full of energy, and his excitement was contagious. I felt my heart flutter at the thought of seeing him again, but I quickly pushed it aside. I couldn't let myself get too carried away with my feelings.

Meeting Dominic, Liam's best friend and roommate, for the first time felt momentous. Dominic seemed to have been instrumental in broadening Liam's horizons. I couldn't help but wonder if Dominic was one of the key reasons why Liam seemed so different from the boy I knew back in California.

"Liam and Dominic want to do drinks at The Smith; you in?" I hollered to Jessie through the music she decided to blare in our room as she danced around.

"What kind of question is that?" Jessie grinned like a maniac. "Of course, I'm in!"

Meeting Dominic wasn't just about being introduced to one of Liam's friends. It was, in a way, getting to know another part of Liam, a part I had yet to encounter. The part of him that had evolved and changed away from home under the influence of this new friend. I wondered whether I'd see a reflection of Dominic in Liam's behavior and whether that would feel familiar or foreign to me.

I decided to test out one of the options I had reserved for a potential graduation dress tonight. After putting a few loose curls in my hair and adding some color to my eyes, I slipped into the strapless, midi-length dress. The high slit on the thigh exposed the tan of my skin against the pink jacquard fabric. I left my hair down and added dainty gold jewelry to my fingers and wrists, finishing with small golden hoops in my ears.

I was sunshine next to Jessie's endless black wardrobe. I helped her zip up the back of her jumpsuit, which had a gentle metallic sheen to the dark fabric. She layered on turquoise and quartz jewelry before we made our way downstairs to catch a cab.

When we stepped out of the cab and into the evening lights of The Smith, I took a deep breath, shaking off my nerves. This was just a casual evening with friends, I reminded myself. But as we entered the warm, bustling ambiance of the restaurant, I couldn't shake off the feeling that this meeting could alter the dynamic between Liam and me forever. My fingers instinctively found Jessie's, intertwining with her digits for a brief moment of reassurance. Then, we made our way toward the bar, ready to meet the guys.

The Smith could only be described as fancy AF. Quiet chatter, soft piano, and thick velvet curtains greeted us as we stepped inside. Vivid blue velvet booths encircled the room and added a touch of luxe, nestled under the gentle radiance of antique iron chandeliers. Each booth offered a view of the grand piano positioned on a small raised platform, set for performances that sprinkled in as background noise every evening.

My eyes scanned the room, looking for Liam, and I spotted him and a huge, broad-shouldered man with jet-black hair sitting across from him. Where Liam gave off golden retriever energy, his friend Dominic gave off rottweiler energy, and I was very curious as to what brought the two of them together.

Liam turned as I stepped past the hostess like he knew I was walking into the restaurant, and his face lit up.

"That boy is in love with you, Em," Jessie whispered behind me, and my face flushed with how excited that made me feel.

As we approached the table, both men rose to their feet, the chivalrous act accentuated by Dominic's unwavering gaze fixed on Jessie. His eyes seemed to be drinking her in, meticulously cataloguing every detail of her presence. Each tattoo that graced her skin, every piece of jewelry that adorned her, was silently etched into his memory for later remembrance.

Despite Jessie's apparent disinterest, she wasn't oblivious to Dominic's lingering gaze. She moved as if each of her gestures was choreographed for an unseen audience, a captivating performance meant solely for him. The subtle lift of her chin, the exaggerated arch in her back, and the smooth slide into the booth; each action was a testament to her self-awareness. She maneuvered with the knowledge of a woman who knew her worth, the way she commanded the attention of men like Dominic. Her silent confidence echoed through her actions, a siren's call demanding to be recognized and respected.

Liam chuckled at the exchange and placed his hand on my thigh as he leaned in and kissed my temple. "Dominic, this is Emma and Jessie." His face didn't leave mine as he spoke, "Ladies, Dom." His head tilted in Dominic's direction.

Dominic extended a hand to Jessie with a grin, then turned to me. "It's great to meet you, Emma; this guy won't stop talking about you, so it's great to see that you actually *do* exist." Dominic's voice came out as a growl as if he were in a perpetual state of annoyance.

I flicked my eyes up at Liam, and he raised his eyebrows and shrugged like he couldn't deny Dominic's claim. Maybe there had been something here the entire time that I just couldn't see.

I felt a flush of heat slide up my neck as I met Dominic's

intense gaze; his dark eyes practically pinned me to my seat. I tried to shake off my nerves, but his presence was overwhelming, almost suffocating.

"Likewise," I managed to croak out, my voice betraying my unease. Liam's hand squeezed mine reassuringly, but I barely registered the contact.

"So, Emma, Liam told me you're graduating soon," Dominic said, finally breaking the uncomfortable silence. "What are your plans?"

I welcomed the change in subject and slid my hand out of Liam's grip, taking a sip of my water to wet my dry throat. "I'm hoping to get offered a position at Spectra Creations," I said, trying to sound confident. "It's been a dream of mine—and Jessie's—to work at their firm. We've been interning there all year, so hopefully, it turns into something."

"Yeah, we can officially apply this week since we finally got our capstone presentation out of the way," Jessie chimed in, pouring herself and me a glass of wine from a bottle that was sitting on the table, not waiting for permission.

She passed me my glass, and we clinked them together, unable to hide the grins that took over our faces. Dominic flagged down the waiter with a simple flick of his wrist, and another bottle of wine was brought to the table, along with some small appetizers. *Fancy.*

After a few drinks coated our bellies, Jessie got nosey, "So, I hear you two have been looking at some big, fancy commercial properties around town." She glanced at Liam quickly but settled her eyes on Dominic, "What for?"

He gave her a wicked grin, and if I didn't know better, they were a match made in, well, I would say Heaven, but knowing

Jessie's beliefs, I'm gonna go with the cosmos. To my surprise, Dom answered, "It's a club. Of sorts."

Jessie huffed a laugh, "Oh my gosh, thank you for all those details; I can almost picture it in my mind's eye just now."

Liam said, "It'll be a place to inspire people, make them feel safe, and bring them joy." The words ring familiar in my head. And they should; I've only been practicing that line for hours on end in preparation for our capstone presentation. I tilted my head over at Liam, and he simply raised his eyebrows and took another sip of his wine.

"Okay, so it seems like we're still workshopping the details then; that's okay." The way Jessie is prodding, I can tell she wants to get more details from the guys, but I'm not sure they're prepared to divulge.

"It's an adult club. For *adult* activities," Dominic added this bit of clarification, and I couldn't help the shock that colored my face.

"Oh, so, like a strip club?" I asked tentatively, trying not to lace my question with judgment. Liam doesn't seem like the kind of guy interested in owning a strip club, but maybe more than I thought had changed about him over the last few years.

"Not a strip club," Dominic said like he was offended that was the takeaway I got.

"Are we just going to keep playing this guessing game here," Jessie cut in, "or are you going to treat us like adults and fill us in on your little boy-preneuer dreams?"

Dominic subtly inclined his wine glass towards Liam, a silent cue passing between them. Liam seemed to take a breath, steeling himself before starting, "It's not a strip club; it's a place where consenting adults can come to explore their fantasies. Either with their partner or with other likeminded individuals."

His voice was steady, confident, and held none of the nervous tremor I had half-expected to hear.

My throat went dry, and I took a gulp of my water, trying to quell the sudden rush of questions. "And how did this idea come about?" I managed to ask.

Liam straightened in his seat, a spark igniting in his eyes as he geared up to share. "As some of you know, my upbringing was . . . constrained," he started. I reached over, letting my hand rest on his thigh in a silent show of support. I knew that delving into memories of his past wasn't easy for him. "I've lived a life where judgment and criticism were constant companions. A life where my desire to express and experience myself freely was seen as wrong."

He paused for a moment, letting his words sink in, "But I know I'm not alone. There are so many others out there, who, like me, crave a safe space where they can freely explore their desires, their fantasies, without any fear of judgment." He shrugged, a quiet intensity emanating from him. "I suppose, in my own way, I wanted to create such a place for them. For us." His final words resonated in the quiet of the room, hinting at a depth of personal experience that added weight to his words.

As Liam's words settled in the air, my mind started spinning. His vision, as unsettling as it was intriguing, jolted a curious fascination within me. His world, one that I'd always assumed was clear-cut and simple, suddenly revealed itself in complex, unexplored layers. There was a thrill coursing through my veins, a tingling mix of apprehension and anticipation.

Jessie's gaze flicked to mine, her eyes a silent query, trying to read my reaction. I could only return her look with a shrug, my mind too absorbed to formulate a response.

Across the table, Dominic was in his own world, his gaze

distant. He seemed to be lost in thought, the red wine in his glass swirling in languid circles as he absently turned it. It was a snapshot of reactions, each of us grappling with the revelation in our own way, all under the warm, muted light of the restaurant.

Finally, Dominic spoke up, his deep voice curling around me once again, "And what about you, Emma? What do you think of all this?"

I took a moment to gather my thoughts, weighing my words carefully. "Honestly, I'm a little surprised," I admitted. "But . . . I can see where you're coming from. And I can understand the desire to have a safe space like this."

Liam's face relaxed into a lazy smile like he had been holding his breath ever since he arrived in the city, holding back this information.

Jessie, never the one to be shy about voicing her opinion, jumped in and said, "So what kind of activities could people do? Is there a dress code? What's the atmosphere like? How will you enforce safety rules so that everyone feels safe and respected?"

Liam laughed and turned to Dominic, "Told you she was always full of questions." He turned back to us, taking our curiosity in stride. He took a deep breath before going into detail of all they had planned for the club.

He talked about how it would be an exclusive membership club open only to those who pass a background check and fill out an extensive application. There would be strict guidelines enforced where everyone must respect one another no matter their relationship status or sexuality. They even planned on having different themed events hosting discussions on BDSM and other kink-related topics hosted by professional sex therapists as well as workshops teaching techniques in rope binding and massage.

It was a mammoth task, one that seemed like it would take a ton of work, time, and money to make happen. As Liam talked, I saw a light in his eyes, an eagerness that I'd never seen before. It's clear he had put a lot of thought into this. In the back of my mind, I can't help but appreciate his commitment and passion for something so unconventional yet so essential to many.

Gradually, the night began to ebb away. Jessie and Dominic were absorbed in a deep dialogue, their words a low murmur that faded into the ambient noise of the restaurant. Meanwhile, Liam and I didn't say much. We sat in a peaceful silence.

My mind was full of thoughts about everything that happened that evening, and from his quiet expression, I could tell Liam was thinking hard too. Our fingers gently brushed against each other on the velvet seat, creating an electrical current that sent shivers up my spine. I caught him looking at me, his gaze soft and full of an emotion I couldn't quite place.

"This was big news," he said quietly, "and I'm glad I could share it with you." I nodded, giving his hand a reassuring squeeze, my mind still processing everything.

"It's huge news," I agreed softly, giving his hand a tight squeeze, the reassuring warmth of his skin grounding me. "I'm . . . I'm still wrapping my head around it all, Liam." The words hung in the air between us, a raw acknowledgment of the weightiness of the revelation.

"I mean, it's not what I expected," I admitted, "but it's . . . it's exciting. And I can see why you're passionate about it. You want to create a space where people can be free, express themselves without judgment. That's . . . that's really something." I took a deep breath, gathering my thoughts before I looked up at him, my heart pounding in my chest.

"It's not the path I might have imagined for you, but it doesn't change how proud I am of you." My voice was steady, but I could feel a knot of emotion in my throat. "This venture . . . it's bold, it's challenging, it's . . . it's very much you.

"I have so many questions," I confessed, my eyes searching his. "I'm curious about the logistics, the ethics, the . . . everything." I laughed, a little awkwardly, a little nervously. "But, I guess we have time to talk about all of that.

"I just want you to know," I said, finally, "that I'm here for you. I'm excited to see what you create, Liam. And . . . I believe in you." My voice was firm, unwavering. I meant every word. This was his dream, and I wanted nothing more than to support him in any way I could.

As we left the restaurant, the city nightlife humming around us, I felt an unfamiliar mix of emotions, a strange cocktail of anticipation, apprehension, and exhilaration. There was so much to look forward to, so much to discover, and as I stepped into the taxi with Jessie, a glance back at Liam standing under the soft glow of the streetlight told me that he was just as eager for this new chapter as I am. Tonight had been a revelation, one that not only changed my perception of Liam but also opened a door to a whole new world, one that I was ready to explore.

NINE

Over the next few days, Jessie and I hunkered down to finish any last-minute to-dos we still needed to complete before graduation and tackled the complicated application for our Spectra positions.

"It should be illegal for the application to be more than, like, three questions long since we've already given them so much of our *free labor*," Jessie groaned as we shelved the application yet again so we could take a break from it.

"Wanna go eat our weight in carbs to take our mind off it?" I asked.

"Absofuckinglutely, I do." Jessie rolled out from under her comforter, and we made the walk to WichCraft, the best-hidden sandwich shop in the city.

WichCraft is a twenty-four-hour establishment, so it was always open for those late nights when school or work collided with a craving for carbs. It's hidden at the back of a small, deserted alley, but enter the door, and the blue-and-white-checkered tiles make a bold statement. The menu is displayed on blackboards behind the counter, as is the motto of the restaurant, "Eat. Repeat." It's a motto that Jessie and I lived by.

I gripped my toasted chicken salad on rye and sighed heavily into my first bite. Jessie's wrap is stuffed to the brim with hummus and cucumber, and she dipped it deeply in tzatziki sauce before biting off a huge chunk.

"We are the picture of refinement and class," I said between a mouthful of bread.

Jessie chuckled. "Speaking of refinement and class . . . did *you* know about the project Liam and Dom are working on?"

She meant the sex club. Or adult club. But not strip club. Club. The place that Liam and Dom have been scouting commercial properties in the city for. Liam showed me some photos of a couple of properties they had on their shortlist, and they are *gorgeous*. Ideally, they'd like to snag a historical property and maintain as much of its integrity as possible. Well, as much integrity as you can when you inevitably install a sex swing inside a 134-year-old building.

I shook my head as I finished chewing and finally said, "Nope, sure didn't."

Jessie's eyes widened to communicate with me as she chewed. "So how do we feel about it? Was this . . . how Liam was when you guys were younger?"

I couldn't help the laugh that escaped me. "No, definitely not. Liam was right; his household was *oppressively* strict."

"Well, then, I guess this makes sense, and honestly, it sounds really . . . lovely." Jessie gave a sly grin.

"Oh yeah? So you would visit then? Partake in the festivities, so to speak?" Jessie was nodding before I could even finish the question.

"And you?" Jessie asked.

"Me? Um, I think I might need to see what one of these clubs is actually like before I can commit either way." I shrugged dismissively like I hadn't been Googling what went on in places like that all night.

"Mmm hmm, yeah. Test the waters a bit. Get your . . . feet . . . wet." Jessie grinned, and I burst out in laughter.

I felt my phone buzz in my tote bag at my feet, and when I pulled it out, I saw Liam had messaged me.

> Liam: I have some appointments to look at some apartments this afternoon, wanna join?

I spun my phone around and showed Jessie the text. She read it with raised eyebrows and said, "Ohhhh, apartment hunting. So he's, like, moving here, for real? Is the place for him or for . . . the two of you?"

"I guess? I shouldn't be surprised if he wants to literally open a business here, but no, with Liam and I just now getting to know each other again, I have no desire to rush into living with a *dude* just yet." I crumpled my sandwich wrapper to throw away. "Besides, aren't we moving into your sister's old apartment after we graduate?"

"That's still my plan; just making sure you're not gonna ditch me." Jessie grinned as she licked hummus off her fingertips.

I opened up Liam's message to text him back.

> Emma: Sure, I'm finishing lunch now. I can meet you at the first apartment in an hour if that works?

> Liam: You the best, Em. I'll text you the
> address.

An hour later, I was walking up to a century-old brick tenement building in the Lower Eastside. Liam was waiting for me, sitting on the stoop, his long legs dangling down to the steps below.

I didn't stop the grin that found itself spreading across my face as I watched him. I still find it surreal that Liam is here in the city that had become my new home for the last few years.

I sat down beside him, and he turned to me, his lips curling into a smile. He was wearing a plain white tee and dark jeans, his hair styled into a tousled mess that looked effortlessly perfect.

"Hey," I said as I tucked a strand of hair behind my ear.

"Hey yourself," he replied, his gorgeous hazel eyes locked onto mine.

We sat in comfortable silence for a few seconds, just enjoying each other's company as we basked in the sun's warmth. I could feel the heat emanating from his body, making my skin tingle with a pleasant sensation.

"So, this is one of the apartments we're looking at," he said, breaking the silence. "Unfortunately, it's on the fifth floor, so we better start the trip; hope you brought snacks."

He reached back to help me up off the stoop, and his hand was warm in mine. He punched the keycode the landlord sent over, and the heavy, glass-paned lobby door opened with a loud buzz. Liam kept hold of my hand as he guided me in front of him to take the narrow stairs.

The old staircase, which wound its way up to the fifth-floor walk-up, was lit up intermittently by dim bulbs that flickered with a warm light. With each step taken, the worn-out treads creaked slightly underfoot—evidence of the many feet that have climbed them over the years. The walls were covered with layers of paint, the corners lifting and peeling back to reveal hints of earlier colors beneath.

We were both out of breath by the time we came to the front door, a sturdy, somewhat scratched, wooden door painted in a muted forest green, with the number "5" in tarnished brass screwed onto its upper middle. A slightly crooked peephole sat at eye level, and an antiquated door knocker looked like it might give you tetanus if you put your hand on it.

The door creaked open, unleashing a wave of thick, stale air that stung my nostrils. My eyes adjusted to the gloom, taking in the chaotic kitchen with trash piled high in the sink and stained counters. The bathroom was no better, with a grimy tub and streaked tiles. The once gleaming hardwood floors were now thick with grime that stuck to our shoes as we walked through the space.

"Based on the look on your face, this isn't the one," Liam said, though the sound was muffled through the t-shirt he'd pulled up over his nose to block out the smell.

I didn't even dare to open my mouth to respond, afraid that I would taste the smell; I simply turned on my heel and made my way back out into the stairwell, now terrified to let myself touch anything in this building.

We both burst out laughing by the time we were out on the sidewalk, gulping down fresh air to clear our lungs.

"No, that was *not* the one." I wiped tears from my eyes as we headed down the block to another apartment. "I didn't even know you were actually moving here. When did that happen?"

"Well, part of it has to do with my deal with Dom. It'll be

easier if I'm not traveling back and forth, and I feel bad for crashing at his place for so long," Liam said.

"And the other part?" I asked when he didn't continue.

"The other part has to do with an old friend that I recently reconnected with. That I would very much like to see more of. And she just happens to live here." He bumped my shoulder with his elbow as we walked.

"Oh really? She must be pretty cool for you to move across the country just to spend more time with her," I teased him as we turned the corner.

"She's *very* cool," Liam emphasized. "And one day, I'm going to convince her to work with me on these cool projects so we can hang out even more. I used to know her really well, but I was kind of a jerk when I was younger and didn't realize what she meant to me."

I stayed quiet, unsure of what to add to this conversation, feeling awkward for one of the first times around Liam. It's not that I hadn't been feeling the same desires; I mean, *I'm* the one who walked away all those years ago after seeing him with someone else made me feel things. Things like jealousy and desire.

Even though we'd technically known each other for over a decade, these feelings still felt new. Uncharted. But what would it take for us to get comfortable?

The next apartment was nestled within an elegant and somewhat weathered pre-war building, painted a basic shade of cream, with a few windowsills decorated with flowerpots. Once inside, the stairwell, wide and gradually winding, with thick wooden banisters, was well-lit. An ancient, hand-operated elevator cage sat in the center, more a relic than a utility.

We made our way up to the third floor and came to a crisp,

red-painted door with a modern black 3A screwed in just under the peephole. Liam used a key he snagged from a mailbox downstairs to unlock the door, and once inside, we could both tell this space felt different.

For one, it didn't smell like death warmed up. But it was the high ceilings and loads of light flooding through the tall windows that did it for me. The studio space was compact, the kitchen tiny, but the exposed brick columns and original picture molding on the walls made the space feel special.

"*That* look tells me this must be the one." Liam smiled as he leaned against the brick column that separated the kitchen from the rest of the space.

"Well, you *have* to check out the bathroom first. That could be a make-it-or-break-it for you. What if all this is for show and the bathroom is really just a Port-a-Potty?" I asked as I turned from the kitchen and headed down a half wall that served as some privacy for the bathroom.

Luckily, there was no Port-a-Potty waiting for Liam behind the wall. It was a simple bathroom that was dominated by a classic claw-foot tub that boasted a handheld shower fixture nestled against an exposed brick wall.

"Oh, this is *lovely*." I put my hand to my chest dramatically. "If Jessie and I didn't already have a two-bedroom to move into, I might fight you for this space. This shower is to die for."

Liam walked over to the tub and fiddled with the silver handheld shower fixture. "I never really understood these things. You just need the shower to stay in one spot, right? No one needs to wield a running stream of water."

"Ohhhh, so you don't know the power of a detachable showerhead, do you?" I teased him as I walked into the bathroom, "Tsk, tsk, Liam. I thought someone who was going to be opening up a *sex club* would know the powers of something like this." My eyes lifted up in a tease in the bathroom mirror at Liam standing in the doorway.

He raised his eyebrows at me, his eyes sparkled with curiosity. "Oh really? Miss Sinclair, do tell me your dirty secrets."

"Maybe I could show you sometime." The statement popped up in my brain, headed right to my throat, and left my mouth before I could even register it. And the surprised expression on Liam's face was guaranteed to match my own.

He swallowed loudly, his eyes locked onto mine in the bathroom mirror, "Would you? Show me? Maybe it could be my moving-in present." His mouth curved into a sexy grin.

I stared back into his eyes just as intently before saying, "I can probably make that happen."

The bathroom felt hot as Liam covered the space between us in just two steps. My back heated as he stood behind me, placing his hands on either side of me on the tiny pedestal sink. I swallowed loudly; my brain went back to the moment our lips first touched. I'd been ignoring my body's demands for more of it ever since.

My eyes followed the movements of his hands in the mirror. They moved from the sink to my hips and up my sides. I rested my hands gently on the lip of the sink to brace myself because I could already feel my head going light. Liam's hands made their way up my shoulders and cusp my neck, gently pushing my hair to one side.

I shivered as Liam's mouth got closer to the sensitive skin on my neck, and my eyes didn't miss how his throat bobbed when he swallowed. *Kiss me, just kiss me, you fool.* My brain yelled it, but my body stayed still.

Liam pressed his nose into my throat and inhaled deeply,

and I tilted my head back to encourage him to keep going. A warm hand touched the skin of my belly as Liam slid his hand slowly up my shirt.

"Is this okay?" His voice came out rough.

"Mmm, yes." I could feel the vibration of my voice against the fingers he had resting on my throat.

He slid a finger along the waistband of my shorts, and I held my breath.

"Is this okay?" He asked again.

"Isn't the front door still open? Will someone come in?" My mind raced, but my body stayed compliant to his touch.

"Maybe." He said it like a challenge. Like a dare. He slid his hand further down my shorts over the top of my underwear.

"Answer me, Em. Is this okay?" He stopped moving his hand.

I arched into his touch as I said, "Yes. Please."

I opened my eyes in time to see him smiling at my reflection in the mirror. My chest was covered in red splotches; my eyes were dilated, my lips parted. Liam's hand resumed its journey further down, this time pressing into my core.

"Open your eyes. I want you to watch us." Liam's voice was in my ear, and I didn't think twice before complying. "Good girl."

Liam kept his eyes locked on mine as he slid his fingers beneath the fabric of my underwear, gently pushing them to the side. There would be no doubt as to how I felt about what was happening once he moved his fingers over just an inch.

I kept my eyes on him so I could watch his face when his fingers found the evidence. I didn't hide the small upturn of the corner of my mouth as his eyes went wild and dark. His hands began to move more frenzied after that. One of his arms wrapped around the front of my chest to hold me upright as his other hand began to stroke my soaking core.

A gasp of breath left my mouth when he finally slid a finger inside. And when he added the rough pad of his thumb to my sensitive clit, my mouth opened in a silent scream. The sounds of the city and other tenants faded into the background as I focused on watching the veins of Liam's hand flex beneath my shorts.

My brain must have shut off all noises because I went to protest when Liam quickly pulled his hand out of my shorts and adjusted himself as he went to inspect the shower. But before a sound could leave my mouth, I heard it, or rather, her.

I spun around, unsure of what to do with myself, as a cheerful, loud voice filled the studio apartment. "Mr. Bennett?" I could hear her heels clicking on the hardwood floor just on the other side of the wall. "It's Laura! The agent?"

I smoothed down my hair just as Liam exited the bathroom to greet her. He bought me a few seconds as he loudly asked Laura about something in the kitchen. I took another peek at myself in the mirror, splashed some water on my chest to cool myself down, and walked out. If we had been given just thirty more seconds . . .

TEN

I kept telling myself that I wouldn't allow any weirdness to creep between Liam and me. Post our unexpected encounter in the bathroom, Liam was not apologetic, but he seemed . . . different. Somewhat reflective, perhaps. There was a lingering weight in his gaze, an intensity that was both thrilling and unsettling. He had had to rush back with the realtor to secure the apartment, so I had made my way back to my dorm.

Now, laying here, my mind slightly hazy and absolutely stunned at my own boldness, I realized there was another emotion threading its way through me. It was elusive, tough to label, but existed somewhere at the crossroads of confidence and euphoria.

I had felt strong, attractive even, in that moment. The power I wielded, the knowledge that my every move held Liam's rapt attention, was intoxicating. I was banking on the hope that our friendship was sturdy enough to handle this shift, this new dimension we were venturing into, without tearing at the seams.

The buzzing of my phone jolted me out of my daydreaming, and I looked down to see a message from Liam. It was a screenshot of his confirmation email that he got the apartment. I checked the time and realized I'd been lying here, dazed, for hours. The sun had almost made its full departure, and my stomach growled loudly.

I rummaged through our small snack cabinet and found a microwavable mac & cheese; I didn't think I had the energy or clarity to leave our room. As it heated, I texted Liam.

> Emma: That was fast! Congrats, you're now an east coaster :)

> Liam: You'll have to show me all the ways to fit in here since you're such a New Yorker now

> Emma: Ha! You'd probably be better off with Jessie showing you the ropes. I still can't get the hang of the subway lines.

> Liam: How are you feeling after today?

How am I feeling after today? It felt like something inside of me just got woken up. It felt like, if I wasn't careful, I could burn with how good being around Liam felt. But I didn't know how to put those thoughts into words, so I typed something else.

> Emma: Mostly just hungry, I'm heating up some mac & cheese now.

> Liam: Ah, the meal of champions.

The microwave chimed its completion, and I carefully

retrieved the heated container, the warmth radiating against my fingers. Steam unfurled from the surface, carrying with it the savory aroma of the golden noodles that had now softened and expanded. I gave them a good stir, the fork slicing through the tangle of noodles, mixing in the seasoning. Then, cradling the bowl in one hand, I retreated back to the inviting cocoon of my bed, the sheets cool against my skin in stark contrast to the heat of my late-night snack.

Emma: But to actually answer your question - I feel fine. A little surprised at myself. How are you feeling? Are you okay?

Liam: Today was probably, no definitely, the best day I've had in this city - ever.

Emma: So, is…watching people…a thing for you?

Liam: Voyeurism? Yeah, it's a thing for me, lol. But watching you?

Liam: I can't figure out how to type the sound my throat just made, so you'll just have to trust me.

Liam: Is exhibitionism…a thing for you?

Emma: I just had to google that. It's never something I've done before, so I don't think I could say it's 'my thing'. And Google calls it 'a compulsive need' and that's definitely not the case.

Emma: But I am feeling a little drunk off power still so maybe

Liam: Anytime you want to feel drunk again, please let me be there

The very idea of baring myself in such a way to anyone else left a cold, clammy sensation settling over me. It was one thing to embrace my boldness, my inner power, when it was within the reassuring comfort of Liam's presence. With him, I felt safe; his calm demeanor was like an anchor amidst turbulent waters. But when it came to Liam, it wasn't just about safety or comfort. There was an undeniable attraction, a magnetic pull that I couldn't ignore.

However, the more I considered his recent revelations, the more questions bubbled up. Liam didn't just wake up one day and decide to venture into the world of adult entertainment purely for the sake of business experience. There had to be more to it, a deeper motive or desire that pushed him in this direction. I needed to understand what that was.

And so, I resolved to peel back the layers of this enigmatic man, to probe deeper into the shadows of his motivations. Not just for the sake of our evolving relationship, but to truly understand who Liam was—beyond the childhood friend, beyond the safe harbor. He was stepping into an entirely new realm, and if I were to stand by his side, I needed to brace myself for what lay ahead.

Emma: So, what else do you, uh, like? I don't know the correct terminology here.

Liam: You can call them 'kinks' if you want, that's what's commonly used. But, yeah, there are a lot of things I like exploring, but I wouldn't say I have one obvious kink, really.

Liam: But to answer your question…I like using toys with partners, a little bit of rope play, group play (if it's the right people)

Liam: ...I don't want to scare you off, Em.

Emma: You're not scaring me. I want to know. How did you learn about all this stuff?

Liam: Well, that question has a million different answers. Let's see...

Liam: There was a time back at UCLA when I wasn't doing well. I was drinking to get drunk, taking home a new stranger every night...I felt like I was constantly chasing some feeling I couldn't ever keep a hold of.

Liam: And then one night, it kind of escalated. Everything was consensual, but I definitely took it too far with this woman who said she was into it. She started freaking out on me, and I got this panic feeling that I would get caught.

Emma: You weren't doing anything wrong, Liam. Sex isn't shameful.

Liam: Yeah, well, years of a cult-like upbringing kind of brainwashed me, you know? I mean, you know how my mom always was. But anyways, I finally spilled my guts one night and confided in Dominic. We'd met Freshman year, and he was so quiet I thought he was the best person to spill my secrets to.

Liam: It turns out he was, in so many ways. His mom is actually a famous sex therapist, and he grew up in the exact opposite household that I did. I had to do a lot of learning and unlearning, but I eventually got to a better place.

Emma: So why a sex club?

Liam: As awkward as it sounds, Dom's mom actually introduced me to a couple back in California. She never took me (that's not one of my kinks 😜). But those places opened up a whole new, controlled environment for me. Those places were really powerful for me, so if I can create that for more people and make them even better, I will.

Emma: Thank you for telling me. This is an entirely new world for me.

Liam: Thank you for not running away, scared.

Emma: Liam, you once made me sit through as you wrote and practiced a song so you could sing it to some girl you had a crush on at school. If I could sit through that, I can sit through anything :)

Liam sent back a scratchy audio message of him flubbing the lines from the song he wrote all those years ago, and I shamelessly saved the audio to my phone. I fell asleep that night, still in a daze, but calmer now that I knew more about how Liam got to this point.

I had fallen asleep before plugging in my phone, so instead of my alarm waking me, I jolted out of bed at the sound of Jessie coming into our room just after sunrise.

"Nice of you to join me," I grumbled underneath my covers as she unsuccessfully tried to sneak in.

"Shh, go back to sleep; you are dreaming," Jessie whispered in the dim light of our room, the first sign of morning barely creeping through the blinds.

"An all-nighter, huh?" I teased, "Work must be *crazy.*"

"I may or may not have accidentally hooked up with my new boss," Jessie blurted out.

This got me to sit straight up in my bed, eyes wide, "You *what*? How do you *accidentally* hook up with your boss?" I shook my head, seeking clarity. "Wait, isn't your boss some old guy? I mean, no shame, but doesn't he have, like, five kids?"

"I did *not* hook up with Nasir, Emma! That's the problem!" Jessie paced around the room, manically organizing her desk.

"Wait, so you *want* to hook up with Nasir?" If we were going to be up this early, we might as well have coffee. I slipped out of bed to put some coffee grounds in our maker.

"No. I don't want to hook up with Nasir." Jessie turned to face me, "Nasir apparently *sold* the bar. And didn't tell us. And the new owner decided to have a little celebratory hangout last night at the bar without telling anyone." She ran her hands over her face and continued, "I was technically off the clock, but I stuck around to order some food."

"And she ordered me a drink, and we just got to chatting, and before I knew it, we snuck away to a spot in the back of the bar, and she's going on about how nervous she is for her first day as the new owner of *my bar*." Jessie let out a huge rush of air and plopped down on her bed.

I decided Jessie needed someone to commiserate in her misery with, so I said, "Well, Liam and I almost got caught by his realtor as he was fingering me in his new bathroom, so there's that."

Jessie flew up in bed with a look of complete shock on her face. "You did *what*?" Her shocked question turned into manic laughter, and we both had tears streaming down our faces by the time the coffee finished brewing.

"Okay, this revelation *definitely* calls for an emergency

horoscope reading." Jessie was already swiping through her phone so she could read me my fate. "Okay, here it is."

Jessie put on the voice she used when reading from her trusty astrology app and said, "Dear star traveler, anticipate the return of a familiar face taking on an unfamiliar role. Trust your intuition—it's singing the songs of truth. Expect a personal revelation, as this person helps unveil new layers of your identity. Embrace the unknown, for it's here where your fullest potential awaits."

"You're a witch, Jess," I said. "A certified witch." I threw myself back on my bed, head swirling with the implications of what she just read. But it was just a horoscope, right?

ELEVEN

The days following our submission to Spectra were filled with an excruciating sense of anticipation. Every buzz of a new email or call set my heart pounding, the suspense of waiting more exhausting than the labor of application itself. In this state of unrelenting uncertainty, life went on, milestones passing like ghosts in the night. Graduation came, cloaked in a flurry of caps and gowns, a blur of relieved smiles and tearful goodbyes. And just like that, we had stepped over the threshold of student life, stepping into the vast, uncharted terrain of adulthood.

The transition wasn't without its charms, though. Jessie and I bid farewell to the dorms that had been our humble abode for years, trading the shared halls and communal bathrooms for the intimate comfort of her sister's old apartment. The beauty of New York was in its hidden gems, the well-kept secrets that native New Yorkers clung onto like precious relics. Jessie's sister was no exception, refusing to relinquish her charming two-bedroom, one-bath sanctuary in the heart of the West Village despite having settled into marital bliss in Brooklyn.

Our first night in the apartment was a cozy symphony of unpacking and decorating. We nestled flickering, flameless candles in the hollow of the faux fireplace, their soft, warm glow casting dancing shadows around the room. Jessie claimed the mantle as her own personal sanctuary, lining it with an array of crystals from her collection. Each one sparkled and shone in the candlelight, casting a mesmerizing rainbow of colors onto the surrounding walls.

Stepping back, I couldn't help but marvel at our new home. It felt like something straight out of a Meg Ryan movie, the very essence of *You've Got Mail* captured within the warm, inviting walls of our apartment. Living in the city was like being a character in an ongoing film. The old brownstone building, the cobbled streets outside, the lively buzz of city life in the air—it all felt surreal, like a beautifully curated movie set. I was now part of this narrative, and I couldn't wait to see what the next scene held.

"Emma, check your email!" Jessie's voice echoed through the apartment, an urgent edge resonating from her room. "Hurry, Noah just texted me!"

In response, I flung my legs over the side of my bed, my heart pounding a frenzied rhythm against my rib cage. Fumbling with my phone, my fingers feverishly navigated through the various screens, finally landing on my email. An anticipatory chill ran down my spine as I saw the email sitting right at the top of my inbox—an email from Spectra Creations.

My eyes darted towards the doorway just as Jessie burst into my room, her hair disheveled and her wide eyes reflecting my own anxiety. Her heaving chest indicated her sprint from her room, the grip on her phone tight with trepidation.

Swallowing the lump in my throat, I looked her in the eyes,

"Okay. We have to look, right?" My words hung in the air, our mutual fear creating an invisible bond between us.

Jessie nodded, a determined glint in her eyes as she managed to croak out, "Unfortunately, yes."

With a shared deep breath, we both bowed our heads towards our screens, our fingers tapping in unison. A heavy silence draped over the room as we each scanned the email, our breaths held hostage by our apprehension.

In the echoing quietness, Jessie's voice cut through like a fragile thread, barely above a whisper: "Oh, my god."

And in perfect synchrony, the words slipped from my lips, "Holy shit."

Our eyes met across the room, the silence echoing with unsaid words. Our gazes spoke volumes, our shared victory reverberating in the quiet space between us. We did it. Both of us had made it. Four grueling years of unyielding work, sweat, and determination were finally paying off. We were inches away from securing our positions at one of the most renowned design firms globally—our dreams teetering on the edge of reality.

"Did Noah get in too?" My voice trembled as I scanned the email again, the incredulous joy making me doubt the words that glowed on the screen.

Jessie nodded, her eyes glued to her phone as she relayed Noah's text, "Yes, him and someone who's an expert in historic preservation. I don't think we've had many classes with him, though." Her voice was filled with a strange mix of excitement and relief.

The adrenaline rushing through my veins gave way to a sense of purpose as I navigated the link from the email, leading to their online system. My fingers danced over the keys, entering my information, agreeing to a noncompete clause, and providing an emergency contact. As I hit the "submit" button, a sense of fulfillment washed over me. I was now officially on the path to joining Spectra Creations.

The thrill of victory was abruptly replaced by the swift return to reality. After setting up our accounts, we received another email, an agenda of what was expected of us. It was clear they expected us to hit the ground running come Monday morning. We were there to absorb knowledge, do the heavy lifting, but also to revel in the opportunity that lay before us.

Jessie's voice pulled me from my thoughts, the echo of her words wafting through the hall, "Drinks to celebrate?" A fitting end to a day of life-changing news, I thought, smiling at the prospect.

A couple of hours later, Jessie and I were making our way down the cocktail menu at PDT, a hidden bar that's only accessible through a phone booth inside a hot dog restaurant. The bar had strict rules on loud chatter, so I kept my tipsy voice quiet as Jessie and I caught each other up on everything going on in our lives outside of waiting for Spectra's email.

"Oh my gosh, how *is* your boss situationship?" I remembered that Jessie had been oddly quiet about the aftermath of accidentally hooking up with her new boss. "Has that gone anywhere?" I whisper-yelled across our table to Jessie.

Jessie took a moment to sip her drink before replying. "Well, she's technically still my boss," she shrugged nonchalantly, a hint of something elusive crossing her face. Then she added, with a smirk, "But considering today's news, not for much longer, I guess."

Seeing the slight hesitation in Jessie's demeanor, I pushed further. "And . . .?" There was clearly more she wasn't saying.

She took another sip before speaking, "Well, yes, we've . . . we've been hooking up a bit more. Still happening, I guess." Her cheeks tinted a lovely shade of pink, and she quickly added when she noticed my shocked expression, "It's really not a big deal, Emma!"

I placed both palms down on the table on either side of my drink, "No big deal?! Jessie Louise—"

"That's not my middle name."

"Jessie Elizabeth Marie Louise." Jessie shook her head no at each one, but I continued, "You have a boss with benefits situation going on. This is major."

She rolled her eyes slightly, but then leaned closer, keeping her voice low. "Don't get me wrong, the sex is amazing. She wears these classy skirt sets that just . . . drive me crazy in this peculiar Girl Boss kind of way, but . . ." she darted a look around the bar, as if fearing being overheard, "I don't know. I feel . . . unsettled. Like there's something else I should be chasing. But the thing is, I'm not sure if even if the right answer came strutting through that door, I'd recognize it." She sighed heavily, leaning back into her seat, looking genuinely bewildered.

As if on cue, I turned and my eyes widened to see Liam, along with Dominic, stepping through the door. Liam must've received my text about joining us for drinks.

Swiftly, I swung back around to Jessie, my eyebrows shooting up into my hairline as a sly grin spread across my face.

"Absolutely not," she denied, but I couldn't miss the flush creeping up her cheeks once more as she hid behind her glass.

"You two seemed to have . . . some sort of connection?" I asked, knowing I could only squeeze in one question before the guys would make their way over to our table from the bar.

Jessie bit her lip, looking slightly uncomfortable, yet there was a sparkle in her eyes, a glimmer of intrigue. "Maybe. I mean . . . he's . . . interesting." Her gaze was fixed on her glass as she traced its rim with her finger. "I just . . . I don't know, Emma. I've got a lot on my plate, and I'm not sure I can handle any more . . . complications right now." She shrugged, her voice a near whisper, "But, I can't deny there's something about him that's . . . captivating."

She whispered the last part as the guys walked up to our booth and slid in, Liam on my side and Dom next to Jessie. He placed his arm on the back of the booth, semi-enveloping Jessie, and I noticed she subconsciously turned her knees toward him.

We excitedly updated the guys about our positions at Spectra, elaborating on the projects we hoped to be assigned. While they didn't fully grasp the prestige of Spectra or the leverage it would give us in the professional world, I remained firm. "Believe me," I insisted, polishing off my cocktail, "in the realm of design, Spectra is the apex. The opportunity to be part of their team is worth its weight in gold."

Jessie explained how well-known designers all got their start at Spectra when suddenly, her voice came to a halt.

I glanced up, and her eyes were wide and locked to the door of the small bar. Her eyes moved frantically as she whispered, "Shit, shit, shit! That's my boss. That's her. Right there. Walking in. Right now."

I spun around and had to lift myself up a bit to see over the high wall of our booth, and sure enough, there was a preppy, blonde, *very* leggy woman walking in right now. "Holy shit, Jessie, she is *hot*!" I looked over at Jessie, who had her head resting on the table, "Jess . . . you might want to look up."

Jessie groaned into the wooden tabletop, "Whhhyy?"

"Because your hot boss is walking over here. What is her actual name, by the way? I can't possibly keep calling her hot boss." I spoke quickly because Hot Boss™ was steps away from our table.

Jessie looked up just in time, fixed her face, and greeted her boss with a smile. "Reagan! Hi!"

She introduced everyone at our table in rapid succession, and after rounds of waves and nods, Jessie inadvertently amplified the tension in the air.

Jessie reached over to tug at Dom's arm and urged Reagan to join us, "Come on in! We can make room!" Dominic said nothing as he scooted closer to Jessie and sat sandwiched between the two women. He leaned back against the wall of the booth as Jessie and Reagan leaned forward to be able to see each other.

Reagan was the very definition of bubbly and preppy, and my eyes darted back and forth between her and Jessie to try and make them make sense. Jessie had never really had a type, so I shouldn't have been surprised to see her attracted to two very opposite ends of the spectrum of hot. She practically had Barbie and Satan sitting next to her, hanging on to every word she was saying.

I noticed a few times that Reagan's hand had landed on Dom's muscled forearm as she spoke. She'd lean forward to speak across the table and rest her hand on his arm, but at some point, I noticed a tight squeeze before she removed her hand. Jessie noticed it, too, and a strange look of conflict spread across her face.

As the night wore on, the tension between Jessie, Reagan, and Dom only intensified. Liam and I exchanged knowing glances as we watched the three of them dance around each other, playing a dangerous game of flirtatious cat and mouse.

Liam's hand stayed rested on my thigh the entire evening, making small circles with his fingertips on the fabric of my dress. Our history allowed us to fall into comfortable ease around each other, and I clung to it like a lifeline.

After what felt like forever, Reagan decided to call it a night. She gave Jessie a knowing look before sliding out of the booth. Our group was silent as Reagan walked through the tiny bar and out the door. I glanced over at Jessie to try to gauge how she was feeling, but her face was set into a confused stare, her brows furrowed, and her hands tight around her drink.

After Reagan left, the energy in the room felt oddly lighter, but that might have been the alcohol setting in, dulling my senses. The night wrapped up on a warm note, and as we departed, I found myself torn. Liam's hand on my shoulder felt so familiar, so comfortable. The kisses he kept placing on the top of my head a new habit I was starting to crave. His laughter rang in my ears, sparking an affectionate feeling I had come to miss.

As the cab pulled away, and Liam's figure grew smaller in the rearview mirror, I couldn't help but question if exploring the territory of "us" again was the right thing to do. His comfort was seductive, but the stakes of losing a friendship were high. And yet, as the city lights whisked past me, I wondered if I had the strength to keep him at arm's length once more.

TWELVE

Jessie and I stepped out of the cab and onto the busy New York City sidewalk, both of us wide-eyed and clutching our portfolios. I had only changed three times before settling on simple wide-leg black trousers and a striped button-up. We glanced at each other and then up at the imposing steel and glass structure that housed Spectra Creations. It was a beautiful building, sleek and modern, its mirrored exterior reflecting the vibrant energy of the city around it. It was our first day, and despite the early hour, the street was bustling with people, each one seemingly just as hurried and determined as us.

As we stepped through the glass doors of the office building, we were immediately swallowed by the frenetic energy of Spectra. There was a weird mash-up of serene design and lounging corners surrounded by the chaotic energy of people speed-walking to their next destination. I looked over at Jessie, her face mirroring my own feelings of being simultaneously overwhelmed and excited.

It was an honor to be here, I kept reminding myself. We had

been chosen to be here. Our internship had been held in one of their satellite offices on campus, so we had never stepped foot into the main headquarters before. It just might knock the wind out of me.

After checking in at the front desk, we were told where to find our respective departments. We stood at the shiny elevator doors, waiting for the doors to open. When I stepped off the eleventh floor, I turned to Jessie, still in the elevator, waiting to go up to the eighteenth. We weren't pulling off the cool, calm, and collected vibe I was hoping we could today. We absolutely looked like newbies, and I hoped we wouldn't be eaten alive for it.

Our first day involved a lot of gawking at the incredible talent shoved into one building, drooling over project updates pinned to the walls, and loads and loads of orientation videos. If I hadn't known any better, I'd have thought we were getting inducted into a beautifully designed cult.

Three facts were hammered into us within the first hour of our employment at Spectra:

1. It was an honor to be here, and we should never forget that. There's always someone ready to take your spot.
2. There was an ironclad noncompete in place, one we'd already signed. Our time and creative energy were for the sole purpose of Spectra.
3. Spectra owned any design or creative concept we produced while working for the firm, whether during office hours or not.

I knew I had no plans other than Spectra, so I happily

signed anything and everything they put in front of me. I would be happy to carry out the entirety of my career here. There were projects lining the walls that might have my name on them one day. This was everything that I had worked for.

Three long days passed before we even bumped into Noah. During a brief break from our duties, Jessie and I managed to sneak off for a quick snack, only to be interrupted by a familiar voice echoing in the hallway. It was Noah, who, predictably, had already latched onto a senior designer to curry favor with. Noah was quite the divisive character—either loved or despised, there was seldom an in-between.

Without missing a beat, he sailed into the room with an air of brash confidence, grabbing each of us by the shoulders and delivering a kiss on each cheek. Then, with a spin on his heel and a flourish, he was gone as quickly as he had arrived. Once he was out of sight, Jessie and I descended into a fit of near-hysterical laughter. Mid-giggle, I hastily stuffed the remainder of my cheese stick into my mouth just in time to notice my manager strolling past the glass walls of the break room.

The inaugural week as full-time designers at Spectra felt like being tossed into a whirlwind. Our days blurred into a dizzying mix of client meetings, concept presentations, and urgent deadlines that reverberated down the sleek hallways. The learning curve was steeper than anything we had ever encountered, and we were expected to adapt instantaneously.

Every evening, Jessie and I would drag ourselves back to our shared apartment in the West Village, completely exhausted, but bubbling with a mix of satisfaction and eager anticipation. The grueling hours and ceaseless challenges were offset by the euphoria of being part of an entity that was shaping the city's architectural landscape.

Over steaming mugs of tea in our cozy living room, we'd unwind from the day, swapping tales of the eccentric senior designers we were learning from, the complex projects we were assisting with, and the little victories we'd managed to claim. Even with the exhaustion seeping into our bones, we couldn't shake off the thrill of being an integral part of something we'd only dreamed of.

By the end of the week, all I wanted to do was crawl into bed and melt into my mattress. My feet hurt from the pumps I had to wear and speed-walk in all day. My face hurt from smiling at new people. My head hurt from nodding in agreement all week, ready to please.

My phone buzzed on the desk beside me, pulling me away from my thoughts. A text message from Liam filled the screen, his name making my heart do a little leap in my chest. It was always that way with him: familiar yet exciting, like coming home but still filled with the thrill of the new.

Liam: Hey, E. Survived your first week? ;)

Emma: Barely. And only because the alternative was death by orientation videos.

Liam: How about you come over in the morning so I can cook you breakfast?

Emma: Oh, yes, please.

Liam: I also owe you. If you're up for that...

Emma: You owe me?

Emma: Oh.

Liam: Goodnight, Em. Sleep well ;)

That sonofabitch. He had to know precisely what he had just done to me. After that day, I might have had to take matters into my own . . . hands, but I also wouldn't be mad at Liam for feeling like he needed to make it up to me.

The next morning, I left a sleeping Jessie and hailed a cab over to Liam's apartment.

"I can smell that bacon from the sidewalk," I said as my way of greeting. "I hope your coffee is just as strong."

Liam flipped a piece of bacon with one hand and handed me a cup of freshly brewed coffee, with just a tiny splash of creamer (just how I like it), with the other.

"Now, *this* is service." I took a deep inhale of the coffee and grinned into the mug.

"Well, I am hoping to get into your pants later, so I do have ulterior motives," Liam said while flipping the rest of the bacon.

I almost choked on my first sip of coffee. "Oh, really?"

"I did a disservice to you the other day." He finally sat the tongs down and walked over to me, cornering me to the counter. "It wasn't very nice of me to let you walk out of here without coming." He kissed the top of my forehead. "It won't happen again."

My mouth opened and shut, but no words came out. Instead, I walked around the apartment, taking in the morning city views outside the tall windows and the severe lack of furniture in his space.

"You know," I took another sip of coffee, needing its fuel in my veins, "I do know some great designers who I bet would love to help you make this . . . come together."

Liam chuckled, "Thanks, Em. But I have a feeling there's only one designer I want to come together with right now."

I blushed but couldn't help but smirk. "Well, let me finish

this coffee and breakfast, and then I'll consider taking on the project."

Liam raised an eyebrow. "Is that all it takes to get you to do what I want?"

I laughed, "No, but it's a good start."

I should've been more annoyed at how good of a cook Liam was, but seeing as I mainly lived off microwavable pasta products, I couldn't be that mad. He'd prepared the bacon extra crispy, but the showstopper was the fresh loaf of sourdough bread he'd made into French toast. He'd drizzled some homemade blood orange and honey syrup concoction, and I had audibly moaned when I took my first bite.

"What can I do to hear that sound again?" Liam winked over his coffee mug at me, and I rolled my eyes but couldn't hide the red splotches that threatened to take over my chest.

"Where did you learn how to cook like this anyways?" I asked as I blushed, trying to steer us back to less sexually charged conversation.

"I lived with a great group of guys back in LA." He turned his attention back to his plate and continued, "We decided to take some cooking lessons one summer to avoid having to go back home. I kind of got addicted to it." He winked as his filled his mouth with a giant fork full of bread.

"Well, aren't you just full of surprises," I said as I licked a bit of sauce off my bottom lip. I watched as Liam's eyes tracked the movement of my tongue.

His voice was low when he said, "From what I remember, you had your own surprise to show me; is that not correct?"

Nerves fluttered in my belly but mixed in with the nerves was a feeling of excitement. I remembered how good his hands felt on my skin, how his touch ignited a fire inside me that I couldn't ignore. I wanted to feel that again.

I stood up from the barstool I was sitting on, and Liam's eyes followed me as I made my way to the bathroom. I felt his gaze on my skin like a caress, and I couldn't help the shiver that ran down my spine.

Liam was standing in the doorway by the time I got the water turned on and the old knobs adjusted so the water would be hot comfortable, and not hot scalding.

Liam's hand found the side of my face, and he cupped my cheek, lifting my chin to look up at him. He grazed the rough pad of his thumb over my bottom lip, and it sent chills down my spine. I arched into his touch, and I swore his eyes went a shade darker.

"Kiss me." I heard myself talking but didn't remember forming the words in my brain.

But Liam complied, happily, greedily—he kissed me.

And his kisses settled into my mouth like they were always meant to land there. The culmination of my daydreams about him and what he could be up to bubbled up to the surface, and I took it out on his mouth.

I had to pull away, or I might have ended up jumping his bones right here on this tiled floor, but I remembered that I owed him a demonstration. I pushed lightly on his chest, and he took a step back, taking in deep gulps of air, his eyes wild.

As my fingers slowly traced their way down the row of buttons on my top, I felt the cold, sharp plastic of each one pressing into my fingertips, offering a minute resistance before giving way. I was acutely aware of Liam's gaze, roving over my form, etching the memory of my silhouette into his mind, memorizing the new terrain being presented to him. His eyes then began their journey upwards, landing back on mine, only this time they held a lingering intensity.

A shiver ran down my spine as I locked onto the raw desire flickering within his eyes, a silent encouragement spurring me on. My top slid from my shoulders, pooling at my feet, and soon, my pants joined it, leaving me standing before him in nothing but my simple black underwear and bra.

Liam's eyes seemed to be magnetically drawn to my body, the flicker in his eyes transforming into a flame. His hands trembled subtly at his sides, a silent battle of desire versus restraint being waged within him. He yearned to touch, to explore, yet he dared not move, as if fearing that any action might shatter the spell we found ourselves under.

Liam's gaze was fixated on my body, and I could see his hands twitching at his sides, wanting to touch but not daring to break the spell. My brain was racing with endless thoughts. But the one at the forefront was an intense happiness that I was here. With him. I was almost happy that I didn't hear him call my name outside of his apartment years ago.

Time needed to pass between us. Experiences needed to unfold so we could be who we are now. For each other. So that we could be given the chance to be ourselves for each other. This moment, this intimate surrender, felt like a crossing point. An invisible threshold that, once crossed, irrevocably altered the path we were on. There was no turning back now, and in that realization, I found an intense happiness.

I reached behind me to test out the water, and it was still hot, so I stepped in.

"Show me how the shower head works." His voice was thick and a little groggy. He stood leaning against the far back wall of the bathroom, far enough away so he didn't decide to get in fully clothed. His face was pained with the restraint of holding himself back. But I knew he wanted this show. He wanted to watch *me*.

I turned around and reached up to detach the shower head. I tested a few of the settings to find a nice but firm pressure. I locked eyes with him as I lowered the shower head down the front of my body, tracing my nipples first, making them pucker. His eyes left mine and watched the slow movement of the showerhead.

The stream hit my core, and I flinched slightly since even just kissing him got me worked up, the nerves sensitive. But the pressure felt good, so I made small movements with the shower head, and a quiet moan slipped out of my mouth. I kept the shower head angled just right since the shower curtain was thrown open and wasn't there to catch the spray.

I pressed my lips together, and a satisfied hum hummed from me, and I could see by the way he shifted that he was holding himself back from joining me. I rolled my head back and reached up to pinch my nipples as I brought the shower head closer to my throbbing center, and I heard Liam suck in a breath.

The pressure was so intense and building deep in my belly. I reached out to place a hand on the wall to steady myself because I knew it was coming. Hell, I'd been wound up since the other day when we almost got caught.

I didn't let my mind wander to how exposed I was right then in front of him. Instead, I took a deep breath, brought the pressure a little closer to my core, and I exploded for Liam.

When my breath and the water started to cool, my brain went into overdrive. Had I just crossed a line that should've stayed firm between Liam and me? I remembered the type of women he'd busied himself with during college. Their petite figures had graced the presence of his social media feeds.

That wasn't me. The similarities I shared with Liam's type started and stopped with the color of our hair. The texture of mine was course and wavy where theirs fell straight. Their skin smooth and light where mine deepened multiple shades the minute I stepped into the sun and had signs of quickly growing curves stretched across it.

My nerves threatened to bubble over the surface as I shut the water off, but when I turned Liam was there, arms wide holding a towel. His hand was held out for mine to grab as I stepped over the edge of the tub. He placed a kiss on the top of my shoulder as he rubbed the soft towel over my skin, drying me off.

"You are unbelievable, Emma. That's going to live in my brain forever." His voice was deep and low.

"I honestly can't believe I just did that." My voice came out a little shaky, both from the nerves and the lingering presence of the orgasm that just came out in full force.

"Did you enjoy it?" He wasn't just asking about the orgasm, but all of it. Did I enjoy doing that in front of him? Did I enjoy taking charge like that and being on display?

The answer was clear even as the flutters in my belly continued. So I said, "Yes."

Liam leaned against the doorframe of the bathroom as I dried the rest of my skin off and slipped back into my clothes. His eyes darted over my body, taking in pieces of me that he'd never seen before.

"Do you think I just ruined us?" I voiced the worry that was sitting heavy in my gut.

He shook his head as if clearing his thoughts. "What?"

"Things will be different now. After that." I titled my head back over toward the shower. "We just got to be friends again and I—" I swallowed loudly, suddenly sad. "We've crossed a line now."

"Emma, I'm sorry that I haven't made this abundantly clear, but let me do that now." He walked over to me and tucked my hair that had started curling up from the steam behind my ear. "I have no intention of losing you again. Back then, when I came home to help you pack, I knew something was different. At least for me."

My heart beat in my chest as he continued, "But I didn't want to say anything that would stop you from going to New York. You needed to be here, and I needed to . . ." he glanced around the room, trying to find the words, ". . . figure myself out. But now that I'm here? I hope we keep figuring this out. Together."

I stared up at him, letting his words sink in. It was hard to believe that he felt that way about me, especially after everything that happened between us. I felt a small smile creeping onto my lips, "I'm glad we're on the same page."

He leaned in, pressing his lips against mine in a soft, lingering kiss. His hands moved down my back, pulling me closer to him, as if he wanted to keep me there forever. I felt his fingers skim over the hem of my shirt, and I pulled away, a little breathless.

"Liam," I murmured, my heart racing. "We should probably stop before we get carried away again."

He nodded, but I could see the hunger in his eyes. "Right. Sorry."

I laughed softly, "Don't be sorry. I just don't want to ruin things between us."

He leaned in, pressing his lips against mine once more. "You won't. I promise."

As he pulled away, I let out a soft sigh. Part of me wondered if we were moving too fast, if we were risking everything we had just found again. But another part of me didn't care, didn't want to think about anything but the warmth of his lips and the feel of his body against mine.

THIRTEEN

Life had a funny way of accelerating when you least expected it. As Jessie and I navigated the whirlwind of life at Spectra, Liam and Dominic were caught in their own tumultuous storm. Days bled into nights as they scouted out potential properties, combed through the city's architectural relics, and incessantly dialed numbers to secure the necessary funding. The pulse of New York became the rhythmic backdrop to their relentless quest.

Liam hadn't exaggerated when he mentioned Dominic's mother's reputation as a renowned sex therapist. I remembered the distinctly captivating voice of Gianna Esposito from her podcast episodes I'd listened to years back. Her radiant face was a familiar sight in the self-help section of bookstores, the back covers of numerous books advocating for open communication as a gateway to improved sexual experiences.

The progress of their venture seemed to rest on the shoulders of Gianna. With her esteemed reputation and extensive knowledge, her involvement could sway the scales in favor of securing the investors needed. Throughout this, Jessie and I navigated a tightrope, treading carefully around discussions about their property, respecting the invisible boundary set by our noncompete agreements. We danced around topics, whispering about the potential shapes the building might take, the vibrant life that might pulse within its walls once chosen and transformed.

Yet, as the days rolled by, it became increasingly challenging to maintain our silence. As designers, we were bursting at the seams with ideas and opinions, especially when it came to the architectural structure and interior design of the space. Spectra's noncompete loomed over us like a dark cloud, stifling us, instilling a constant anxiety. There were times when I found myself apprehensive about even contemplating their club's design, as though Spectra might somehow pluck those thoughts straight from my mind as I slept. I started to see Spectra not just as a golden opportunity but also as an iron cage, tempering our enthusiasm and creativity.

Even if Dominic's family was ready to throw in all their considerable wealth, working with Spectra would be off the table. Spectra wasn't just about the money, it was about the image, reputation, and the scale of the projects they undertook. They dealt with monumental, prestigious designs—sprawling airports, state-of-the-art hospitals, illustrious libraries, and grand university buildings. A venture like Liam and Dominic's, no matter how promising or innovative, simply wouldn't align with Spectra's portfolio.

As much as Liam was hoping to dismantle some of the taboos around sex positivity, the shame for most was still there. But the shame must not exist in the Esposito household because from where I sat at Liam's kitchen counter, I could hear

Gianna, Dominic, and Liam excitedly talking about what was coming next.

Gianna would ask about the privacy that could be created in both public and closed-off spaces, and Dominic would chime in to comment on the amount of space available for demonstrations. Liam had sent them the top three contenders he had in mind for the final location, and he excitedly pointed out the historical aspects of the building he wanted to keep.

The conversation turned to funding, and my ears perked up when Gianna suggested a Fourth of July party at their home in the Hamptons for the guys to chat up some investors. Dominic's parents would ensure the right people, with the deepest pockets, were invited if the guys made sure they had their pitch down.

Liam ended the call, and I couldn't help but feel a flutter of pride in my belly for their progress. Slowly but surely, the safe space Liam wanted to create would come to life. Liam stood and stretched his arms over his head, causing his shirt to ride up, and my eyes couldn't help but trace a line from the hem of his shirt down to the top of his pants.

He winked at me, like he knew what I was watching, and said, "Wanna go to a party with a bunch of rich people?"

"Hmm, let me think about that." I pretended to ponder my options before shrugging. "Okay, I guess I can make that work. Do you guys have your pitch down?"

Liam groaned and made a face, "No, we don't even have a name for the space yet."

"Well, that could be an issue. You and Dominic must be on the same page for the project." I got up to stretch my legs and refilled my coffee. "You'll need a name, a mission statement, a brand vision, a growth plan, and a potential timeline for your opening."

He carried his mug to the sink and rinsed it out, "Okay, yeah, that's a lot. I think Dom and I need a little planning session." Liam clapped his hands together. "Wanna head up to the fancy party of the city? Dom's place has some of the best views of central park."

We took a cab over to Central Park Tower, stopping to pick up Jessie on the way, and when we stepped out in front of the building, my jaw dropped. The building loomed over everything around it, its mirrored surface reflecting the sky and park in its large panes.

"How in the world?" My question didn't need to be complete for Liam to understand what I asked.

"Coffee filters, babe." He slid his hand in mine as we headed toward the doorman waiting for us, "And sex therapy."

Jessie trailed behind us, mouth agape at the structure of this building. As designers, we'd definitely learned about the prowess that is Central Park Tower, but to be here at its feet was surreal.

The doorman allowed us in—apparently, Liam was on the list of approved visitors—and my ears popped as we ascended to the sixty-eighth floor. My shoes felt cheap as I walked over the polished marble floor to Dominic's door. Liam knocked twice and twisted the knob, the door opening gently.

Jessie and I were speechless as we walked inside. Dominic's corner unit boasted north and west park views, and it was almost dizzying to look down at the city below.

"We are in the *wrong* business, Em," Jessie whispered as she trailed her hand over the cool stone kitchen countertop that faced the park.

Dominic came out of a room from down the hall, wearing nothing but athletic shorts and rubbing a towel over his wet hair. I heard Jessie suck in a breath next to me and watched her as she watched him, her eyes glazing.

"Are you going to make it?" I teased Jessie under my breath as we made our way into the living room filled with low, comfortable couches.

"Shut up. I don't know what you're speaking of." Jessie couldn't hide the slight twitch of her mouth as she lied.

Jessie and I decided to give ourselves a self-guided tour of Dominic's apartment as the guys settled in to figure out their pitch for the club. The apartment seemingly had endless views of the city; each window offered its own special glimpse into the bustle below. I could only imagine how magical this view would look at night with the city lights glowing.

I could picture Liam and me in one of these guest rooms with the lights off and the only light coming in from the city below. I would walk over to the window and lift the hem of my dress up as an invitation. He would stand behind me; his body would press mine into the glass, and his hands would grip the flesh at my hips.

I would ask him to—"Emma!" I heard Jessie's voice call for me from down the hall, and I shook my head to clear my thoughts. The teasing that Liam and I had done over the last few weeks was making me go crazy.

I found them all back in the living room, pizzas that the guys must have ordered stacked on the edge of the kitchen counter. Liam's eyes found mine, and a smirk appeared on his face. Could he tell what I was thinking? Was it that obvious by the look on my face that I wanted more of him?

"You look delicious in this dress," Liam mumbled in my ear

as I flipped open the lid of one of the pizzas. My face heated, but I smiled. Liam wasn't shy about his thoughts, and I wasn't mad that I seemed to occupy his just as much as he did mine.

"So," Liam said, now down to business, "we've made a lot of progress, but I think we'll button it up faster if we talk it out loud with the two of you. Let us know what's missing or if you're confused."

I glanced over at Jessie and raised my eyebrows; we had talked about how we weren't going to get involved with this project because of how strict Spectra was about outside work. I didn't want to put Jessie in a situation where she felt like she was crossing a line.

"Well," Jessie said, "brainstorming the initial brand stages doesn't really count as design, right?" I could tell Jessie wanted to have a say in this just as much as I did.

"Right." I took a bite of the gooey pizza. "It's just conceptual at this stage anyways. There's no harm in hearing their pitch; it's not like *we* wrote it."

Dominic and Liam looked between the two of us, but it was Liam who asked, "Are you sure? We don't want to put you in a bad position."

Jessie and I exchanged one more look, and I nodded just once. "We're sure. Let's hear it."

As Liam began to share his and Dominic's vision, the room seemed to quiet, every little ambient sound fading away. His words began to paint a vivid picture in my mind, creating scenes from a place not yet birthed. A sanctuary where societal pressures of what's normal and acceptable evaporated, replaced with an atmosphere of acceptance and openness. A haven where individuals could dive deep into their desires and fantasies without a hint of shame coloring their cheeks. A gathering place where connections, deep and meaningful, were born from shared interests and shared experiences.

The image swelled within me, filling my thoughts. It made me reflect on our multidimensional selves that we keep carefully hidden beneath our public personas. It's almost like a kaleidoscope, with each turn revealing a new pattern, a new side. Every one of us chooses which facet we present to the world, while the rest stay buried, seen by a few or none. It was an ambitious goal, to create a place where all these hidden facets could be celebrated and accepted. But seeing the spark in Liam's eyes as he passionately described their vision, I felt the stirrings of a new reality forming.

Dominic cut into the mounting tension, providing a reprieve from the intensity of Liam's vision. "So, with all that being said," he paused for a moment, letting Liam take a breath and grab a slice of pizza, "we still haven't landed on a name."

Suddenly, the pizza and the brainstorming felt mundane in the wake of the world Liam had crafted with his words. I found myself standing, feeling the need to distance myself from the table, to process. I crossed over to the windows, the setting sun casting long shadows over the city. It was that magical time when day began to cede to night, the sky a canvas of crimson and gold.

Beneath, the city began its metamorphosis into the world of night, small buildings sinking into darkness, their outlines barely visible against the encroaching night. Streetlights flickered to life, their glow wavering as they fought back the darkness, a silent battle waged daily. And as the smaller lights struggled, other high-rises began their display, winking into existence like distant stars.

A glint caught my eye. A prism of light, riding on the dying waves of the day, had found a reflective surface on a neighboring building. In that split second, it exploded into a spectrum of colors, vibrant and mesmerizing. And that's when it hit me. I turned around, the idea practically bursting from me, "What about The Prism Society?"

The moment I suggested the name, a sudden silence filled the room, only broken by the distant hum of the city outside the window. The three of them exchanged glances, weighing the name, rolling it on their tongues.

Liam was the first to respond. He leaned back in his chair, crossing his arms, a slow smile spreading across his face. "The Prism Society," he echoed, seeming to test the words. "It's unique. It has a ring to it." His gaze met mine, eyes sparkling with a certain excitement. "It captures the essence of what we're trying to build here."

Dominic, ever the more analytical of us, tapped his fingers against the table in thought. "It's catchy," he admitted. "And the prism . . . it's a good symbol for the diversity and variety we're aiming to celebrate. Plus, it gives us plenty of scope for the visual identity."

Lastly, Jessie spoke up, her tone thoughtful. "It sounds inclusive. Like a place where everyone's welcome to explore the colors of their identity. A society. Yeah, it works." She smiled, her eyes meeting mine with approval.

Their reaction was unanimous, an echoing agreement rippling around the living room. The Prism Society—it wasn't just a name, it was a symbol, a representation of the spectrum of identities, desires, and fantasies Liam and Dominic aimed to cultivate. It was a promise, a declaration of acceptance, exploration, and diversity mirroring the spectrum of identities held within each of us as humans.

FOURTEEN

"Holy *shit*, Dom," Jessie muttered the curse under her breath as we pulled into the long drive off Meadow Lane, one of the most prestigious streets in Southampton (thank you, Google). "Hanging out with you sure has its perks." She punched him softly on the shoulder, and I could have sworn I saw a *blush* creep up Dominic's neck.

My eyes scanned the property through the backseat window, and it looked like there were acres of landscaped grounds tucked behind iron gates flanking the property. The mansion was classic Hampton cottage style with grey shingles and sculpted hedges. With wide eyes, I glanced at Liam, and he shrugged like he expected this more than I did.

Our tires crunched on tiny pea gravel as we pulled up to the wide staircase leading up to the double front door painted a robin's-egg blue. The inside was a luxurious beach style, and Jessie and I couldn't help but gape at the unique interior design, from the nearly black hardwood floors to the jam-packed library on our right. Oversize white furniture filled the living space, and it would have almost looked shabby chic if the walls weren't covered in beautiful modern art.

In their generous spirit, Dom's parents had provided their Hampton home for our Fourth of July celebration. Even though the party wouldn't start until the following afternoon, preparations were already in full swing. As the scent of fresh flowers mingled with the savory aroma of snacks, it was evident that this wouldn't be your average soiree.

Amid the preliminary hum of activity and anticipation, there was an undeniable undercurrent of strategy. Among the crowd of friends and revelers that would arrive tomorrow, a select few had been invited with a particular motive—to interest them in the prospect of investing in The Prism Society.

"You can go pick whichever room you want upstairs." Dom turned to head to what must be the staff quarters. "I'm going to make sure the tables showed up for tomorrow. Make yourselves at home, seriously." He walked away before Jessie, and I could utter a word, our mouths still on the floor at the expanse of this home.

My hand glided over the dark wood railing as I took the stairs to pick a bedroom. Apparently, there were seven to choose from. Jessie was bouncing on her toes, going from room to room, assessing each to pick her favorite. Liam pulled my hand towards a room with double doors and put a finger to his mouth with a quiet "shhhh."

The door clicked open, and my mouth somehow fell further open. Liam must have picked the primary bedroom because it was massive, with a clear arched window view of the ocean. Besides the vast bed, there was our own living room that was bigger than my entire apartment, a fireplace, a private balcony, and a bathroom that could rival most spas.

"Do you think it's okay if we pick this one?" My voice came out as a whisper, thinking we might get in trouble if we were caught in here.

"Dom said to pick whichever one we wanted, so," he extended his hand, palm up over the space, "I say we go for it." He walked over to wrap his arms around my waist, "Let's pretend to be Mr. and Mrs. Esposito for the weekend."

I leaned into his touch, his embrace warm, "Okay, but if he says we should pick another room, let's do that."

"Deal." A knock and Jessie's voice interrupted us.

"Em, did you see the freakin' pool? We *have* to get in." I heard her humming to herself as she unpacked her bag.

I turned to Liam, his hands on either side of my face as he leaned in for a deep kiss. "You and Jessie go ahead; I'm going to see if Dom needs any help." His lips left mine, and I already missed them. I considered pulling him back in and locking the door. Wanting to go further with Liam was all but eating up my every thought.

I found Jessie already lounging at the pool by the time I made my way back downstairs, through the gardens, and onto the deck of the infinity pool that looked like it spilled directly into the ocean.

"Jessie, this is *fucking* insane," I whispered, not wanting to be overheard by any of the staff scattered about.

"I *know*, I feel like we got dropped in some celebrity's life for the weekend. But I am not mad about it, girl." She shrugged off her worn Tori Amos world tour concert t-shirt and dipped her feet in the pool. "Heated. Just like I expected."

I snagged some sparkling water from the refrigerator in the outdoor kitchen and met Jessie in the pool, resting elbow to elbow on the edge, facing the ocean.

"You look happy." Jessie leaned her head on her forearm and squinted at me through the sunlight.

"Your horoscope was very enlightening today." Jessie cracked open her can of Key Lime LaCroix and took a sip. "Here, let me read it." She heaved her body up over the ledge to grab her phone and came back to me to read it.

She cleared her throat before she read from the app on her phone, "An unexplored depth of emotional connection beckons you, inciting an eagerness to plunge into the mysterious waters of a new relationship. The universe whispers encouragement, nudging you forward." She winked at me before continuing, "But remember, dear one, every path has its puddles. As harmony blossoms in your romantic sphere, be vigilant. Rocky happenings loom in another area of your life. Watch your steps carefully, for the universe provides both challenges and comfort."

"Well, that's pretty fucking ominous. Couldn't they just stop at the encouraging part?" I rolled my eyes and dunked my head underwater in hopes of clearing the racing thoughts that were running laps in my mind.

When I surfaced, I noticed the pool lights had turned on since the sun was starting to set, and Liam and Dom had made their way out to the pool. Music filled the outdoor speakers, and the guys jumped in, creating a small tidal wave of water that sloshed over the edge. Liam walked through the water to me, his large hands scooped me up, and I let out a yelp as he settled me on his lap.

"Are you okay?" His voice was soft as we glided around the pool. Somehow, Liam was able to tune into my moods even if I hadn't said a word. In the background, Jessie and Dom argued over the playlist. She wanted indie, and he wanted rock—my bet was on Jessie.

I let out a deep breath and nodded, "Yeah, it's just. All this," my eyes scanned the pool and the property surrounding us, "it feels so different than what I'm used to, even in LA. I think I'm still getting used to the mystery that is Dominic." I ducked my head. "And you."

"Me?" He leaned back and tilted my chin up to look at him.

"Yeah, you. You're just . . . I don't know. Different. And I don't know where I fit in with this new version of you." I let out my breath, afraid to look him in the eye, knowing his response could burst the bubble we've built around ourselves.

"I think the thing that I've realized," Liam talked softly as he carried me around the pool, "is that it would've been my childhood *dream* for us to have been a thing back then."

I leaned back and looked at him, confused. "Oh, don't think, for one second, that I didn't think about you and me back when we were younger. I just also knew I would most likely fuck it up."

"What I realized," he continued, "is that I had some growing up to do. I had to detangle myself from my upbringing and really figure out what *I* wanted."

"I think that's what worries me," I cut in, my voice quiet. "I'm worried that I'm just some relic from your childhood who hasn't gone through this growth journey like you. I'm just—me."

"Well, I really like *just you.*" Liam leaned down and gently kissed my mouth. He smelled like citrus, and I could taste the salt from the sunflower seeds he had on the car ride down.

"Do you remember that first night your mom let me sleep over?" Liam asked, and I nodded; I remembered it well. His dad had decided to go on an hours-long sermon at dinner, and when his dad started beating his fists against the table, shattering plates, Liam had fled.

He'd only been fourteen to my twelve, and even then, I had felt the shift in Liam. His lack of trust in his parents exploded around him. He'd come to our back door, thinking he could quietly sneak in, but my mom was sitting at our kitchen table and saw him wide-eyed and scared.

She brought him in without a single question, a mother's instinct speaking to her, and she poured him a bowl of cereal. I'd heard movement from my room and snuck downstairs to see what was going on.

"What are you doing here this late?" I'd asked, my childhood brain having no filter.

My mom had answered for Liam, "He just needs somewhere to stay tonight. So he's going to stay here." This happened countless times over the next few years before Liam could finally move out to LA for school.

"Well," Liam continued, "your house, your mom, *you* gave me so much security back then. Being at your house was like a reset for my entire system. Whenever I felt like raging back at my dad, I came to you."

My brows furrowed at his confession, and he continued, "I guess I still seek you out whenever I want to feel that."

"You deserve to feel that always, Liam," I said.

He nuzzled his forehead against mine. "Yeah," he said, "lately, it's all I've been feeling."

For now, I wasn't going to let myself overthink what was unfolding between the two of us. At this moment, I felt a sense of belonging I had never experienced before. With Liam, I didn't have to pretend or put on a façade—I could just be myself. And for the first time in a long time, I was content.

"Okay, who wants to play a game?!" Jessie's voice carried across the pool and startled me back to reality. I gave Liam a soft smile and dropped from his lap to swim over to Jessie.

Jessie started up a game of two truths and a lie which revealed that Dominic was randomly allergic to kiwi and Jessie had, in fact, hooked up with someone in a bathroom stall before.

A few canned cocktails in, and Jessie started to get curious, "So, what, exactly, is up with the two of you, huh?" She held her can and pointed at Liam and Dominic. "You two seem to be polar opposites but act like brothers. Why?"

I watched as the guys gave each other a glance like they were silently arguing over who had to tell this story. Dominic, with his menacing glare, of course, won.

So Liam started, "Well, we all know my time at UCLA was . . . adventurous." He finished his cocktail and sat the empty can on the small side table in between our loungers. "I wasn't exploring the things I wanted to do in a super safe environment. Everything I was doing was consensual, but," his voice trailed off like he was choosing his words carefully, "it would've just taken one wrong person, and things could've gone south."

Dominic spoke up, "We'd been sharing a house with a group of guys at this point, so I'd been watching him nearly fuck up his chance even to graduate." Liam nodded as Dom continued, "So I shared some resources my mom had given me, and we . . . worked through some things."

Dominic wasn't a man of many words, so I was surprised we got that much out of him. Liam picked up where he left off. "Dom is being modest. He stepped up when I felt really lost and unsure about who I was and ashamed about what I liked." He clapped Dom on the back, "When I shared my idea of opening up a club, he was all in, no questions asked."

"And soon, The Prism Society will be born," my voice cut in, and the group smiled; even Dominic's mouth turned up into what might be considered a grin.

"Yeah, and now, you've somehow suckered us into joining your scandalous adventures," Jessie teased as she stood and stretched her limbs; Dom's eyes followed her every move.

"Well, not officially joining," I cut in to correct. "As much as I wish we could, Spectra is on our ass about our noncompete."

"There *has* to be a way around, though, right?" Jessie moaned as she wrapped herself in her towel like a makeshift blanket. "I mean, is it even legal to say they own our ideas even outside of work projects?"

I didn't know the legality behind the forms we signed, but I was anxious even to skirt the line of potentially breaking their rules. We had worked so hard to land our dream jobs; we were honored to work there, and yet the feeling of wanting to contribute to something as special as The Prism Society weighed heavily on me.

It was almost two in the morning when Liam and I finally decided to call it a night, leaving the twinkling poolside lights behind us. Jessie and Dom remained, locked in an animated debate about whether Batman was, in fact, an accurate representation of "toxic masculinity."

I could still hear Jessie's laughter from the pool as I slipped between the covers and turned to face Liam.

"Do you want to know another truth?" Liam's whisper cut through the dark.

"Yeah, tell me." His hands met mine in between us.

Liam hesitated for a moment, his eyes searching mine as if he were hunting for the right words. Finally, he took a deep breath and spoke, "Being around you is the most comfortable, easy thing in the world. And I'm afraid that one day you'll wake up and realize that you don't like what's standing in front of you." He paused, his fingers tracing patterns on the back of my hand. "And maybe that won't be enough."

As his words settled into the space between us, I felt their weight, heavy with emotion. But instead of pulling away, I leaned in closer, pressing my hand against his.

"Hey," I whispered. "Look at me."

When he met my gaze again, I could see the fear and uncertainty in his eyes.

"You are more than enough," I said firmly. "And not because I say so but because you *are*. I know there are some aspects of you I'm excited to learn more about, but I *know* you, Liam. And you don't scare me."

We drifted off to sleep, our breathing heavy in the dark. Maybe tomorrow will bring the clarity we both felt we needed.

The next day Jessie and I spent most of it together exploring the grounds, getting lost in the maze of hedges, and walking the beach. The guys ensured all the details were coming together for the party that night and were busy checking in with the food delivery, the music, and the drinks. Liam said there would be about thirty or so people coming, all people from Dominic's family's inner circle who wouldn't turn away from an idea like investing in The Prism Society.

When the sun began to set, I stepped out of our room in a lavender minidress with sheer long sleeves. I saw Jessie from across the hall in a pale green t-shirt minidress with iridescent fringe tickling her thighs. We looped our arms in each other's and headed downstairs.

As we made our way to the pool, I couldn't help but feel a bit nervous. This was a big night for Liam and Domnic. Tonight's success could mean the difference between securing investors for The Prism Society or it falling apart before our eyes. I took a deep breath and looked over at Jessie, who raised her eyebrows as if to say, "Let's do this thing."

FIFTEEN

As the summer sun began its slow descent over the lavish Hampton estate, the Fourth of July party was pulsing with life. Laughter and chatter bounced around me in rhythmic waves, keeping time with the sultry jazz music playing softly through hidden speakers.

Clusters of well-dressed guests dotted the sprawling lawn, their laughter carrying on the gentle sea breeze. Waitstaff deftly navigated the scene, balancing silver trays topped with flutes of champagne and a medley of artful hors d'oeuvres.

Amid the crowd, I spotted Jessie and Dominic, deep in conversation with a stylish older woman, likely one of their targeted potential investors. Well, Jessie was doing the talking, and with her hand squeezing his arm every so often, Dominic would take it as his cue to smile and nod. I smiled to myself at their odd pairing, wondering what, precisely, kept bringing them together like magnets.

My fingers felt cold against the dewy glass of my champagne flute, and I took the last sip, the fizzy liquid cooling and scratching my throat. I walked back through an open set of French doors into the warmth of the house.

I saw that Liam had basically been held up in the same spot all evening. He was in deep conversation with a pair of chuckling business folks, his face radiating a fervor that I recognized from our recent moments of solitude. Yet, this wasn't the laid-back Liam I'd known growing up. This was Liam, the entrepreneur, the visionary, commanding attention in a world I'd never imagined him in, yet one where he seemed to thrive.

Seeing him like this solidified just how much I wanted to watch him succeed. I knew he had dived into the real estate world even before he graduated from UCLA, but this would be the biggest project he'd ever tackled. Seeing him like this was as if I was meeting the grown-up version of my old friend, seeing the man he'd become.

I wandered deeper into the house, seeking a quiet reprieve from the bustle of the party. I walked down a darkened hallway, seeing a soft spill of light come from a door that was slightly cracked open. I pushed on the white wooden door and found myself inside a small but stuffed home library.

The room was a trove of stories, its shelves boasting an array of worn spines, the aged parchment smell of old books blending with the musky scent of leather armchairs. Scattered amongst the books were trinkets and curios from Dominic's mother's work. Piles of signed books and a thick manuscript sat stacked on the edge of the desk, and an old cup of tea sat forgotten on a side table.

The pop of the first firework caught my attention, so I opened the doors at the back of the library and found myself on a small, private terrace with perfect views of the colors lighting up the sky. I plopped down on the wide couch on the balcony outside the library and tilted my head back to watch the show.

"Am I interrupting you?" Liam's voice came from the double doors leading back into the library. "I saw you sneak away. It shouldn't surprise me that you found the library." He grinned as he sat down at the end of my lounge chair.

I smiled back at him. "You're not interrupting me; but don't let me hold you back from chatting up the people you need to tonight." His hand squeezed my knee as I said, "It looked like it was going well?"

"It's okay; I need a break from sucking up to so many rich guys anyways." The light from the bursting fireworks danced across his face. "How are you doing? With all of this?" He wrapped an arm around my knee and rested his chin there to look up at me.

I took a deep breath before responding, "It's different, that's for sure. Sometimes it feels like you've done much more growing up in the last few years than I have." I looked up at the sky as fireworks continued to pop off. "I feel like I'm just getting started figuring out what I want."

Liam pulled back and sat up, looking quietly up at the sky. "Why did you leave? You were keeping my legs warm." I extended my arm to reach out to pull him back.

"Sorry," he rubbed his hand down my leg to warm my skin. "I don't want you to feel like I'm roping you into my world if you're still figuring out what you want. You had your whole life planned out before you moved out here, and you're making it happen." His eyes found mine again. "I don't want to mess that up for you."

"What makes you think you're messing it up? All of this is

new and exciting—different, yes—but exciting." I took his hands in mine and squeezed tightly, "Can I tell you a secret?"

Liam just nodded, so I continued, "I don't love working at Spectra." Before he could say anything, I added, "I mean, I'm sure one day I will. I'm really grateful to be there, but . . ." he didn't interrupt me as I paused to gather my thoughts. "It's really cutthroat there, and I can tell I'm going to have to learn how to play 'the game' of the corporate world."

I glanced back up at the sky and whispered, "And I'm realizing that maybe I don't want to play that game. But this was my dream *forever*. It's all I've been thinking about for years, and I don't know how even to entertain the idea of doing something else. But part of me already feels stuck, and I hate that."

"Come work for us. Design for us." Liam said it like it was no big deal. Like it was easy to leave my lifelong dream for a brand-new project that wasn't even funded yet.

"I can't do that. I don't have the experience; I have no insight into what one of these clubs is supposed to even look like; I—" This time, Liam did interrupt me.

"First of all, you're the most talented, detailed, and creative designer I know. So we don't even need to talk about the experience." Liam held up a finger to make his point, but I looked at him curiously.

"How do you know about my design work?" I asked.

"I told you I crept on your socials." My brows furrowed, knowing I didn't share much about my school projects there. "And maybe I found your portfolio online." I raised my eyebrows at his confession. "And maybe," he continued, "I saw that your work was going to be featured in a showcase, and maybe I came to see it."

My brain cycled back through all the work I'd completed

over the last four years, and it clicked, "You saw my designs for the co-working space, didn't you?"

Liam nodded. "And that is why I know you could design for The Prism Society. You know, the club that *you* named."

I ignored his last comment and asked, "You said 'first of all.' What are your other points?"

He smirked. "And two," he said, lifting another finger, "I can take you to a club so you can see what it's like." His eyes roamed my body as he added, "So you could get the full experience."

I wet my lips, eyes locked on him. "I can't just leave my job. This was my plan. I always follow the plan." I said it like I was trying to convince myself too.

"Fuck the plan." My eyes widened at Liam's declaration. "I mean," he continued, "keep the job if you want. I will fully support you if that's what you do. But don't let a decade-old plan dictate what you want to do *today*."

My chest was warm from the champagne, from the thought of visiting a club with Liam, and from his undeniable confidence in what I could do. It was nice to be believed in so unequivocally.

We sat in silence for a moment, eyeing the sky and the fireworks still lighting it up. I let his words sink in, and I allowed myself a moment to dream. What if my life went on a different path? Would that be so bad? But to be the designer for a club as salacious as what I imagined The Prism Society would be would basically seal my fate in the industry.

I would go from a freshly hired junior designer at one of the more prestigious firms in the country to a small business owner and designer of a literal sex club. I wasn't sure if I was ready to cut ties on my long-held dream.

My voice cut in through our daze, "I don't think I can leave Spectra, Liam. I don't think I've given it the chance it deserves. Maybe it's supposed to feel hectic and cutthroat."

"I get it." His voice was reassuring and safe. "I really do. You're going to do incredible no matter where you are."

His hands found my thighs, and they squeezed. "But that still means I need to take you to a club so you can fully understand what I'm hoping to create."

"Now tell me," he continued, "what experience would *you* want to create at the club, hmmm?" I threw my head up to the night sky as his tongue made its way down my throat. "A little exhibitionism, maybe? Where we sit outside at a party, and I slide your panties down to leave you bare for me?" His fingers slid up my thighs, and he hooked his fingers in my panties and tugged them down.

His hand moved up to my chest and up my throat, "Maybe you like it a little rough and want to scream so loud other people hear you?" He squeezed slightly, and I let out a moan.

His fingers trailed back down the front of my dress and dipped under the fabric. He hummed when he could feel my wetness coating the insides of my thighs. He danced his fingers along the inside of my thigh, "Or maybe you want me to bring you to the edge and not let you come?"

"No, definitely *not* that." It's the first thing I said in a couple of minutes, and my throat was scratchy.

He leaned forward and took a deep inhale of my skin, wrapping his large hands around the sides of my hips and squeezing gently. "Emma, you are the epitome of every dirty fantasy I've ever had."

I sighed, my mind racing at the implication of that statement, leaning further back into the lounger as he climbed up on his knees. He sprinkled kisses up my belly and tugged my dress down over my breasts—his touches were slow, like he was trying to memorize every pore of my skin, every mole that scatters my chest. His hand came up to palm my breast, and my head rolled back because he felt so good.

My mind raced with a thousand thoughts and feelings as I watched Liam's hands explore my body. The scent of his skin, a gentle blend of orange and cedar, once a reminder of lazy summers by his pool, would now be forever linked to this moment. I never noticed the way his hair curled beneath his ball cap until it lay between my fingers, and I never fully appreciated the way his hands flexed until he used them to touch me.

His hand trailed up my thigh getting closer and closer to my core, and I sucked in a breath at the anticipation of feeling him again. His fingers gently trailed in the crease of my legs and danced over my belly button.

I release a small moan as he puts his fingers everywhere but where I wanted them, and he chuckled, "So greedy for me, Emma."

I leaned into his touch just as he slid a finger down, finally feeling how ready I was for him. I didn't think it was possible to get this wet with only his soft touches and stares. He hummed his approval and dipped a finger inside. His other hand gripped my backside, and the sharp dig of his fingers in my skin made me lean in more, and his finger sank deep.

"Oh my god, Liam," my breath was already coming out in moans, and it was almost embarrassing the effect his man had on me.

He added another finger and started to slide them in and out as I sunk deeper into his touch. I was convinced this man had magic fingers. I rested a knee on his thigh and leaned closer so he could plant his mouth on my breasts; I gripped the back of his head, tugging him closer.

"I want to taste you." His teeth pulled at my nipple, and I hissed from the pain, knowing I'd be back for more. He removed his fingers, and I already craved the fullness again. He came down on his knees in front of me, and his face dove in without hesitation. Even though Liam is not my first, he is my first to do *this*. I've never felt comfortable asking for it before, and no one else ever brought it up. I certainly didn't think it could feel this good.

His tongue made lazy circles and wide laps at first before he tensed his tongue, and the pressure had me shoving the back of his head to my core before I could stop myself. Holy shit. He hummed, and the deep vibrations had my hips coming off the edge of the bed, but Liam's hands held me down as he continued to feast. Like, truly feast.

He placed a forearm against my lower belly to hold me in place as he added his fingers back inside, and I was going to explode from the pressure. He hooked his fingers deep inside and pressed as his tongue was firm against my clit.

"Liam, oh my go—" my voice trailed off in a stutter as I tried to catch my breath.

"Breathe, baby," he mumbled to my core and placed a quick kiss on the inside of my thigh before continuing.

My skin was hot, and my toes were starting the tense up, and I knew what was coming, and oh my god, I was going to come on his face. Liam growled into me as my insides clenched around his fingers, and that's all I needed to fall over the edge. It came out in waves, my skin still hypersensitive to his touch as he stayed in place to feel it all.

I smiled but grabbed his chin firmly in my hand, turning his face to look at me and giving him a taste of his own medicine, "I *need* you inside me this time. No more playing."

He smirked up at me before quirking a brow, "And what if I want to play in this sweet little pussy of yours?" He moved closer and nipped my thigh.

I wriggled against him, ruffling the dark waves of his hair as my eyes found his, "Then play, but please, just do it inside of me."

He smiled and leaned up, gently kissing me before his hands reached for his zipper, and he pulled himself out, stroking himself. My eyes locked onto the movement of his hand.

He was hard and throbbing, the tip of his cock pressing into me, stretching it. My stomach was tight as I watched it part my lips, the warm throbbing tip that felt better and better with each short breath.

"I'm gonna go slow, okay?" he whispered, and I nodded, the sound of my heartbeat hit the drum of my ears as my breathing grew deeper and deeper, waiting for him to fill me.

When he pushed inside, I felt the weight of his body shift. His weight on my body, the length of him pushed into my core. When he pressed past my entrance, I rested against him, bracing myself. My fingers dug into his back, his skin warm to touch, my breaths heavy.

"Are you doing okay?" He looked up at me as he paused.

I nodded, "Yes, yes, I want more. I'm ready for more." I reached for his back to pull him towards me. Liam slowly inched in, and I felt myself widening to fit all of him; once he'd pressed all the way in, we both stilled, taking a breath before he dared to move again.

"Fuck, you feel so good. I can feel you squeezing me, baby." Liam brought his forehead to mine as he kept his pace slow.

"I want you to fuck me now, okay?" My eyes stared into his. "I'm good. I'm ready."

He growled and slammed his mouth to mine; his tongue skirted over my teeth before diving in. I could taste myself on him. He picked up his pace and gripped my thighs tightly in his hands, and I knew I'd see bruises there tomorrow.

The couch scooted across the balcony floor and finally bumped against the wall as Liam grabbed my legs and tossed them both over one of his shoulders. He gripped my hips for leverage and wrapped an arm around my thigh to dance his fingers over my clit, his fingers spreading me wide.

"Fuck, Emma, you were made for me; you know that, right?" he asked.

Sex with anyone else wouldn't ever be this good. It felt like this because it was Liam, and it was me, and I could only hope that we'd keep figuring out how this could work because I'm not sure I ever wanted to go back. Our breaths mixed with each other, and it felt like the entire terrace steamed up. He brought a hand up to dance on my clit, and I started to hum. The light tickling sensation of his fingers mixed with the deep fill of his cock inside me was enough to bring the warmth back to my belly.

"Liam, I think I'm gonna co—" and my body started to shake, and I didn't need to finish my sentence for him to know. He groaned loudly as my insides clenched around him tightly, and he found his own release, shoving deeply inside me.

He brought his face to mine, "I could live inside you for the rest of my life, and I'd die a happy man."

My heart caught in my throat at his words, and I watched as he folded himself back into his pants and snuck back into the library to find some tissue, and came back to help me clean up.

He held his hand out to me to help me stand and helped my feet step back into my panties, "Shall we go back to the party, my dear?" I chuckled as I slipped my hand into his at what we just did *outside at a party*. Maybe Liam would corrupt me after all.

SIXTEEN

Weeks had passed in a blur of hectic design drafts, client meetings, and coffee-fueled late nights at the Spectra office. Each day, the harsh fluorescent lights cast long, unforgiving shadows as I found myself knee-deep in a sea of fabric swatches. The fine line differentiating various neutral tones became a relentless puzzle, while the sharp scent of hot lamination and the metallic tang of freshly printed architectural plans underscored my growing disenchantment.

The reality of being a designer at Spectra was proving to be a far cry from my once idyllic dreams of boundless creativity and inspirational design. The cutthroat atmosphere, the mad scramble to meet impossible deadlines, and the constant need to impress the senior designers who reveled in the ensuing chaos felt more like a battlefield than a haven for design. The coveted badge of honor of working here was slowly morphing into an invisible cage, confining me within its rigid walls.

However, surrender was not an option. I was here, after years of relentless pursuit and countless sacrifices. I owed it to myself to see this through, to face the challenges head-on, and ultimately, to conquer them.

Liam's offer to design his club lingered in my mind, a tempting escape. But I wasn't ready to jump ship. I did, however, agree to help him scout locations. Over the weekend, we had narrowed down the options to two stunning old buildings in the city. I found myself looking forward to those outings, my heart thrumming with excitement as we envisioned how the dusty, forgotten spaces could be transformed into a vibrant, glamorous club.

Jessie ended up finding me in my cubicle, a fresh, hot latte for me in her hand. "Oh, thank you, my brain is turning to mush over here."

"No problem, I needed an excuse to stretch my legs; I've been sitting in the sketch room all morning." Jessie rubbed her temples and sat on the edge of my desk. "You were out pretty much all weekend; what were you up to?"

I glanced around our open-concept workspace, double-checking for eavesdroppers before spilling the weekend's details to Jessie. "I mean, they were gorgeous, Jess," I whispered, blending my voice into the consistent hum of the office. "In a fixer-upper kind of way. But I'm really hoping he goes for the one in Brooklyn. It's a massive brick building with these stunning arched windows on two sides." A dreamy sigh escaped my lips as I envisioned the potential transformation.

"It'll be a fun project," she added, her gaze shifting to a spot above my head, "for whoever gets to work on it." Her voice took on an unusual high-pitched, punctuated tone that signaled incoming company.

"Good afternoon, ladies." Noah had somehow materialized over the wall of my cubicle.

"Hi . . . yes! Definitely a fun project for someone," I replied, my cheeks flushing a touch too pink.

Noah tapped his fingers rhythmically on the edge of my cubicle divider. "What are you two up to?"

"Just chatting," Jessie answered smoothly.

His brow quirked, "Sounds pretty project-based for 'just chatting.'"

I darted a quick look around the office floor before answering, "An old friend asked for some feedback on a property he's considering. I thought I'd help him out."

Noah hummed thoughtfully, "Just remember our noncompete clause, Emma. Don't want any issues."

I held his gaze, not backing down, "I'm aware, Noah. I was merely advising an old friend. Nothing more."

"Mmm, hmm," Noah hummed again, "I suppose if I hadn't been assigned to the Franklin Library project, I'd be looking for extra experience too."

My frustration bubbled over. I wanted to remind him that he hadn't been the only one who fought to get a place at Spectra. But I bit my tongue, knowing it would do more harm than good.

He continued, oblivious to my frustration, "Anyway, Shea wanted to schedule a meeting with Thompson Textiles. Could you organize that for her?"

"Sure thing," I replied, managing a professional smile despite the increasing desire to roll my eyes.

As Noah sauntered away, I turned back to Jessie. "You think he heard anything?"

Jessie watched his retreating figure before responding, "I don't think so. God, he can be insufferable."

I didn't have much time to dwell on Noah's intentions,

though, because work at Spectra was relentless. As a new junior designer, I found myself buried under a mountain of menial tasks, including scheduling meetings and coordinating with unreliable vendors. The job was not too different from my time as an intern, and I was eager for a more challenging workload.

As the summer rolled into fall, I felt like I was living a double life as I sat buried in administrative tasks at Spectra, but then it would shift when I would meet up with Liam and Dominic and secretly sit in the lead designer role. I couldn't help but give my opinion about which building I thought they should choose or how the front entrance could look.

By this point, Dominic and Liam had secured tremendous funding for The Prism Society. Gianna had chosen the right people to invite to that Fourth of July party, and nearly all of them had financially committed in some way.

Jessie and I had even snuck in a trip to the location I was crossing my fingers for. Inside was musty and dust-covered, but the potential in those high ceilings and brick walls created a buzz inside me. The guys were in negotiations for this building, and I held my breath every time Liam was on the phone with the lender. Hearing him work his magic on why they should let him buy the building was sexy.

Eventually, the four of us fell into an unspoken agreement. Jessie and I wouldn't leave Spectra, but that didn't stop us from moonlighting with Dominic and Liam after hours. Jessie and I didn't acknowledge the major Spectra rule we were breaking, but if we stayed focused and clear on our work projects, then it wouldn't become a problem.

"I'm struggling to figure out what the private floor should even look like," I interrupted our quiet working with my question. Jessie and I had made a habit of heading straight to

Dominic's apartment after work, where he and Liam were usually already working. Tonight, I had hoped to sketch out what the second floor and private quarters could look like.

Dominic had gotten some demo crews over to the building earlier this week, and they were opening up all three floors for us so we could start from scratch. I could literally design this space from the ground up, and my mind whirred with ideas.

"I think that means a visit to The Oasis is in order," Liam said slyly, glancing over at Dom.

Dominic just nodded once. Jessie asked, "What's The Oasis?"

Dominic answered, "It's a private club in Chicago. Their model is the closest to what we want to create here."

My eyebrows raise with curiosity, "And we could just go? Without, like, being members or whatever?"

"It's run by some old friends of my mother," Dominic added. "They would let us tour it, sure."

I glanced over at Jessie and saw curiosity on her face. I shrugged once, a silent question for her. *What could it hurt?*

Jessie tilted her head slightly as if to say: *we might as well check it out.*

"When could we go?" I turned to Liam and watched as his mouth turned up into a silly grin.

"I'll message them now, see if we can get in soon," Dominic answered, his phone already in his hand.

"So what actually goes on in these places?" Jessie asked bravely. "I mean, it's not just all *Fifty Shades* shit, right?"

"I mean, if you're into that, you can find it there," Liam said, and I watched as Dominic's eyes landed on Jessie.

"Hmm," she pretended to contemplate her options, "and

what about nudity? Are there just going to be naked people caught up in orgies everywhere?"

My eyes went wide, hoping to Dumbledore that wasn't the case. Liam chuckled before he answered, "No, it's not a sex *party*; it's a sex *club*. The Oasis, specifically, really just feels like a high-end spa. You just choose your own adventure for what you're up to behind closed doors."

"Spanking. Group sex. Bondage. Whatever you want." Dominic listed off a few of the club's features, and I couldn't help the warmth that spread to my cheeks.

I stood up to carry our takeout containers to the kitchen, needing space for a breather. "You are deliciously flushed right now," Liam's warm voice tickled my ear as he walked up behind me at the sink. "I can practically feel your heartbeat from across the room."

His hands trailed over my lower back, and I shivered at his touch. "I like it when you get worked up. It makes me want to know what's going on in your mind right now."

I swallowed loudly as he slipped his hands up the back of my shirt and around my belly. "Do you want to know what's going on in *my* mind right now?"

I could hear Jessie grilling Dominic about what else The Oasis had in store from the living room, so I said, "Tell me."

Liam grinned wickedly. "My mind is picturing you at The Oasis. You'd be wearing that blue and white dress that I like. I don't know if you know this, but when the sun hits that dress just right, I can see the shape of you underneath."

His breath heated my neck as he continued, "What I want to do with you there . . . I'm not sure if you're ready for."

I turned to face him, my chest red and cheeks flushed, "Do you want to know what's going on in my mind right now?" He nodded, so I continued, "I keep thinking about the views from one of those guest rooms down the hall." I trailed my fingers down his forearm. "I keep thinking about how I bet the skyline looks great as I'm pushed up against the glass."

Liam didn't let me elaborate as he grabbed my hand and led me down the hall, sneaking away as Jessie and Dom chatted away in the living room. The guest room I had sneaked into on my first visit sat quiet and empty. The door clicked shut behind us as Liam ushered us inside.

His mouth crashed into mine as we stumbled further into the room, the back of my knees hitting the edge of the bed. I wanted him, needed him, *now*. I pulled away for just a second so I could shed my layers, and Liam used that time to do the same.

We both let our breaths catch for just a moment as we stood naked, staring at each other. Liam's large hands gripped my waist and spun me around forcefully; a moan escaped my mouth as I reached back up and tugged at his hair. I could feel him pressing into my backside, and I took steps forward toward the floor-to-ceiling windows.

The city lights shown below, the brake lights of cars blinking, the traffic heavy even at this late hour. My hands found the glass, and the heat of my palms felt cool against the thick pane. I pressed my palms against the glass, pushing my waist back into Liam.

A low groan came from his mouth as his hands gripped the skin at my hips tightly. This was the version of Liam that was rough and frenzied, and I craved more of it. I stepped my feet out wide and slid my hands down the window and dared a look over my shoulder.

Liam's eyes were dark, his breathing deep. He lifted his eyes to mine, feeling me watch him, "I'm going to fuck you where everyone in this city can see you."

And right before he pressed my entire body against the glass, I only whispered, "Please."

I hissed at the coldness of the glass against my breasts but obediently pressed against it and brought my arms up over my head. Liam gripped my waist and placed himself in between my legs, tapping himself against my wet core.

He was so hard, so warm, and I moaned as the head of him pressed against my swollen clit. Liam took one hand and intertwined his fingers in mine, holding them in place as he sunk himself deep inside me in one long push.

I held my breath, so I wouldn't scream as he rammed back and shoved himself deep inside me. My skin stuck and pulled against the glass, and my breath made large circles of fog. I could feel the heat from Liam's chest as he moved behind me.

He slid his hand down from mine and placed it gently at my throat while the other hand guided my hips forward and back.

"Touch me," I begged through panted breaths.

And he obliged; he moved the hand from my waist around to the front and lightly swirled his fingers at my heated bundle of nerves. I bucked myself on him, the sensation almost unbearable. He moved the hand at my throat to cover my mouth right before he pinched my clit gently, and I moaned loudly into his palm.

He didn't let up on the frenzy of his fingers at my clit or the depth of his cock as he continued to shove himself inside me. His palm stayed over my mouth as I cried out into it as my orgasm took over my body. I squeezed him tightly, my body now shaking and cold. He quietly grunted as he found his release, spilling himself deeply.

Our breaths came out ragged as he slowly slid out of me, grabbing a tissue off the nightstand to quickly catch the liquid dripping down my inner thighs. He helped me back into my clothes, placing soft kisses on my skin as he did.

"Why don't you want to tell me what you want to do at The Oasis?" I asked the question as Liam was pulling up his jeans.

He took a deep breath before responding, "I don't want to scare you away. I don't want to lose . . . this."

"What if I want it too?" I asked as I ran my fingers through his hair to help smooth it back down, "I know I'm not as . . . experienced as you, but I trust you."

Liam looked at me for a few seconds before he decided to respond, "Watching you explode . . . does a lot for me. I'd love to be able to get to watch the whole process." He tucked a strand of hair behind my ear, "And I think having someone watch you is a thing . . . for you."

"So what would that mean, exactly? Do you want me to, what, just masturbate in front of you?" I was surprised to hear the confidence in my voice as I asked the question; these conversations were getting easier.

Liam smiled, "That, or . . ." He took a deep breath, the real depth of his fantasy on the tip of his tongue. "I'd like to watch as someone else makes you come. I want to be in the room and just get to watch you be fully immersed in the pleasure of it all."

My eyebrows raised at his confession, a little surprised but not fully against the idea. "Hmm, so your kink is my pleasure, huh?" I smiled up at him, wanting to reassure him that I wasn't scared. That I wasn't turning away.

"One of them, yes." He leaned down and kissed me deeply,

a silent thank-you. "I think we should probably get back out there they might be wondering where we ran off to."

"Or Dominic finally decided to make a move with Jessie," I said, half-joking.

"Oh, that would be something, wouldn't it?" Liam said as we tried to turn the knob as quietly as possible.

It turned out no living room hookups happened, which is probably for the best as we walked out to Dominic and Jessie in an intense discussion about the psychology of colors and the paint choices they should make for the club.

I smiled to myself, proud of the odd little friend group that the four of us had formed. I was anxious at all the boundaries Liam and I had crossed, but I had to remain hopeful that everything would unfold precisely how it was supposed to.

SEVENTEEN

The screeching of the trains and the chatter of commuters filled the air as Liam squinted at the map, his finger tracing the tangled web of colored lines. The acrid scent of stale coffee mixed with the metallic tang of the turnstiles as we swiped our cards and squeezed into a crowded train car.

The four of us had decided to fly out to Chicago together; a tour of The Oasis was on the agenda. Being in a space that had inspired Liam even to explore opening his own club would help Jessie and me wrap our heads around the design.

After getting off at the wrong stop twice, our New York brains unequipped without directional streets, we finally made it to our hotel downtown to freshen up before we headed over to The Oasis.

Where the vibe I hoped the guys would decide for The Prism Society to have was classic, vintage, and moody, The Oasis was light, airy, and modern. Vast white walls covered with teak wood slats in geometric patterns drew your eye up the two-story lobby to the giant, brass globe lights hanging in the center.

A random passerby might confuse this space as a high-end, members-only spa and never guess what went on behind closed doors.

The owners, Zara and Kai Sterling, found us waiting in the lobby, my face still set in wonder as I glanced around the beautiful space. Zara led the tour, highlighting the areas for spaces she wanted to add upstairs, her bracelets clinging together as she waved her arms around her body. I easily got sucked into her excitement as we traveled across the slated catwalk that connected the two sides of the room over the lobby.

After doing a walk-through of the spaces that weren't marked by plaques labeled *"private,"* we ended up in the downstairs bar. It turned out clubs like this limit patron drinks to two. They understood the need for the calming effects of alcohol but were intentional about keeping the clarity of choice at the forefront. This was something I was hoping Dominic and Liam would implement at The Prism Society.

I ordered Jessie and myself a glass of white wine each, and Liam sat down in a high-top chair and opened his arm wide for me to step into; his fingers drew circles on my hip as he talked to Kai about the progress they're making back in New York.

After a while, Zara spoke up, "Kai, we should leave them now so they can enjoy the space." Zara's voice was calm and relaxing when she wasn't bubbling with new ideas. "They've traveled so far to see it; now, let them relax."

"You're absolutely right, my love." He turned back to Liam and me, "The spa is yours to use as you wish; you can check in through those double doors over there." He pointed to giant teak slated doors.

Jessie and Dominic opted to stay at the bar; perhaps she wasn't quite ready to explore things *in that way* with him. I could tell, however, with the glint in her eye and the way she swirled her glass of wine that she'd still find a way to get Dom riled up.

Inside the teak doors was a true oasis; ethereal music with Tibetan bowl sounds played through the speakers, and a beautiful water feature sat in the middle of the room. The bodies, which were in various stages of intimacy, clued you in on the fact that this was no ordinary spa; they were spread around the ample loungers that formed a semicircle around the fountain. It turned out that there *were* naked bodies around; they were just all behind these double doors.

There were sheer curtains that hung around each of the loungers, so you were unable to make out anyone with total clarity. But even with the filter, I could still see knees spread wide or make out the repetitive movement of slow thrusts. I could still see a woman arch her back and watched as her breasts bounced as she slid down her partner. I caught a glimpse as two women and a man claimed another lounger and crawled into the space. I could only imagine how anyone working the desk beyond the fountain could get any work done all day.

The music and the public displays had an immediate effect on us as we walked in. I was calm but eager to go deeper into the space to find a place for us to settle into. My belly was already warm, and I was curious about what we'd get ourselves into here at The Oasis.

We were greeted by two cheerful faces at the lobby check-in desk and given an overview of the spa and a list of options we could experience. There were private and couples massage rooms, a large grotto where everyone was welcome, the loungers up front, steam showers, saunas, and even a large relaxation room filled with loungers. I got the feeling that the ooze of sensuality wasn't reserved just for this space and that we'd find activity around every corner.

We decided to start with a couples massage in a private room because both of us could actually use one. Unlike other spas we were used to, for this massage, we had to fill out a checklist of sorts of what we would allow in the massage and what we didn't want. But this checklist wasn't about pressure or lotion preferences.

We took our forms over to a small bench. "So . . ." I nervously looked over the sheet of paper in my hand, "what are you thinking about marking on your list?"

"I'm open to exploring whatever you want to explore. We can simply go in and get an excellent massage, or," Liam glanced down at the list, "we can add in some additional features." His grin was a little shy when he looked up at me.

I stared down at my list, suddenly clammy and anxious about what to select. I knew I had the full support of Liam next to me; I just had to voice what I wanted. Why was that so hard?

As I stared at the unchecked boxes on my sheet of paper, I turned to Liam. "You told me that *my* pleasure was one of your kinks?"

"Mmm hmm, I did." He placed his hand on my knee and rubbed gently.

"And you said that," my eyes skirted around the room, "you would like to watch someone *else* pleasure me?"

"I also said that, yes," his face turned from sensual to firm, "but by no means do you have to explore that now or ever if you don't want to."

"But that *could* be something we explored. Here?" I asked anxiously.

"It is," Liam said. "The staff here are professional, calm, and have your safety and consent as their number-one priority. No one would do anything here that you didn't explicitly sign up for."

I nodded and glanced down at my sheet, checking a few of the boxes. We're here at The Oasis, after all, and the feeling of sensuality is heavy in the air.

After changing into thick, soft robes, Liam and I met in the hall and made our way down to our private room. Inside was dim, with candles flickering around the space. Two massage tables rested in the center, just a few inches apart, and a comfortable-looking lounge chair angled toward the tables. It felt good to know we'd be so close to each other. We settled on the tables; the warm blankets fell heavy over our bodies.

Our therapists entered the room shortly after, and pretty soon, warm lotion and oil spread over my back. We left our checklists in a slot outside our room, so I was confident that they knew what we were open for and where our boundaries lay. The tension started to fade as firm hands worked out the knots in my shoulders. My entire body began to melt into the table as my therapist continued working the oil into my skin.

Hands and fingers trailed sensually down my thighs, never touching anywhere privately but rather skirting right around the edges. By the time we were ready to flip over to our backs, my entire body felt like a loose noodle, but my belly was warm with excitement. Liam sat up from his table, put the robe on, and took a seat in the chair facing me. My heart beat heavily in my chest.

Liam had told me all I had to do was hold my hand up, palm out, and all action would cease—I didn't even need to explain. I glanced over at Liam, and he smiled as the sheet slid down from my chest, only covering my middle. Oiled hands reached up from my hips to span across my belly and cover my breasts; my back arched as thumbs flicked over my hardened nipples.

"Are you ready for me to remove the sheet?" A soft voice cut through the air, and I glanced at Liam. I was anticipating hesitation at the idea of watching someone else's hands on me, but his face was dark with lust, and instead of feeling nervous, I felt powerful.

I said yes, and Liam's eyes trailed my entire body as the sheet was removed, and I lay naked on the table. The oiled hands of both therapists worked their way across my belly and hips, down my thighs, over my feet, and my breasts. Liam sat back further in his chair, his eyes never leaving my body.

My skin was shiny with oil in the candle-lit room, and every nerve ending in my body was ignited. Large hands began to grip the skin of my inner thighs, and I knew it was their way to let me know what was coming next. My eyes closed as a warm finger trailed through my middle; the oil mixed with the excitement that was already there. My body was on sensory overload, and I widened my legs subconsciously.

The therapist must have taken the cue because next pressure built as a finger slid inside me. I glanced over at Liam, and his eyes were fixated on my core, his lips parted. I watched as he slid his hand in between the folds of his robe.

"Can you move the robe? I want to watch you." My voice came out breathy, but my request was approved, and I watched as Liam gripped himself tightly. A moan escaped my lips as another finger was added inside me, and they began to slide in and out. Pressure from the palm of their hand was added to my clit, and other hands pinched and tugged at my nipples.

Every nerve ending in my skin was firing, and I knew I

wouldn't be able to hold on for much longer. "Come for them, baby; let them see how beautiful you look when you explode." Liam's voice was thick with desire as his hand gripped tighter and tugged faster.

His demand was all I needed to go over the edge, and my thighs tightened, and my feet drew up as I found my release. Liam wasn't far behind, and I heard him finish beside me as a warm towel was being wiped over my skin. I took a couple of deep breaths and dared a look over at Liam. Did he regret sharing this moment with others? Did he feel weird after watching someone else touch me?

The goofy grin on his face pushed any anxiety I might have had away, but his response was confirmed when he said, "Fuck, Em, that was so hot. I love getting to watch you like that. Did you like it?"

I sat up from the table and slid my legs into the small space between us. I rested my hands on his shoulders, his skin shiny from the lotion still covering his skin, "I loved it because you were right here. It felt like you were still a part of it, you know?"

He sighed deeply and rested his forehead against mine, "I'm glad you enjoyed yourself."

I reached down and trailed my nails up his inner thigh, "Wanna go see what else we can get ourselves into before we leave?"

We decided to head to the relaxation room to see what we could find there. The room was large and oval-shaped, with curved walls and flickering sconces above large loungers. It was very dim, and when we first walked in, I couldn't see much of what was going on.

We made our way down the center aisle and claimed a lounger for ourselves. After a minute, my eyes adjusted, and I saw that the room was nearly empty, with just one other couple at the other end of the room.

Liam found us some spa water and sat down beside me as we cozied up on the lounger. The other couple was too far away to see clearly, the room too dim for details. But the sounds that trickled up from their corner gave away the nefariousness of their actions.

I tugged open Liam's robe and trailed my hand down his chest. His chest was hard, and his skin was tan from when he went on runs, and I wondered when he shifted into someone so *sexy*. The hard lines of his body were the antithesis of the softness and curve of mine. I reached further down to feel the weight of him in my hand, his hardness already back.

He pushed a hand into the flaps of my robe and grabbed a handful of my breasts, and they rested heavy in his hand, the desire making them swell. He leaned down and captured a breast in his mouth, his teeth grazing my nipple softly. I tugged his face closer to my chest, silently begging for more of his touch, and he complied.

I scooted back and leaned against the pillows that lined the lounger, and Liam tugged gently at the tie, holding my robe closed and letting it fall open on either side of me. His eyes took a survey of my skin and the rise and fall of my chest before he dipped his head down between my thighs and inhaled deeply.

A low hum came from his throat as he said, "You are the most beautiful woman I've ever laid my eyes on."

I used to be nervous about the way previous guys would stare at my body; my own insecurities would float up to the top of my brain as they would grip the skin on my hips or smell my arousal. But now I had learned to lean into the power that my body possessed, and my legs widened for him.

I was lost in the feel of Liam's tongue exploring when my ears perked up at the sound of more people coming into the room. My eyes opened slightly to see two couples come in together and watched as they claimed one lounger in the middle of the room. They wasted no time in dropping their robes and settling in together against the pillows.

Two women lay facing each other with, presumably, their partners behind each of them. I watched as they unabashedly started touching each other, hands roaming over bodies, tongues dancing together, fingers disappearing into mouths and other places.

Liam must have caught that my attention was elsewhere because his voice vibrated up from between my legs, "You like watching them, don't you?"

I nodded my head, afraid to trust my voice.

"Then let me make you come while you watch them, baby." Before I could even respond, Liam's face dove back down, and his tongue darted inside me. I gripped the back of his head and pressed it to my core. He was right: watching those couples got me way more turned on than I could've anticipated.

My gaze went back over to them, and I watched as one woman slid down to taste her friend, her own ass up in the air. One of the guys came to her and slid his fingers inside her, making her wiggle her hips for more. So he gave her more; he tapped his hardness at her core before sliding it in slowly, filling her up. His thrusts pushed her forward as she continued to devour her friend.

My eyes widened at the display, still in disbelief that there were places where things like this could go on behind closed doors. I kept my eyes on them as he slowly kept pushing into her.

Her friend must have found her release beneath her because a soft moan filled the air, and the other woman leaned back to kiss her partner. Their sex was slow and drawn out; none of them were in a hurry. Liam matched their pace and slid his fingers inside me slowly, using his thumb to circle my clit.

I watched as the other guy got on his knees and placed himself in front of the woman's face. I watched as the thrusting sped up from her partner as she took in her friend's thick cock deep in her mouth. My eyes widened at the sight, baffled that there were couples who shared like this, in public of all places.

But the sight also warmed my core, and I was soaking wet as Liam's tongue continued its dance. The soft sounds of skin smacking against skin and slicks of wetness filled the air. I felt like an improper queen, laying back and getting devoured while getting to watch the private moments of others.

My release was building deep inside my belly as Liam found the rhythm that he knows will be my undoing. I watched the friend group again just as one guy slid his cock out of her mouth with a pop. He moved to his partner and settled deep inside her, her thighs thrown up over his chest. Everyone was close now; the speed picked up, and the breaths quickened.

I reached down to tug Liam up because I needed to feel him inside me. I gripped his hardness and guided it to my center, getting it wet. Liam pressed inside, and he slid into my warmth. He pulled out only to press right back in, and I knew we wouldn't need long. He reached his hand around to squeeze my clit, and that was all I needed for my muscles to tighten tightly around his cock as a deep pulse ran through my body.

I let out a moan, knowing the other guests in the room could hear me. And I didn't care.

Liam chased my release with his own, and I could feel him

twitch inside me as he came down. The other couples had gone back to soft touches and kisses and must have been prepping for round two because I saw both guys grip their cocks to bring them back to life as the women kissed.

Liam brought me a warm towel, and we exited the room, leaving more people behind us that we hadn't even noticed come in. The Oasis had put a spell on us, and it was hard to shake the lust that buzzed around my brain. I came here expecting just a small tour of the space so I could draw up some concepts for The Prism Society, but I was leaving with its imprint on my soul.

EIGHTEEN

"*Of course,* you look cute in a hardhat." Liam tapped his knuckles on the top of the white hardhat that sat on top of my head as we unlocked the doors to the future home of The Prism Society.

I smiled up at him, gripping his hand as we stepped inside the construction zone. We were finally allowed inside after the demolition crew had come in and torn down as many walls as they could, leaving the floors open and dusty.

The first floor of The Prism Society, even in its skeletal form, promised to be a marvel. Stripped down to the bare essentials, the expansive lobby-to-be still had an air of grandeur. A wide, sweeping staircase invited you upstairs, its railings a ghostly echo of the opulence that would soon manifest. You could already imagine the visitors, swathed in their evening best, stepping into a spacious area dotted with high tables and plush seating. A marble-topped bar could soon stretch along one side, soon to host some of the finest cocktails this side of the city.

Liam and I climbed the unfinished staircase, which I imagined would later be covered in a vintage carpet runner. The second floor would eventually house private rooms for members to live out their fantasies. Even without the polished wooden floors, the ceiling-to-floor windows, and the classic crystal chandeliers, you could feel the room's anticipated elegance.

On the top floor, we were greeted with a blank canvas destined to be the event space for workshops and classes. With its high ceilings and planned skylights, I could already envision the room filled with streams of sunlight by day and sparkling under the city's twinkling lights by night. This space, designed for exclusive gatherings, would breathe an air of understated luxury and refinement.

As we wandered through the unfinished space, I couldn't help but feel a pang of longing. I envisioned myself poring over blueprints and swatches, deciding on lighting fixtures and the exact shade of paint that would perfectly match the bespoke furniture. Yet, I was constrained by the noncompete clause I signed with Spectra. Instead of being at the heart of the design, I had to resign myself to being a spectator on the sidelines, giving my opinion only when I couldn't hold back.

"You sure you don't want to take me up on my offer?" Liam interrupted my daydream, gesturing around at the raw space. He'd asked before, and each time, it was more difficult to say no. "I know Spectra has been the dream, but dreams can shift."

I sighed, looking at him with a sad smile. "I appreciate the offer, Liam. Really, I do. But I can't." My heart ached at the refusal, but I had my reasons, all professional and personal, tangled up into a knot that was hard to untangle. He nodded, understanding but clearly disappointed. I wished things were different, but for now, they simply couldn't be.

"Oh!" I said. "Speaking of Spectra. Our annual design

showcase is coming up. Would . . . you wanna be my date?" I rushed into an explanation before he even had a chance to respond. "It'll be fancy and boring, but you'll get to see our latest projects, meet super-rich clients, that kind of stuff."

He raised an eyebrow, taking a moment to pretend to mull over the information. "A chance to see you in action, huh?" he said, a playful smile dancing on his lips. "Count me in."

Seeing Liam excited about my work, even after I told him every day how stressed out that space made me, was nice. He knew how to push me in a way that let me know he believed I was capable, but he respected my decision to stay with Spectra. After working so hard the last four years, it was a dream I wasn't ready to give up on yet.

"Tell me about the rooms." I turned the conversation back to the space. "What themes are you thinking?"

Liam smiled slyly. "Well, I think we might have room for five on each side. I want to make sure we leave plenty of room for the reception desk and the lounging area."

We walked down what would become a large hallway, and he continued, "I want to make sure we have room for some light BDSM, so some ropes and blindfolds. I want a room stocked full of a treasure trove of toys people can purchase, use, and take home." He spun around and pointed to the other side of the hallway, "I think having a room with a *huge* bed is necessary; oh, and I always thought it would be fun to have everyday scenarios set up for imaginative play."

"Everyday scenarios?" I asked. "Like what?"

"Imagine walking into a room that's set up like a private office. A large oak desk in the middle, chairs facing it, shelves lined with books. A little bit of boss-employee fantasy going on." He winked at me, and I couldn't help the grin that spread across my face.

This was a weird world we existed in together. Certainly, not one I would've ever predicted to be on my bingo card of life, but here we were. I walked us back to where the reception area would be.

"One thing I saw at The Oasis that we didn't use, but I imagine would have been helpful, was their semi-private lounge area outside reception." I walked in circles around the space, imagining what it could all look like.

"Maybe," I continued, "we could have large loungers with curtains over here. And if anything needed to be set up in their room or they just wanted to wait, they could use those spaces." An idea popped into my head, "Oh, and when their room was ready, a small light could turn on in their lounge, letting them know."

Liam smiled at me as my brain kept bursting with ideas. "What else do you see?" he asked.

"I keep picturing the design as dark and moody. Almost like a Parisian art salon." My voice came out in a hurry, excitement bubbling in my chest. "I think you should work with artists and hang their work down this hall in big frames. I'd use flickering sconces on the walls to case a nice glow down the art. For colors, I'm thinking deep jewel tones and—"

I cut myself off, realizing I was rambling. "Sorry. That's just what I keep imagining. I'm sure you have other ideas."

"I love your ideas." Liam's words made my heart flutter, and we exchanged a look, our eyes locked in mutual understanding. But after a moment, I turned away, taking in the room once more.

The construction still had plenty of detail work to be done, but the vision seemed almost tangible now. It was something that we could all have a part of, and for one moment, I almost forgot that I couldn't stay on as a partner.

Even in its unfinished state, the club was starting to take shape. The skeletal structure was there, waiting to be fleshed out into the vision we were creating. It was something we were all contributing to, and for a moment, I let myself forget about the restrictions that barred me from being a permanent part of it.

But even as a temporary contributor, I could see the potential of The Prism Society. A place of exploration, where people could push the boundaries of their desires. A place of connection, where individuals could meet others on the same journey. A place of expression, where everyone was free to be their most authentic selves.

I envisioned the numerous lives that could be touched, the countless connections that could be formed, the infinite discoveries that could be made about oneself. How many people were out there, just like me, hoping to understand themselves better? To uncover what really made them feel alive, fulfilled, truly seen? Why has society made it so difficult, so taboo, to explore our own bodies, our own desires, our own identities?

And in that instant, it dawned on me. The Prism Society was not just a place, it was an idea, a concept that could start a revolution, dismantling archaic societal norms and replacing them with acceptance, understanding, and love. It was a safe haven that might just help me find myself, too.

NINETEEN

The night of Spectra's annual design showcase arrived faster than I'd expected. As I prepared for the evening, I felt a mix of nerves and excitement tingle in my stomach. I applied a final coat of mascara, eyeing my reflection critically before deciding I was as ready as ever.

My dress was a deep emerald-green silk that fluttered to the floor and traveled high up my neck, leaving the back open. The fabric caressed my skin like a whisper, reminding me of the day I bought it. It was the first purchase I made with my Spectra paycheck, a luxury I allowed myself to indulge in to celebrate my achievement. I'd decided to keep my hair up tonight, and it sat loosely pinned in a low bun at the nape of my neck; a few strands fell loose around my face.

A tap on my doorframe revealed Jessie, her petite frame made taller in silver stilettos. She was wearing a strapless black velvet dress and smiled mischievously as she glided into my room. "I just came over to steal your lipstick," she said, her eyes twinkling as I slid tiny gold hoops into my ears. With graceful fingers, she plucked a deep red lip stain from the top of my dresser and leaned in closer to the mirror, carefully applying it to her mouth.

A soft rapt at the front door caused us to turn toward each other, allowing us to give ourselves our last-minute check before heading out. I grabbed my small beaded clutch, dropped my phone and lip gloss inside, and headed to open the door. Liam stood in the hallway, looking effortlessly handsome in a sharp, navy-tailored suit. A soft gasp escaped my lips at the sight of him, and I saw his eyes widen as he took me in.

"You look . . . absolutely stunning, Emma." The words were barely a whisper, but the warmth in his gaze told me he meant it. I could feel a blush creep onto my cheeks at his compliment, but before I could say anything, he extended his arm, a small grin tugging at his lips. "Shall we?"

Dominic had let us use his car service for the evening, so there was a sleek black car waiting for the three of us outside my apartment. Jessie had decided to attend tonight solo, not quite ready to invite Reagan (yes, Hot Boss™ was still a thing) or comfortable enough to invite Dom as her date. As the city lights whisked by us, I couldn't help but feel an air of dreamlike unreality surrounding us. It felt like we were characters in a glamorous movie, heading off to some grand, romantic adventure.

When we arrived at the Spectra Design Showcase, it was as if we'd stepped into another world. The event space was a symphony of sparkling lights and sophisticated elegance. The room was divided into different sections, each displaying a unique design project. The walls were adorned with high-resolution images of the projects, alongside glass cases filled with miniature models, sketches, and fabric swatches, each telling the story of the design journey.

Liam, ever the gentleman, disappeared briefly to fetch us

drinks. He returned holding three flutes of champagne, the bubbles shimmering under the soft lighting. We clinked our glasses together, his warm gaze never leaving mine before we began our exploration of the displays.

We weaved our way through the various exhibits until we reached a small corner where my own work was showcased. It was a humble section—just a few sketches and miniature models that I'd been allowed to contribute to larger projects. As I explained the design process behind each piece, I couldn't help but daydream about what it would be like to have my own design front and center.

"I hope, one day, I'll be able to design more than just fragments of these projects," I confessed, feeling a little vulnerable as I shared this part of my journey with him. "When I joined Spectra, I had such grand plans. . . . But I suppose I should be grateful. I'm part of something big, even if it's not exactly how I imagined it."

Liam squeezed my hand reassuringly, his smile warm and understanding. He didn't say anything, but he didn't need to. I knew there was probably so much more he wanted to say about how my time at Spectra was unfolding, but for tonight, he kept them to himself.

We lost Jessie to the crowd and eventually had no choice but to mix and mingle ourselves. Alone together, we claimed an empty high-top table at the edge of the mingling crowd. It was while standing there, picking over the remnants of the tiny appetizers on our plates, that Ben from my interiors team at Spectra made his approach.

"Emma, delightful as ever," Ben greeted warmly, brushing a light, respectful kiss against my cheek. "You have some fine work on display tonight. Just the beginning, I'm sure."

I swallowed and pasted a professional grin on my face. "Thanks, Ben. One day, hopefully . . ." Turning to Liam, I quickly made introductions, "Ben, this is my good friend Liam. Liam, Ben."

Ben's eyes lit up with recognition as he shook Liam's hand. "Of course, Liam. Your face did seem familiar. How's the historic project in Brooklyn going?"

Liam's expression remained calm, but his eyes betrayed a glimmer of surprise. He started to answer, but I intervened, unable to stifle the prick of curiosity. "Wait, how do you two know each other?"

"Oh, I sit on the New York City Landmarks Preservation Commission," Ben shared, his chest puffing up slightly with the revelation. "I was on the committee that gave the green light for the changes on the Whittier building."

A knot tightened in my stomach. My neatly separated spheres of life were colliding far earlier and more publicly than I was ready for. I had hoped to keep the ambitious dreams of our little Prism Society Crew more covert for—how long, I didn't know—maybe forever.

Liam began to respond, but again, I cut him short. With a forced brightness, I said, "That sounds exciting! Liam and I were actually just about to refill our drinks . . ."

I shot Liam a pointed look, desperate for him to pick up on my frantic need to extricate us from the conversation. But Ben was undeterred, his curiosity piqued. "What's the business that's taking over the space, anyway? We only supervise the facade changes, but the actual operations always intrigue me."

I felt a cold prickle of perspiration breaking out along my spine. The words tumbled out in a rush, preempting Liam's response, "Oh, it's just an event venue, really. A cocktail bar and lounge, quite low-key."

Liam's gaze dropped, a disappointed shadow crossing his face. His smile was tight as he nodded along in agreement with my underwhelming description of his vision. I could feel the sting of my words as I watched Ben's reaction.

"Well, best of luck to you, young man. A cocktail bar in such a historic building seems ambitious, but who am I to say?" His laughter echoed hollowly in my ears as he gave Liam's hand another shake, and then he was gone, swallowed by the crowd.

Liam and I were left in the wake of our shared awkwardness, the unspoken hurt simmering between us, a grim reminder of the careful balance we were yet to strike. I avoided the eyes that I knew were zeroed in on my face.

The rawness of the conversation with Ben weighing thick around us, Liam took my hand and guided me to a secluded corner away from the vibrant chatter and clinking glasses. He wore a calm exterior, but I could see the hurt and confusion lurking in his eyes.

"Emma," Liam began, his voice soft but firm. His eyes, usually full of warmth, bore into mine with a steely intensity that made my heart flutter with anxiety. "What was that about?"

I struggled to find the right words. I was caught off guard by his question, but it was a fair one. "I . . . I don't know, Liam. I just . . ."

Liam cut me off, his grip on my hand tightening. He was silent for a moment, gathering his thoughts, and when he finally spoke, his voice was rough with disappointment.

"You made it seem like I'm just some kid wanting to open another bar in the city. Like The Prism Society is nothing more than a whim, an ego trip." His words stung, and I instinctively tried to pull away, but his grip remained firm, grounding us in this difficult conversation.

He looked me in the eye, his gaze searching my face for answers. "Are you embarrassed? Ashamed?" The question hung in the air, heavy and accusing, his eyes reflecting the hurt his voice tried to hide.

"I'm sorry," I stammered, desperately trying to find the words that would explain away his hurt. But he was shaking his head, his anguish radiating from him like a furnace.

"They always judged me for what I wasn't. Who I wasn't. What I liked and didn't like. I thought you'd be the person who embraced me—not the one to shut me out, make me feel ashamed of who I am." His voice cracked as the pain of my rejection flooded his eyes.

His words hit me like a punch to the gut. I wanted to defend myself, to explain that I didn't mean to make him feel this way, but the look in his eyes told me that my intentions didn't matter right now.

He continued, "Look, I know I've had more time to process this world than you have. I can appreciate that." He dropped his grip on my arm and took a step back and the space between us felt massive. "But I need you to know that I want someone who is okay being in this, out loud, with me."

I said nothing, unable to form the jumble of thoughts going on in my brain into coherent sentences.

The car ride back home was tense. Jessie, oblivious to our conversation, was chattering about the event, about the conversations she'd had, the people she'd met. Liam and I sat in silence, the invisible wall between us growing with every passing minute. We nodded at the right moments and laughed when it was expected of us, but the air was thick with unspoken words and unvoiced regrets.

I wanted to reach out, to break the silence that hung over us, but the words wouldn't come. When we finally pulled up to our apartment, I turned to Liam, a shred of hope still on my face that he would come upstairs so we could talk more.

Liam spoke in a mere whisper, his hurt still evident in his eyes, "Goodnight, Emma." And with that, he stayed seated in the car, leaving me with the haunting echo of my regrets.

TWENTY

I had experienced my fair share of moments of shame. Like the time I had lied about where I lived when the other girls in sixth grade were giving grades to neighborhoods around their school. Mine would've, rightfully, been given an F. So I'd lied and mentioned some neighborhood that I'd seen my mom drive by, and the girls had ooo'd and ahh'd and given my neighborhood a B+.

But that had felt like a small white lie that was okay to tell in order to protect my fragile teenage girl heart from shattering at the judgment of girls whose names I couldn't even remember now.

The shame that was lining my belly now felt heavy. It felt personal. This shame was wrapped in a barbed wire of guilt with Liam's name etched into the metal. I'd decided to give Liam space after that night, but every time I closed my eyes, all I could hear was his disappointment.

"Honey, oat milk latte for Emma!" The barista's loud voice broke through my daze, and I reached for my mug. I made my way through the crowded coffee shop to find where Jessie had sat. Our normal, street-side seats were currently occupied by a distracted parent and their toddler, who was spinning on the stool about to fling off into the table nearby.

I settled into a worn leather sofa against the rear wall, turning my knees in to face Jessie. I listened half-heartedly as she filled me in on her latest escapades with Reagan. Jessie had decided that it was okay for them to keep hooking up since she didn't work at the bar anymore, but she definitely still referred to her as Hot Boss™.

Jessie's voice fluttered in through the recess of my mind, ". . . and then Hot Boss™ asked if I wanted to call in Dominic for a threesome—"

"Wait." My brain caught up, and I interrupted her, "What did you just say?"

"I knew you weren't listening!" Jessie exclaimed, "I was just trying to get your attention."

"Sorry." I shook my head to try and physically clear my thoughts. "I messed up with Liam. I don't know what to do about it."

Jessie face softened. "What happened?"

I looked down at my hands, the weight of that night rushing back. I filled Jessie in on everything that happened the night of the showcase, about how I all but shunned his idea for The Prism Society and shut him down from talking about it with people from work. About the immediate look of panic that flooded my system when they might find out about the project. About the hurt look on his face as he realized I was no different than his judgy parents or people from back home.

"Oh, Em." Jessie's voice was sorrowful, and her tone only solidified more how much I'd royally fucked up.

"It's just a lot to take in, right?" I tried to find a way to get some sympathy back on my side. "I mean, it's a *sex club*, for goodness' sake."

"And?" Jessie asked. "People have been having weird sex and will continue to have weird sex until the end of time. That's not new."

"Yeah, but doesn't it make you into, I don't know, a certain type of person when you engage in the *business* of sex?" I asked.

"A certain type of person?" Jessie turned to face me more directly. "A type of person that cares about the well-being, happiness, and safety of others? Yeah, would *hate* to become that kind of person."

I sighed, cupped my hands around my mug, and took another sip. "Well, when you put it like that."

"Emma," Jessie started, "you yourself said that design can create spaces that inspire people, make them feel safe, and bring them joy. Don't you think that's what The Prism Society is trying to do?"

I breathed a heavy sigh as Jessie's words sank in. She was right, of course. I realized that I had betrayed not just Liam but also my own belief in what design could and should do. This wasn't about my colleagues or my noncompete. It was about believing in my own capacity to create something meaningful and important.

But what could I do now to show Liam that I wasn't judging him or his ideas? That I did want to see The Prism Society come to life; in fact, it's what I kept daydreaming about. My gut was laced with regret, but a plan was beginning to take shape in my mind.

The following days were a blur. I found myself in a state of constant thought, my mind circling back to The Prism Society again and again. Even in sleep, I was flooded with visions of the space: how the lights could play off the high ceilings, how the acoustics could be perfectly tuned to foster intimacy while maintaining privacy. In the daytime, I sketched mindlessly, filling up pages with patterns, textures, and layouts, each drawing reflecting the essence of The Prism Society. It was as if the project had ignited a creative fire within me, one that I couldn't put out no matter how hard I tried.

As I walked through the city, I found myself peering into boutique stores, elegant restaurants, and even opulent hotel lobbies, gleaning inspiration from their designs. The richly detailed woodwork of an old library, the playful elegance of a rooftop bar, the subtle drama of an art exhibit, and every environment seemed to offer a piece of the puzzle.

I was caught in a tug-of-war between excitement and apprehension. What if Liam rejected my ideas? What if he felt that I was encroaching on his vision? What if he'd already shut me out from being a part of it altogether? But at the same time, I could feel the pull of the project, its potential consuming my thoughts and fueling my determination.

One night, as I was sitting alone in my room, I realized I couldn't ignore it any longer. The Prism Society was more than a potential project for me now. It was a manifestation of my belief in the power of design, in its ability to create spaces that inspire and uplift. It was a testament to my faith in Liam's vision, and it was time for me to show him that.

In the quiet of the night, with only the soft glow of the city filtering in through the window, I worked like I hadn't in years. Sketches became blueprints; ideas morphed into design concepts. The Prism Society wasn't just a cocktail bar in a historic building; it was a sanctuary, a beacon of acceptance and celebration.

Finally, when the first light of dawn started to seep in, I stepped back to take in my work. A large vision board stood in front of me, covered in drawings, fabric swatches, inspirational pictures, and even a digital 3D model of the front lobby. This was The Prism Society, not as it was, but as it could be. It was a tangible expression of my belief in the project and in Liam.

Now, I just needed to show him.

TWENTY-ONE

The day had been marked by an undercurrent of nervous anticipation. The apartment had transformed into a war room of design ideas, mood boards, sketches, and written proposals. The normally tidy living room was a sprawl of fabrics, paper, and paints. Pinned to the walls were renderings of The Prism Society's potential space alongside storyboards of imagined experiences. Our coffee table had become an island in the sea of design work, offering a spot for the now lukewarm coffee I'd forgotten to drink.

As the sun began to set, I finished the final touches. Our apartment was a tableau of my feelings and intentions. My conviction to show Liam that I was serious, that I cared about him and The Prism Society, had never been stronger.

When my phone buzzed, signaling Liam's arrival, I felt a flutter of nerves. I hadn't seen him since our argument, and the days of silence between them had felt like a chasm. Empty check-ins had replaced our usually easy, flirty banter, the rawness of their disagreement still lingering in their conversations.

With a steadying breath, I buzzed him in. I tried to quiet my nerves, reminding myself of the hours I'd spent pouring my heart into this project.

Liam walked in, his usual confident swagger dampened by a tinge of awkwardness. His eyes darted to the flurry of sketches and designs before meeting my gaze.

"Emma," he started, his voice filled with confusion as he took in the scene before him. "It's been . . ." He trailed off, the words hanging in the air.

I stepped in, offering a small smile. "I know, Liam. And I'm sorry for how I reacted. It wasn't fair, and it wasn't what I believed in. But before we talk more about that, I have something to show you."

I led him to the living room, where my vision for The Prism Society was laid out in its most tangible form. It felt as though I was introducing him to a part of me he had yet to meet—my passion, my commitment, my belief in the transformative power of design.

"I've spent the last few days," I started, my voice slightly shaky, "thinking about The Prism Society. About what it could mean and the potential it holds. Though I've always recognized the beauty of the concept, I allowed my apprehensions and the fear of societal judgment to blind me. And I'm really sorry for that."

As I started walking him through my ideas, my sketches, the mood boards, and the storyboards, I felt my nervousness fade away. Each detail, every stroke of my pencil, and every word I had penned down was a testament to my commitment. It wasn't just a design presentation; it was a declaration of my understanding, my support, and my willingness to dive head-first into this venture with him.

"And now," I said, my eyes meeting Liam's, "I'd like to show you what I see for The Prism Society..."

Liam sat quietly on the sofa as I walked him through every detail. He didn't say a word as I clicked through the digital rendering on my laptop and walked him through what the front lobby might one day look like. He only nodded as I let him feel the soft fabrics of the velvet curtains and boucle sofas I envisioned in the space.

Liam absorbed every detail with rapt attention, the soft glow from the laptop illuminating his face. As I concluded my presentation, a heavy silence hung between us. Then, he finally spoke, his voice soft, filled with surprise, and touched by the gravity of my efforts.

"Emma..." he began, a hint of disbelief laced in his voice. He traced his fingers lightly over the fabric swatches, his gaze lingering on the digital renderings, taking in the intricate details of my design. "This... is more than I could have ever imagined. The time, the detail, it's... incredible."

His gaze then met mine, the vulnerability I had seen that night at the gallery returning. He smiled, appreciating my efforts but also seeking something deeper, something more personal in my eyes.

"This design, it's beautiful, Emma," he continued. "It truly embodies the essence of The Prism Society. But while this all is really great..." He paused, locking eyes with me, the question hanging heavy in the air.

"Where do you stand, Emma? I want to know how you feel. Are you in this with me, truly? Because as brilliant as this design is, I need to know that you understand and support the purpose of The Prism Society. Not just as a design project, but as a place for freedom, expression, and acceptance." His words were a plea, a hope for clarity beyond the design, beyond the physicality of the space. He was seeking my genuine commitment to the philosophy of The Prism Society.

I took a deep breath, matching his earnest gaze. I felt a surge of honesty rise up in me, a need to let my own vulnerability shine through. My hand reached out, instinctively seeking his, a tangible connection as I navigated through my feelings.

"Liam," I began, my voice a quiet whisper that filled the silence. "I need to be honest. The fear of judgment, the fear of stepping outside the norm, terrified me. I let that cloud my vision. I let it make me forget what I truly believe in—that design is meant to inspire, to foster community, to bring joy, and provide a safe space."

I paused, swallowing back my fears, and continued, "The Prism Society, your vision, it does exactly that. It provides a space that's accepting and safe. It allows for freedom of expression and celebration of oneself. And yes, it's unconventional; it's different. But that doesn't make it wrong."

My grip tightened on his hand, a silent plea for understanding. "I see the beauty in The Prism Society. I see the beauty in what you're trying to create. And I am sorry that it took me this long to admit that to myself . . . and to you."

Then, looking directly into his eyes, I made my declaration, my voice steady and my resolve unwavering. "I am with you, Liam. I support The Prism Society, and I am not afraid of any judgment that may come my way. Because I believe in this. I believe in you.

"And if you'll have me," I continued, "I'd love to take you up on your invitation for the design position. At this point, I truly don't think I could leave it in anyone else's hands."

A wide grin formed on Liam's face. "I couldn't imagine any better for the project."

The shadow of my iron-clad noncompete lurked ominously in the darker corners of my consciousness, a malignant phantom that could manifest at any moment to lay waste to everything I held dear. Every moment that passed, every word I spoke, I could feel its icy breath at the nape of my neck, a chilling reminder of the precarious tightrope I now dared to walk.

I would need to juggle the dual responsibilities and balance the precision of it all like an expert acrobat. But this wasn't just about mere survival; this was about striving for more, reaching for something meaningful beyond the mundane.

Yes, I could gain invaluable experience as the lead designer of The Prism Society, pushing boundaries and challenging conventions. And I could also learn the ropes by taking the scraps they chose to throw at me at Spectra.

I was willing to gamble, to roll the dice, and hope that the numbers fell in my favor. Because, when it came down to it, I could do both. And I would.

TWENTY-TWO

"I've got a big job for us," Liam yelled from the kitchen as he heaved something heavy onto the counter. "You up for it?" After deciding to go all in on designing The Prism Society, I'd resolved to spend nearly every night at Liam's apartment. It was easier for us to work through designs and ideas than having to travel back and forth. Plus, waking up to him and the things he did under the sheets wasn't a bad trade-off.

I could feel the excitement bubbling in my veins as I strode into the kitchen. Liam was standing by a giant cardboard box, his eyes bright and full of mischief, hands resting on top of it like he was guarding a great secret.

"What's inside?" I asked with a skeptical look on my face.

He shifted to block the box from me and wore a mischievous expression when he said, "Let me ask you a question before I show you what's inside. We wouldn't want to put anything inside the club that we didn't know was perfect, right? We wouldn't want our clients to experience something we hadn't first tested ourselves, right?"

"Liam," my tone was teasing, "*what is in the box*?" I laughed as I tried to reach around him and grab the edge of it to peek inside. But it was too high on the counter, and Liam was too big to push past. He then stepped aside as if presenting a treasure to me, revealing the contents of the mysterious box. The room fell silent as I knelt and pulled open the flaps of the worn cardboard.

Inside was stuffed with box after box of sleek packaging. Smooth, almost velvet, black boxes of all shapes and sizes fit like a puzzle inside. I picked one at random and pulled it out, and my mouth dropped open. I ran my fingers along it, feeling the indention of the letters embossed on the top. I could feel Liam behind me, his presence radiating heat and excitement. I scanned the rest of the boxes, flipping some over to see the cover. Inside, was filled to the brim with a variety of vibrators, dildos, butt plugs, lube, handcuffs, eye masks, feathers, and things I'd never even heard of before. Like, what the fuck is a *chin dong?*

I looked up at him, my face asking the question I didn't need to form, and he answered, "We've already got vendors reaching out to us wanting us to feature their products in the club," Liam said, standing over me. He shrugged nonchalantly, but his enthusiasm was evident on his face. "This is more exciting than sheets or brands of liquor. We have to test these for quality assurance purposes since this is The Prism Society."

My brain raced with all the possibilities that lay inside these boxes, and my cheeks burned with embarrassment as I realized what he meant by testing. "Oh my god, Liam, this is insane," I breathed out.

"So what do you say, babe?" He dropped down beside me and started looking through the box, "How about you dig through here and pick something out you've always wanted to try?" He stood. "I'm gonna go for a run, but you spend some time deciding." He winked as he headed to the room to change. Soon he was out the door, and I was left with a risqué box spread open in front of me.

It couldn't hurt to try something new, right? Maybe we wouldn't lead with the *chin dong*, but there was a nice variety of vibrators in there. I sat cross-legged on the kitchen floor and started unboxing everything.

After I sorted all the unopened boxes into piles of "absolutely never," "maybe one day," and "let's try it," I decided that maybe I had time to have a little fun myself before Liam got back home. For quality assurance purposes, obviously. I settled on a purple, palm-size flower-looking device that was supposed to provide *incredible* stimulation.

After washing it and gathering the batteries I needed, I headed to the bedroom, propping up some pillows and slipping off my panties. I browsed through some smutty stories on my phone and found one that promised five chili peppers worth of spice. Holding the buzzing device in my hand, I cautiously pressed it against my core and felt it latch onto my swollen clit with its soft suction motion. A moan escaped my lips as an overwhelming pressure built inside me before finally crashing through me in waves of pleasure.

My vision returned just in time to see Liam standing in the doorway, watching me intently from afar. His voice was rough but barely audible when he asked if there was another one at the counter that I wanted to try. Without a word, I nodded and watched him go to unbox it and clean it for us.

He entered the room with his hair still damp from his run, a mix of body wash and sweat filling the air. He sank into the end of the bed, his eyes taking their time to trace over my bare skin and leaving me feeling both exposed and adored.

"I could watch you do that every day," he murmured before pulling my mouth towards his in a passionate kiss. I returned it hungrily, and he smiled against my lips.

"I can officially give that one my stamp of approval," he said softly as he pulled away again.

He grabbed hold of the light blue vibrator I had chosen from the box earlier, getting it wet before slowly pushing it inside me. I opened wider for him, letting out a deep breath as my body adjusted to its presence.

"Can I turn it on?" His gaze met mine as he asked this, his hands curling around the base while another hand traveled up to cup my exposed breasts. With a heavy breath, I nodded in response, and he switched it on. An involuntary moan escaped my lips at the sensation, and I was grateful for having picked this particular toy—ridges ran down its shaft that sent pleasurable ripples through me with each thrust. Still, it was the vibration that made me want to pick it out of the box. Liam kept an arm around its middle, using his free hand to caress my nipples.

"Oh my god, Liam." He pressed and pinched again, my muscles pulsing tight in my core.

He pressed the button once more, increasing the thrusting speed and pushing me closer to pleasure. I gasped in delight, and my moans became louder as I neared the edge. Liam placed his hand on my swollen clit, adding a gentle pinch that sent shockwaves of sensation through my body. I threw my head back in bliss as he continued to press and pinch, each touch pushing me over the edge in an explosion of pleasure.

My whole body quivered as he quickly moved me onto my belly before tugging my hips up into position. He slid inside me without hesitation, filling me with pleasure as he began mounting me with rough, swift movements. He groaned as I leaned down on my elbows, changing the angle to give him even more pleasure. His breathing increased before his muscles tightened around me in a powerful orgasm. We stayed connected for a few moments before separating and collapsing onto the bed in exhaustion.

Liam chuckled softly and ran his arm across my back. "I guess you can give your seal of approval for two of the toys now, huh?" he said, smiling at me. Embarrassed but elated, I blushed and hid my face with my hands.

"Let's hope your anxiety around it leaves by the time we get through that entire box then, 'cause I hope you *never* stop doing that." He got up to wash off and came back with a warm cloth and began to rub it down my thighs.

Being with him was encouraging a new side of me to come out, and it felt equally amazing but terrifying to meet this new version of myself. It's like I was shedding an old skin and revealing a new, more confident version of myself, with a vulnerable center that scared the shit outta me.

TWENTY-THREE

An adrenaline-fueled whirlwind encapsulated my life. By day, I was the dutiful junior designer at Spectra, swallowing my pride and seeking solace in the scraps thrown my way. My time was spent creating color schemes for boutique hotels, designing trendy co-working spaces, and even handling the layout of a new tech start-up's headquarters. It was work, indeed, but it lacked the soulful connection I craved. My designs were creative, yes, but they felt hollow, like beautiful shells devoid of deeper meaning.

My colleagues noticed a change in me, an almost insatiable hunger for more work, a zeal they hadn't seen before. I laughed it off, attributing it to a newfound sense of responsibility and desire to make my mark. Little did they know that my passion was ignited elsewhere, in a project they had no inkling of.

By night, I transformed. I was no longer the underappreciated junior designer; I was the visionary behind The Prism Society. I hunched over blueprints and renderings, my hand gliding across the paper as I sketched out detailed designs that seemed to flow straight from my heart. Every piece of fabric, every hue I chose, and each piece of furniture was selected with meticulous care, embodying the freedom, safety, and acceptance that The Prism Society stood for.

In the mayhem of devoting all my time to my shapeshifting duties, my normal, tidy life was fraying. Dirty coffee cups had multiplied like rabbits, settling in random nooks, while discarded blueprints played hide-and-seek under the couch. My slow weekend coffee catch-ups with Jessie became scarce, and there was a running tally of at least three phone calls I needed to return to my mom.

Meanwhile, at The Prism Society's headquarters, Liam was neck-deep in the initial building phase alongside Dominic and our contracted builder. His days were spent huddled over construction details, his fingers tracing the lines of the blueprints I had poured my soul into. He was translating my interior vision into reality, and with each passing day, the building was taking shape. The skeletal structure was already up, and excitement was building in my belly with every visit to the site.

Fear, however, was a constant companion. Every email I sent and every phone call I made had me wondering if I was leaving a trace for my bosses at Spectra to follow. I was terrified that one wrong move might unveil my secret venture, that the whispers of a daring new designer making waves in the city would reach their ears. But the thrill of what I was doing, the weight of the change I could bring about, kept me going.

And yes, the fatigue was relentless. There were nights when I could barely keep my eyes open, my body protesting the lack of sleep, the nonstop flurry of activity. There were days when I had to splash cold water on my face to keep from dozing off during meetings at Spectra. Coffee became my lifeline, caffeine coursing through my veins to keep me alert and on my toes.

In the quiet moments of the night, the soft glow of my desk lamp illuminating the sketches before me, I would wonder if I was spiraling down a path of self-destruction. But the doubts receded as I traced the outlines of what The Prism Society would be. This was more than a design, more than a mere building. It was a testament to my resolve, my ability to seize my destiny, and a monument to my courage.

Navigating the dynamic maze of Spectra was becoming increasingly complex, a chess game I wasn't prepared to play. The office thrummed with the usual cacophony—the mechanical rhythm of keyboards clicking, hushed conversations scattered across cubicles, and the sharp, sporadic laughter that punctuated the drone. Amongst this common ensemble, there was a shift in the harmony that irked me. A shift named Noah.

Noah had always been just another colleague—jovial, hardworking, a companion in the trenches of junior designer duties. However, there was a sudden surge in his presence that felt off-kilter. His name was cropping up in places it never had before on projects that were beyond his grasp, according to the hierarchical ladder of Spectra. He was suddenly shadowing senior designers, sitting in on high-level meetings, and even presenting pitches to clients—an opportunity that was considered a golden ticket for us junior designers.

One particular day, the office was buzzing with the energy of an impending meeting. The entire design team was huddled in the glass-walled conference room, the air thick with anticipation. Our lead designer, Clark, was presenting a new hotel project, an account that could be a potential game-changer for

Spectra. After the introductions, the spotlight shifted to who would shadow Clark on this venture.

I found my heartbeat escalating. After all, wasn't this the chance I had been vying for, working late nights, pushing the boundaries of my creativity? I saw Clark's gaze sweep over us, the tension coiling like a spring in the silent room. Then he said it.

"Noah, I think you'll be a good fit to shadow me on this one." He closed his laptop, a clear sign this wasn't up for discussion.

The room echoed with scattered applause, but I could hear nothing over the rush of blood in my ears. My eyes met Noah's, his usual jovial expression replaced with feigned surprise. A bitter taste filled my mouth. What was happening?

The uneasy feeling gnawed at me over the weeks as Noah's ascent continued. I was buried under mounting paperwork while he was sketching designs alongside Clark. It felt unjust, a deranged version of our office reality that left me bewildered and frustrated.

As I settled into my role, the glossy veneer of Spectra began to chip away, revealing a harsher reality. I found myself teetering on the edge of burnout, weighed down by long hours and a workload that seemed unending. I felt dwarfed in an organization that often overlooked my efforts, treating me as a replaceable component in a well-oiled machine.

The expectation of my role as full-time designer had included a substantial share of demanding tasks, but also the prospect of mentorship and development. I craved the opportunity to demonstrate my creativity, to leave my mark. But instead, I found myself swamped with the administrative work that reminded me a lot of my time as an unpaid intern.

The imbalance was stark. Noah, who seemed to have the senior designers wrapped around his finger, appeared to be the only one landing prime assignments. Watching him ascend while Jessie and I grappled with menial tasks was frustrating, especially since we worked just as hard as he did to get here.

I decided I had to confront Noah. The mere thought made my stomach churn, but I had to let him know how it was going for Jessie and me. I found him in the break room, sipping coffee nonchalantly. I approached him, my heart pounding in my chest.

"I need to talk to you," I stated, trying to keep my voice steady.

The smirk he gave me sent a chill down my spine. It was the face he had given his competition when we were all still in school, and now he was using it on me.

"Oh really? About what?" he asked, feigning innocence.

I held my head high and my voice steady as I outlined how it was going for Jessie and me. The lack of invites to important meetings and after-hour meetups. The to-do lists that consisted of mostly administrative work with little to no design work whatsoever. I was hoping he could help right the ship. Put in a good word for us. Open the door a little bit.

"Do you remember, Emma, that one night about a month back?" Noah had a grin on his face I should've been more afraid of. "You were here late, long after everyone else had left."

My heartbeat spiked, but I kept my face neutral. "I've stayed late on several occasions, Noah. It's part of the job."

"No, not just staying late," he corrected. "You were hunched over the drafting table in that secluded corner of the office, with blueprints that weren't any of our projects."

A cold knot formed in the pit of my stomach. How did he know?

"Why were you even here that late, Noah?" I tried to redirect his focus, stalling for time to gather my thoughts.

He shrugged nonchalantly. "I'd forgotten my phone in the office. When I came back to get it, I saw you. You looked so engrossed in your work that I didn't want to disturb you."

"And why are you bringing this up now?" I inquired, attempting to keep my voice steady.

He tilted his head, studying me. "Because I know what it looks like when someone's working on something they're passionate about, and those blueprints, they weren't related to any of Spectra's projects, were they?"

I swallowed. "I don't know what you're talking about."

He smirked, "Of course you don't. All I'm saying, Emma, is that we're all just trying to climb the ladder here. And we should be grateful for what we've been given, don't you think?"

His insinuation was clear: he had information that could compromise my position at Spectra, and he wouldn't hesitate to use it if necessary.

With that, he turned on his heel and left, leaving me standing in the middle of the break room, my heart pounding and my mind racing. I had to be more careful. Noah had initiated a precarious game of cat and mouse, and now I was left scrambling to keep up.

In the coming days, I resolved to tread more cautiously, to find a way to maintain my dual commitments without rousing suspicion. It was a tall order, but I was willing to do whatever it took.

I was optimistic that with a little more determination, a little more effort, I would find a way to balance my responsibilities at Spectra with my dedication to The Prism Society. I believed, perhaps naively, that if I could just hold on a little longer, everything would fall into place.

But as it would turn out, the universe had its own designs. And they weren't quite what I had in mind.

TWENTY-FOUR

"I was thinking this one here," I suggested, my arms outstretched as I held up a swatch of wallpaper that boasted a bold black and cream stripe pattern. I stood in the spacious downstairs lobby of The Prism Society, the undecorated wall serving as a blank canvas for my vision. "And this one," I shifted my gaze and motioned to my second choice, a wallpaper sample with a subtle geometric design, "in this hallway."

The installer, a nimble woman with sharp eyes, jotted down my specifications in the small spiral notebook she always tucked into her back pocket. Giving me a nod of acknowledgment, she quickly got to work, ready to transform our decisions into reality.

It was an intense period of transformation for The Prism Society, as each day brought noticeable changes. The once bare skeleton of the club was gradually becoming vibrant and filled with character. There was the low hum of voices and the rhythm of work in every corner: walls receiving fresh coats of paint, wallpaper breathing life into hallways, light fixtures being hung, and the carefully chosen furniture being delivered and arranged.

The space was evolving, taking on a new life, and I was at the heart of it, orchestrating the transformation. I darted from one floor to another, monitoring the progress of each element. Ensuring that the paint matched the color schemes we'd painstakingly chosen, that the wallpaper adhered smoothly and enhanced the desired ambiance, that the light fixtures illuminated the space as intended, and that the furniture harmonized with the overall aesthetic.

Everywhere I looked, my designs were turning from paper sketches into tangible experiences, like a maestro conducting a grand symphony. It was a mammoth production, and I reveled in the chaos, the creativity, and the satisfaction of watching my vision materialize before my eyes.

I took my near-daily walk through the space, starting at the front door, which would eventually be replaced with arched double doors with beautiful carvings in the wood. As I strolled through the still-transforming space, I perceived it from the perspective of an incoming member. What greeted me now was a landscape of partially set up seating spaces, a skeletal reception desk that awaited its stain, and hollow light fixtures hanging eagerly for their bulbs. Despite its incomplete state, I could clearly visualize the impending metamorphosis that would occur over the next few weeks.

The reception desk, the lounge area, the imposing bar, the mystery-filled hallway—all these spaces seemed like parts of a larger orchestra, each waiting to play its part in the grand symphony of The Prism Society. As I walked through, envisioning each element falling into place, my phone buzzed, breaking the silence and stillness that had engulfed the room.

Jessie's name flashed on the screen, her timing impeccable as always. I found a quiet corner in the semi-finished lounge area, sinking into an upholstered chair as I swiped to answer.

"Hey Jess," I greeted, her name a sigh of relief in the bustling chaos.

"Hey Em," her familiar voice echoed from the other side, carrying a hint of mischief. "Got your horoscope ready. You want the cosmic lowdown?"

I chuckled, not surprised anymore that Jessie called to solely share the latest astrology prediction. "Sure, hit me with it."

Jessie cleared her throat dramatically. "Okay, it says, 'You are in the midst of a transformative phase. Remember to remain true to your vision and do not be deterred by the enormity of the tasks at hand. Embrace the chaos as it will lead to clarity. Your creativity is your compass; let it guide you through the storm.'"

A shiver ran down my spine. "Jess, are you sure you didn't write that one yourself?" I joked. The reading resonated almost uncannily with my current situation.

Jessie laughed, "Swear on my tarot deck. So, how goes it at The Prism Society?"

I filled Jessie in on the progress we'd made, describing the space's transformation and the excitement and trepidation it brought with it. I hadn't let Jessie come to the space often. I already knew I was skirting the line—well let's be honest, I was over the line—regarding Spectra's rules.

I worked really hard to keep my name off of order forms and only gave my opinion verbally and never in writing for fear that it could get traced back to me. As much as working at

Spectra wasn't what I had dreamed it would be, it was still *the dream*. I figured the grunt work I was still doing, the exact work I thought would stop once I transitioned from my internship to full time, would end soon. It had to.

There was a pause on the other side before Jessie spoke, her voice serious. "You know, Emma, you should do what makes you happy. Life's too short for anything less."

I wasn't sure what life without Spectra would look like. It had been the goal for so long, the only marker I'd given myself for the finish line. And I had gotten it. I had it. And it didn't feel like I thought it would.

"That's the thing, Jess," I confessed. "I'm not sure what that is anymore."

We talked a bit more, Jessie's comforting voice and encouraging words serving as the tether I didn't know I needed. When the call ended, I found myself staring at the semi-transformed space of The Prism Society, Jessie's advice echoing in my mind. What did I want?

I had two very different futures grasped between my hands and I wasn't sure which one I wanted to grip tighter. Because, deep down, I knew I wouldn't be able to keep both for that much longer.

Shaking off the nerves, I turned my attention back to the club. There was still so much to do, so much to achieve. Jessie's words had provided a moment of respite, a reminder of why I was here. Her words, strangely prophetic and comforting, ignited a renewed sense of purpose within me. And with that, I was ready to dive back into the whirlwind, to continue shaping this extraordinary vision.

Glancing up, my gaze fell on the vast ceiling. Though now bare, it would soon hang plush, heavy velvet drapes, an elegant barrier to obscure the tantalizing views of the club's interiors until members were officially welcomed behind the curtain.

I then ventured into the semi-private lounge area, the heart of the first floor. It was envisioned as a cocoon of intimacy for members to engage in hushed conversations and quiet moments of solitude. The space would soon be filled with high-back, oversized loungers swathed in creamy boucle fabric. Arranged carefully, none would face another, cultivating a sense of private comfort despite the communal setting.

I meandered towards the sprawling bar stationed along the imposing back wall before making my way through to the staircase leading up to the second floor. Though it was barren now, I could almost hear the clinking of glass and the hushed murmur of conversation that would soon surround it. My footsteps echoed in the still-exposed concrete of the steps, but I couldn't help but feel giddy as I walked out into the lobby.

The desk here was much smaller, simply needing to serve the purpose of members checking in for their experience. A plush lounge corner that held capacious seats was designed as a restful pit stop for members to gather their thoughts before they ventured into the hallowed privacy of their personal spaces.

However, the true centerpiece of this level was the mysterious hallway painted in a sumptuous oxblood hue. Once the black-and-white marble tiled floor was polished, the rugs laid, and the lights wired, a curator would bring in the art pieces Liam and I had picked out. The hallway, a journey in itself, would soon serve as the silent storyteller of The Prism Society.

It wasn't just one element that made this space special. Everything had been designed and selected to create the feeling of being cloaked in a cocoon of secrecy, of being privy to something special. I walked down the hallway, noting how the oxblood walls seemed to pulse and breathe with life, a testament to how the space was coming alive.

Framing both sides of the hallway were ornately paneled doors, each fitted with polished brass handles that gleamed under the soft, atmospheric light. These elegant portals stood like silent sentinels, their austere exteriors cloaking the secrets and wonders they held within their confines. Behind each door, a bespoke experience awaited the curious visitor, each meticulously chosen by Liam and crafted with the intent to inspire exploration and self-discovery.

As everything seamlessly progressed, I was eager to add the final touches and finally unveil The Prism Society to a hand-picked group of guests. We planned a soft launch, more of a rehearsal with our core team and a modest guest list, intended to serve as a sneak peek into The Prism Society's enchanting world before we welcomed our growing roster of waitlisted members.

Liam and Dominic had filled the waitlist much sooner than I had thought possible. The salaciousness and high cost of the membership apparently did not deter many. A whirlwind of dinners and phone calls had ensued as Liam passionately painted the allure of The Prism Society, fanning the flames of interest and excitement amongst potential members.

As the waitlist began to swell, I found myself taken aback each time another enthusiastic individual enrolled, thrilled to be a part of the clandestine world we were creating. I was well aware this hush-hush society existed, but seeing such enthusiasm reminded me of the potential impact it could have. It was an unspoken endorsement of the possible impact and reach The Prism Society could have, and the awareness washed over me. This was happening. We were creating something of consequence, something people were actively seeking. The astonishment was overwhelming, but more than anything, it kindled my drive to bring this vision to life.

I made my way back to the staircase, leaving the partially assembled second floor behind. I found myself on the third floor, where a different kind of assembly was taking place. Half of this floor wouldn't be open to members as it would hold private offices, but the other half was a skylight-filled open area where we could host classes and workshops for members. You never know when you might need to freshen up your bondage skills.

I heard the hum of a conversation before I rounded the corner. Liam was there, naturally, holding court amongst new faces—the newly hired public-facing staff. I watched from the edge of the room as he introduced them to the core values of The Prism Society, his face serious as he let them into our little world.

There was Maureen, a silver-haired woman with a radiant smile, who would command our reception desk with her years of experience in hospitality, welcoming our members with her warm demeanor. Then, Leo, our resident mixologist with a flair for creating exotic cocktails, would be behind the bar crafting signature drinks that would help our most timid members loosen up.

In the shadows, ensuring the members' experiences were seamless, was a team just as vital. For them, Liam and Dominic had scoured the city, their networks, and even overseas for uniquely talented individuals.

Arlo was an imposing figure, towering over most with his height. Despite his physical stature, he exuded a gentle aura that was disarmingly comforting. His cropped black hair and slate grey eyes held a deep quietude that was somehow both mysterious and inviting. He would be one of our in-house talents, an essential figure to those members who craved a unique experience within The Prism Society's walls.

Sierra was a striking redhead, her fiery hair cascading down her back in wild curls, perfectly mirroring her vivacious personality. Her sparkling green eyes held an indomitable spirit; her confidence was as palpable as it was infectious. She would join Arlo as an in-house talent, an exciting addition to the team that would add a whole new layer of intrigue to our members' experiences.

Finally, there was Jules. Her petite stature and shock of electric blue hair made her stand out from the crowd. She had an infectious energy, and I could tell she was already forming a commitment to our members' experiences. Her role as the upstairs receptionist was more than just a job; it was a mission. She was there to ensure that every interaction within our space was not just safe but entirely consensual and built on respect and trust. Her meticulous approach to her work would be instrumental in crafting the incredible experiences we promised our members.

I watched as Liam described the member's journey, painting vivid pictures of what they would experience, what role each individual would play, and how it all came together to form an unforgettable experience. The staff listened with wide eyes, hanging onto each word, already feeling the weight and privilege of their roles.

Finally, Liam's eyes twinkled as he spotted me and beckoned me over. "Ladies and gentlemen," he announced with a grand gesture, "our very own designer of dreams, Emma." Amidst the friendly laughter and encouraging applause, a wave of anticipation washed over me. This was the moment. We were all assembled, united in our mission to bring The Prism Society to life. Despite the hurdles we'd jumped and countless sleepless nights, the sense of accomplishment and exhilaration made every challenge worth it.

TWENTY-FIVE

My fingers were cramped as I flexed them around my coffee mug, the evidence of a long night of wrestling with Allen wrenches and furniture assembly instructions still fresh. After endless reassurances that our furniture would arrive in plenty of time for white glove delivery and professional assembly, we had been left standing in an empty downstairs lobby with just two nights to go before our soft launch.

The distinct echo of screwdrivers against wood, metal clanging against metal, still rang in my ears. My limbs ached, a physical reminder of the time spent hauling, lifting, and maneuvering furniture off the delayed shipment that had finally arrived. The delivery had caused a frenzy.

When we'd finally resolved to pushing the launch date back, the beep of a truck backing up to our building's dock caused us to rush outside. There, at nearly midnight, was a truckload of loungers, side tables, and barstools. Dominic, Liam, Jessie, and I had all been there, walking around the open space, willing a miracle, and it had come.

We had been left with no choice but to roll up our sleeves, order pizza, and dive into the mountain of flat-packed furniture ourselves. As the night turned into dawn, we cranked up the music, the pulsating beats echoing through the empty yet-to-be-filled halls of the club.

Laughter and playful banter filled the air, masking the desperation and tiredness that clung to us. Despite the arduous work, there was an unmistakable air of camaraderie, of shared purpose. We were in this together, making the best of the situation, and somehow, the urgency of the moment only amplified the closeness that had begun forming between us all over the past year.

I had begun having more than just the "Sunday Scaries" when it came to Spectra. After having so much creative freedom and control over The Prism Society design, walking the halls of Spectra, where my voice still didn't hold weight, felt empty. I simply worked through the motions during the day and allowed myself to light up after hours. It was here, surrounded by these people I cared deeply about, that I could be myself.

"I feel like I could've slept for a week," Liam said sleepily as he walked over to top off my cup of coffee, both of us needing the caffeine desperately.

"I'm not sure there's enough concealer in all of New York City to cover up the bags under my eyes." I squinted up at him, the morning sunlight harsh on my eyes.

"Maybe we could tell everyone there's actually a theme tonight; we could make it zombie themed so you'd fit right in," he teased as he leaned down to kiss me on my forehead.

"Ha, ha, you just wait to see the miracle I can make once I slip on that dress," I said.

Liam's eyes flickered over to the zippered bag that had been hanging on the back of his bedroom door for days. I asked him not to look, to not ruin the surprise, and as far as I knew, he'd listened.

Tonight for our soft launch, I'd chosen a rust-colored dress that plunged deeply down my chest. It hung tight against my middle and flowed out slightly once it reached the floor. It would fit in perfectly with the jewel-toned rooms and black-and-white decor of The Prism Society.

While I had made sure everything looked perfect inside the club, Liam had worked to make sure every detail was taken care of to make tonight happen. The invitations, an embossed card stock sealed with a crest that he had designed for the club, went out to a select few. Tonight, investors, friends, and owners of some of Liam's favorite clubs, including Zara and Kai from The Oasis, would be in attendance.

It was our chance to work out any kinks (pun intended) before we would fully be ready to open in our public launch a few weeks later. Tonight was all about rewarding ourselves and welcoming others into what felt like our secret club. I had every intention of dipping my toe into what The Prism Society offered, and I could only hope that Liam would like what I had planned.

Later that morning, as I was debating on whether or not I had the energy to get myself in the shower, my phone buzzed with a text from Jessie.

Jessie: Put your shoes on and come downstairs! I have a surprise for you :)

My curiosity piqued; I let Liam know I'd be right back and headed downstairs. There, waiting on the curb, was Jessie, with two large coffees from Urban Brew in hand and a town car behind her.

Jessie didn't even wait for me to ask the question that showed on my face before she excitedly said, "We have a whole day of treating ourselves on the agenda. First a massage, then we get our nails done." She handed me one of the coffees, and I took it as she continued, "Then hair and makeup before we're dropped back off at our apartments to get dressed."

"How?" I couldn't even form the entire question.

"Dom." Jessie shrugged and opened the car door for me to slide in.

I fired off a text to Liam as the car door shut behind me, letting him know that Jessie had kidnapped me to get pampered for the day. As our driver navigated the city traffic with ease, I couldn't help but bubble with curiosity. "Jess, how did Dominic even set this all up? I mean, a spa day this fast? It's New York!"

Jessie laughed lightly, taking a sip of her coffee. "I honestly don't know, Em. I just mentioned in passing that something like this would be really helpful, especially given how exhausted we've been lately. You know, with us women having to prep and all before such a big event. The next thing I know, he's showing me the confirmation emails and telling me the time it all kicks off. It's like he had it all set up in minutes."

I stared at her, my mouth agape in astonishment. Dominic had always been efficient, but this was on another level. This was . . . thoughtful. My gaze drifted over to Jessie, a knowing look crossing my face. "Seems like he cares about you, Jessie," I said, my eyebrows raising in a tease.

At my words, a pink blush bloomed across Jessie's cheeks, her gaze flickering out the window at the passing building to avoid my probing stare.

Clearing my throat and trying to rein in my amusement, I changed the topic, rummaging in my bag to grab my phone. "Alright, since we're on the road, how about you read me my horoscope for today?"

Jessie nodded, her fingers moving quickly over her phone screen as she searched for today's predictions. I settled into the leather seat, allowing the city sights and the rhythm of the journey to calm my excitement. Today was a big day, and we were about to begin it in the best way possible.

"Okay, here it is," Jessie began, her voice filling the quiet car. "'Your journey has taken you to surprising places, and it appears you've found your passion in the most unexpected of arenas. As you step into a new chapter, remember to trust in yourself, even if it means venturing into the unfamiliar. Embrace the unfamiliarity as a chance to learn and grow. Soon, a significant revelation is set to change your perspective, shaking the very foundation of your world. Embrace this shift, for it is a harbinger of a remarkable journey ahead.'"

As she finished reading, a hum of anticipation filled the car, the words of the horoscope resonating with both of us. Something big was coming, and we could both feel it.

I arrived back at Liam's apartment, being dropped off by our driver after Jessie, feeling like a totally new woman. My hair hung loose over my shoulders, my skin smooth, and my muscles loose after the massage and pedicure. I'd had the makeup stylist add a shimmery yellow to my lids and a darker lash than I was used to. I was far from the zombie I felt like this morning; now, I appeared like a sultry vampire.

The glamour of my look felt out of place with my baggie t-shirt and sweats, so I couldn't wait to slip on the new dress I'd gotten just for tonight. As I unlocked the door to Liam's apartment, I could hear soft music coming from inside and smell the scent of his cologne, a spicy aroma I'd come to associate with him.

Liam was in the living room, half-dressed in a pair of tailored black trousers, his shirt still unbuttoned, revealing a tantalizing glimpse of his chiseled chest. His hair was tousled just right, making him look devilishly handsome. A citrus aroma clung to him, mixing with his cologne, and I felt a flush of heat sweep over me. It was unsettling how this man made me feel.

He gave me a half smile, the one that reminded me of when we were younger, and said, "Damn. I don't think you even need the dress; you could go just like this." He wrapped his arms around my waist; his eyes took in all the new details of my appearance.

"Oh, trust me," I said softly, "you're going to want to see this dress." I placed one kiss on his lips, sharing my lip gloss with him, before tucking away in his bedroom to finish getting ready.

I unzipped the garment bag to reveal the shimmery fabric of the dress inside. As I pulled it over my head, it slid down my body like a second skin, hugging the curve of my belly and settling in over my hips. The deep V-neck showed off skin that was rarely seen, and the soft shimmer of my lotion caught ride light as I turned.

I added a pair of diamond studs to my ears and a delicate, long gold chain around my neck that lay gently in between my breasts. Slipping into my black heels, I checked my reflection one last time, my transformation complete.

Stepping back into the living room, I watched as Liam's gaze met mine. His eyes widened slightly, a flicker of surprise passing over his face before it was replaced by a slow, appreciative smile. He looked me up and down, his eyes lingering on me a little longer than necessary.

"God damn woman," Liam said as if I dressed intentionally to make his life difficult, and I guess in a way, I did because I glanced at the clock, and if we didn't leave this minute, we'd be late.

"I think our car is waiting for us downstairs," I reminded Liam. Dominic had again sent private cars, but this time for us and each of our guests, and I'd gotten the notification that our driver was a few blocks away a few minutes ago.

"Mmm hmm." Liam didn't appear to care as his hands traced the way the fabric hugged my curves and teased his fingertips where the edge of my dress met my skin. "I know tonight is to show off for our investors, but god, I want to see what this dress looks like bunched up around your waist."

My face flushed at his brash honesty like it always did, and I grabbed his hand to steer him toward the front door as he asked, "Are you ready to enjoy the world you helped design tonight?"

I felt entirely prepared for the night ahead. During our ride over, Liam's hand remained a comforting weight on my thigh, the city's transformation from day to night unfurling around us. The Prism Society's building, nestled among the city's towering structures, looked no different from its neighboring buildings on the outside. However, the attention to detail was clear in the refurbished historic arched windows, the meticulously repaired red brick, and the gleaming black window frames.

The Prism Society's raised prism logo was etched into a marble plaque to the right of the double doors. Jessie had sourced those doors from an old salvage yard and had them restored to fit our space. The arches matched the arch of the windows that lined the building on both the front and the side, and the carvings engraved on the surface gave the impression we were walking into a rather *unholy* sacred space.

A curated playlist of quintessential New York music flooded the speakers, and I smiled when eyes found our friends across the room, and I swiftly snagged a chilled champagne flute on my way over. Jessie was breathtaking in her slinky deep red dress. I couldn't help but notice Dominic's hand lingering on her lower back before quickly retracting and being hidden in his pockets. Despite his constant presence, Jessie didn't appear to be uncomfortable; it seemed like they'd found a compromise that suited them both.

I stifled a squeal of excitement as Jessie and I clinked glasses, the exhilaration of reaching this milestone threatening to bubble over. After a moment to compose myself, I inhaled deeply, bracing for the inevitable chitchat that lay ahead before Liam and I could steal away upstairs.

TWENTY-SIX

"Seems like you're having a good time." Liam's hand found its familiar place on the small of my back, his breath a warm whisper against my neck.

"My cheeks ache from all the smiling," I confessed, sucking in my cheeks and letting out a long, weighted exhale. "But just look at how incredible everyone looks in this space." I turned to take in the scene in the downstairs lobby.

People were engaged in chatter with Leo at the bar. Couples were cozily tucked away in the lounge chairs we'd assembled just days prior. Even future members were going over intricacies with Maureen. A photographer milled about the space taking photos for a feature they'd be running on Liam and Dominic, highlighting the club as the first of its kind in the city.

"Emma, you should be exceptionally proud." Liam's words pulled me back from my observation, refocusing my attention on him. "None of this would have been possible without your hard work. I know you've been pulling double duty for a while, and I hope I can help you relax tonight."

Flushing slightly at the compliment and the promise of later plans, I turned to him, "And what about you, Liam? You've managed to bring your vision to life. How does that feel? Is this what you had in mind?"

Liam paused, surveying the scene before answering, "The impact we could have with this space . . . it's beyond what I initially imagined, truly. I know it was no small task I asked of all of us, but we did it.

"The part that makes it unbelievable," he continued, "is that you're here. Right here—" he squeezed my backside playfully. "If my teenage self could only see me now." He chuckled and nuzzled in my ear.

"I'm glad I got to be a part of this." I reached for his hand and squeezed. "Thank you for trusting me with this part of your life."

"I would go out on a limb and say it's also part of *your* life now, too." His gaze darkened a bit. "I asked Sierra if I could reserve a room, and she told me you'd already done it." His eyes raised curiously.

I wet my lips, excitement for what was to come building inside me. "I did, yes. Let me know when you want to head upstairs."

Liam released a quiet groan and said, "Let me go check in with Dominic about membership." His eyes stared intently into mine, "Then I'll come to find you."

He walked away before I could respond, and it was probably best that he did because heat was building in my core, and I might have threatened to take him right then and there, my plans for tonight disregarded.

Instead, I made my way into the lounge area, eyeing couples and guests sitting tucked away. Every square inch of this club was designed with pleasure in mind. Around every corner was an opportunity for you to enjoy yourself, alone or with others, and upstairs was where you could take things to the next level. Our space was created for unabashed enjoyment, and I was happy to see so many of our guests partaking in that mission so freely.

I felt like the queen of a sultry underworld as I walked through the lounge with my cold champagne flute in my hand. I saw tender couples sitting close in chatter, a hand resting high up on a thigh. I watched as a guest nuzzled their partner's neck as their eyes glazed over and their head leaned back. The further I got through the lounge, the more confident the couples were.

My body was tingling with anticipation for later, the champagne bubbles coating my tongue. I ran a finger subconsciously across my collarbone as I watched Liam finally make his way back over to me. With one long stare from across the room, we both left our posts and headed for the stairs.

The second floor would always be my favorite, regardless of what went on behind closed doors. It was like stepping back in time to nineteenth-century France when art salons existed to bring people together to discuss art and enjoy themselves. Large, gilded frames with gorgeous artwork hung from picture wires all over the wall and wall-mounted candle sconces give off a glow to guide you down the long hall. Tucked away between picture frames were lacquered oxblood-painted doors, and behind those doors were the private rooms designed to give our guests the night of their lives.

We made our way to the private nooks that lined the front hall, and I stepped into the alcove. We had designed a custom U-shaped sofa with deep cushions and a high back that took up all three walls of each nook. Each space was made private with thick velvet curtains, which hung on a track at the entrance.

I sat back on the bench as Liam came in with two glasses of champagne. Any sounds from the lobby were muffled as he slid the curtains closed.

"Have I told you how incredible you look tonight?" Liam sat next to me, rested his elbow on the top edge of the sofa, and turned to face me.

"Yes," I smiled at him, "but you can tell me again." I reached out to gather the edge of his shirt fabric and rubbed it between my fingers.

"You look good enough to taste," he paused, and I watched as his tongue wet his bottom lip, "and, boy, do I plan on getting a taste."

My breath quickened, and I felt heat travel to my core. Liam hadn't tried to hide his obsession with me, and now I was addicted to hearing it. It was funny how someone else's undeniable feelings for you could help shape your own confidence and mindset.

"Do you want to share what you have planned for us this evening?" he asked. "Or do you want it to be a surprise?"

Nerves fluttered in my belly both at the idea of verbalizing what I'd planned for tonight and for him to actually see it. But one thing I've learned in the last year is communication is sexy. Communication is consent. And there was nothing wrong with expressing what you want to experience with your partner.

"Remember our time in the relaxation room at The Oasis?" I asked. "And the . . . people that were there?"

"In the room with us? Where I dove deep into your pussy while other people could see?" My face blushed at his blatant recall of our time together. "Yes, Emma, I remember it well."

"Well—" I started, but the small light inside our lounge area flicked on, signaling that our room was ready for us. We both caught it at the same time, and our eyes found each other's, and I shrugged, raised my eyebrows, and smiled.

Liam chuckled, "Oh, Em, I *cannot* wait to see what you have in store for us." He stood, held his hand out, and helped pull me up from the sofa. His eyes roamed down my body and appeared to take a mental note of my flushed chest, my hardened nipples, and my deep breathing.

He rubbed his rough thumb over the fabric of my dress, covering my nipple, and my breath caught. His eyes were hooded, his vision focused, and I locked this to my memory as one of my favorite faces. I let him lead me down the main hall and waited as he used the code to unlock the door to our room.

Inside, the lights were dim, and the gold threads weaved into the floral of the wallpaper shone as the flickering light caught on the detail. In front of the bed sat a low, long chaise, and across from the chaise was a small raised platform. An upholstered daybed sat in the middle of the platform, positioned where its occupants could see the middle of the room.

We headed toward the daybed, and I gathered the hem of my dress in my hands as I stepped onto the platform. Liam trailed his fingers down the deep v of my dress, causing goosebumps to prickle all over my skin and my nipples to harden. His fingers continued their light touch all over my chest, down my arms, and up my neck. His fingers barely skimmed the surface as they made their journey, making me crave more of his touch.

Liam circled me, coming around to my backside to slide the zipper of my dress down. His hands slid in between the fabric as he helped push it down over my hips, and I felt a soft flutter of silk as it pooled at my feet. I heard the low hum of approval vibrate in his throat as he stared at me, standing in the red lace I wore underneath.

"I'm so glad you're here with me," Liam's voice came out husky and quiet.

I walked over to him and placed my hands on his chest, "Me too."

At that moment, a door I had designed to remain hidden in the wallpapered wall clicked open. I looked up at Liam and smiled with my eyebrows raised as Arlo and Sierra walked in and headed toward the large bed across the room.

The excited curve of his mouth told me he approved of my surprise, but it was the hardness of him that I felt as he pulled me tight to his body as he kissed me deeply that confirmed it. The Reflection room back at The Oasis was my first experience in the world of voyeurism, and it was something I'd been itching to recreate ever since. The thrill of watching others explore their bodies and find pleasure while I got the same attention from Liam heightened everything for me.

Watching others was exciting but distracting enough that it helped to keep my orgasm at bay so I could stay in the moment longer, and by the time I would be ready for Liam to fill me, I knew it would be intense. Liam walked to the edge of the daybed and sat down, softly tugging on my arm to stand in between his legs.

I knew as I stood there, with Liam's hands on my hips and mouth on my breasts, that Arlo and Sierra were exploring each other behind me. My breath was heavy by the time Liam gently pushed on my hips, spinning me around. He brought his face down to my backside and used his teeth the nip at the lace of the fabric.

Over on the bed, Sierra was laid back as Arlo had his face

buried between her legs, her hands gripped tightly on his hair. I watched as her back arched when he found a sensitive part, and a soft moan escaped her lips. From behind me, Liam tugged down my underwear, leaving me exposed in the dim light of our room. This was part of it, for me, the idea that others could also watch me as Liam played.

Liam brought me down on his lap, his own knees pushing mine out to spread them wide. And as I watched Sierra buck her hips into Arlo's face, Liam ran a finger over my clit and slid it deep inside me. I moaned as he pulled it out, only to add a second, and the fullness caused me to lean further back into his chest. His other hand palmed my breast and tugged at my nipple, and I could feel myself dripping down Liam's hand that was buried in between my legs.

Across the room, I watched as our guests made their way off the bed and onto the chaise that lay low in front of it. Sierra sat perched on the back edge as Arlo opened up a small wooden box that they must have had here waiting for them. From inside, he pulled out a soft blue vibrator that I recognized.

Liam continued the lazy slide of his fingers inside me, keeping me warm but not bringing me close to the edge. My eyes were fully locked on the scene before me as Arlo covered the vibrator in lube and ran it down Sierra's middle before teasing her entrance with it. He stood to the side so we had a full view as he finally pressed it inside. Once he let her get used to the fullness, he pressed the button on the end and turned it on.

She started bucking into it nearly immediately and used her hands resting on the back of the bed as support to hold herself up. Arlo kept one hand on the toy as its automatic thrusting pushed itself in and out of Sierra, and his other hand was fisted around his cock. Liam used his thumb to add pressure to my swollen clit, and I moaned loudly.

Liam used his other hand to start unbuckling his pants, and I needed him to move faster because I needed him inside me. I felt his warmth on my backside as he pulled himself out of his pants, the tip of him sliding between my legs. He pulled his fingers out of me and instead used them to make circles on my clit. He tilted my hips just slightly as entered me from behind.

The room was full of the soft sounds of pants, a light vibration from the toy, the slickness of Arlo's cock in his hand, and of Liam pushing himself inside me. We were a group of unlikely partners, finding pleasure together.

I moved to my hands and knees on the daybed behind us, arching my back and spreading my legs as Liam shoved himself back inside. His hands gripped my hips tightly as they tugged me toward him over and over. I was close, and I could tell Liam was too.

My eyes found their way back over to Arlo and Sierra, and I watched as her face contorted and her mouth fell open as she found her release. Arlo came with her, hot streams coating her belly as he tugged. Liam's arm curved around under my belly, and his fingers found the spot where I needed him most. He pressed deeply and rubbed. My body tensed up, and my insides clenched around him tightly. Before my orgasm was even over, I heard Liam groan from behind me and shove himself deeply inside me as he came.

He slid out of me, and I laid back on the daybed to catch my breath. Our guests had snuck out in the midst of the frenzy, so it was just Liam and me as he used a warm washcloth to clean me.

Liam's voice held so much care as he said, "You are incredible, Em."

I smiled, my breathing almost normal. "Thank you for inviting me into this world. I had no clue what I was missing."

He nuzzled my neck as he helped me back into my dress, "Oh, baby, we're just getting started."

TWENTY-SEVEN

Life had returned to its relatively regular rhythm now that The Prism Society was open. The once insurmountable mountain of work that had been consuming my time and energy had receded into the background, and my schedule was starting to feel more manageable.

Yet, there was a stark contrast between the joy and fulfillment I found working on The Prism Society and the monotonous drudgery of my daily job at Spectra. I yearned for a project that would reignite the spark I'd felt while working on the club, but alas, the thrill seemed elusive in the confines of my corporate job.

But I reminded myself that this was just part of the process, part of the journey of working my way up the design ranks at such a prestigious firm. I was ready to finally be able to focus on playing the corporate game because I was tired of seeing Noah get win after win. His project roster was unheard of for someone with his experience, and there was no reason why I couldn't have a piece of that.

If I could only show my bosses everything I'd done, on my

own, with The Prism Society, I knew it would open doors for me. But as quickly as they could open, they would slam shut. The Prism Society was my own dirty secret, and not because I wanted it to be, but because my job depended on it.

Liam and Dominic had been busy working on continuing to grow the club membership; the network of these unconventional societies was heavily supportive of one another. I was jealous that they got to live and breathe The Prism Society when I could only do so after hours. I had ideas for workshops and events that we could host that could really open us up for growth.

At Spectra, I was trying to stay off of Noah's radar. He wanted only the best for his corporate growth, no matter the cost.

We had all met in the conference room one day to get an update on a project. As Caroline spoke during her presentation, Noah boldly cut her off. He'd violated the unwritten rule that says those with seniority shouldn't be interrupted, and yet he did it with no regard for those around him.

"Your idea isn't doable, Caroline," Noah spat. A wave of tension washed over the silent space as Caroline's eyes widened in shock.

But Clark stepped in before she could respond. "Let's hear Caroline's ideas out fully before getting into feedback," he said kindly with a wide smile across his face, directed at Noah.

It was subtle, but it was enough. The room eased back into rhythm, but eyes had scattered over Noah, wondering how he'd gotten away with it. Confusion had creased the foreheads of plenty of people at the table, but Clark had dismissed it quickly enough that none of us dared speak up.

One afternoon, as I was laboriously archiving blueprints

and mentally constructing an event concept for The Prism Society, the soft chime of an incoming email broke the rhythmic silence of my routine. My eyes flicked over to my computer screen. I noticed the sender's name, briefly displayed in the top-right corner before fading away, was that of my boss. A brief flutter of anticipation coursed through me—could this be a new project opportunity?

With a rising sense of intrigue, I promptly shifted my attention from the physical blueprints sprawled across my desk to the digital landscape of my inbox. The anticipation of what this could be about prompted my fingers to navigate the mouse and click on the new message quickly.

The email opened to reveal a simple calendar invite for an impromptu meeting with my boss. The subject line read "Quick Chat," and the body read just as concise: "Can you swing by my office when you get a moment?"

Immediately, my mind started racing with possibilities. Maybe this was the moment I had been waiting for, a chance to be assigned to an exciting project. Yet, there was a nagging sensation that I couldn't quite place—a slight tension that caused my stomach to twist.

Pushing the thought aside, I composed myself and rose from my desk. I could feel the low hum of the office around me, the hushed conversations, the tapping of keys, and the distant hum of the printer. But at that moment, it was all just background noise.

The sense of anticipation grew with every step toward my boss's office. My heart echoed in my ears, matching the rhythm of my footsteps on the corporate carpet.

Shea was leisurely flipping through the pages of a glossy magazine as I walked in, a picture of nonchalance. Something about this action put me at ease. I couldn't let the anxiety her curt email created overcome me. Everyone was anxious when they got called to their boss's office.

"Emma," she greeted, her eyes still scanning the pages. "Come in, sit."

I settled into the chair opposite her, taking note of the stark contrast between her relaxed demeanor and my own mounting anticipation.

"How are you finding Spectra so far?" Shea asked, glancing up from the magazine, a cheerful grin on her face.

I mirrored her smile and said, "It's really great, honestly. This is where I've always seen myself ending up, it's—" I glanced around her office, views of busy Manhattan multiple stories below, "everything I've ever wanted."

My mind flashed back to the countless nights spent in my childhood bedroom, surrounded by sketches and floorplans, my eyes burning from lack of sleep and the soft glow of my desk lamp. My room was my canvas, a tangible testament to my evolving passion for design. It was a space that transformed as often as my whims dictated, bearing the brunt of my late-night bursts of creativity.

"I remember being up at odd hours of the night, rear-ranging my room for the umpteenth time, driven by this insatiable urge to create something new, something meaningful," I continued, my hands instinctively mimicking the motion of shifting imaginary furniture.

Shea smiled back at me. "I know. You wrote about that in your application essay, and it's one of the reasons why I wanted you here." She stared out the windows as if she was lost in thought. "I did that a lot when I was younger, too. Rearrange. It drove my parents crazy."

I smiled, let out a breath, and settled more into my seat. This was good, Shea and I hadn't gotten a chance to connect yet, but this would change things.

Shea laid the magazine on her desk, finally giving me her full attention. "Emma," she began, "this is an opportunity that many people out there would lie, steal, and cheat for." I nodded, my brows furrowed, confused about the direction this was heading. "We have strict requirements for our team, but we also have the best team. And we get the best projects because of it."

I could feel a surge of pride rush through me; this was it. This was my chance to step into the spotlight. The validation I had been craving was within my grasp.

"When you first started here," Shea continued, "do you remember the agreement you made? The rules we uphold are stricter than most in the industry but crucial to our success. Do you remember?"

A sinking sensation abruptly replaced the rising tide of hope. A chill ran down my spine as I racked my brain, the memory of the agreement slowly creeping back into my consciousness. The three cardinal rules we all had to abide by. Suddenly, my double life seemed dangerously close to exposure.

"Emma," Shea said, picking up the magazine and sliding it across her desk towards me. "Explain this to me."

My eyes fell onto the glossy cover of the magazine, a feature of The Prism Society tucked between the pages. My eyes scanned the feature; this must have just come out today; we hadn't even seen it yet. I turned the page, and there I was. My heart plummeted. A full-page photograph of me, champagne glass in hand, beaming with pride as I walked through the lounge of The Prism Society.

But what made it worse, what sealed the nail in my proverbial coffin, was the small write-up next to my photo. If I'd been in any other position other than the one I found myself in, I'd have beamed.

"Emma Sinclair: A Rising Star in Design," the title read, and beneath it, a brief but impactful description followed:

"Striking the perfect balance between provocative and comfortable, Sinclair takes an antiquated, ruined structure and breathes vibrant life into it. Her imaginative design of The Prism Society, a controversial private club in Manhattan, is a testament to her talent. Exemplifying the transformative power of design, Sinclair emerges as a dynamic force in the field, artfully challenging traditional boundaries with her unique approach."

As much as I yearned to bask in the glowing praise of the writer's words, the dread gnawing at the pit of my stomach left no room for pride or satisfaction. Instead, a sense of impending doom seemed to swallow any positive emotions that tried to bubble up. I was featured as an independent designer, a role I played in a secret life that was no longer secret.

"I . . ." I began, struggling to find the right words, my voice barely a whisper. My heart pounded in my chest like a drum, echoing the fear that resonated through me. "I . . . I'm sorry, Shea." The sting of unshed tears pricked my eyes, threatening to spill over. My gaze drifted upward to the stark ceiling of her office, an attempt to keep them at bay.

"It wasn't like that . . ." The excuse felt feeble, even to me, but it was all I had. "They're friends of mine. . . . They needed help setting up their new club. I was just lending a hand."

Shea's expression hardened further, if that was even possible. "I don't give a damn if you were doing it for the pope!" She stood up abruptly, her hands slamming down onto the surface of her pristine desk. The force of her anger made me lean back in my chair; she was a storm threatening to consume everything in its path.

"A sex club, Emma?" She turned the magazine back a few pages, pointing at the photo of Liam and Dominic with a harsh jab of her manicured finger. "These are the 'friends' you risked your job for?" The words hung heavy in the air between us, each one a slap to my already frayed nerves.

"You're just lucky they didn't reference Spectra in your little write-up," she said the words mockingly, "or legal would be up my ass." She took a deep breath, her hands still splayed out on the glossy surface of her desk.

I had nothing else to say to try and defend myself, so I stayed silent, my eyes cast down at the carpet. I noticed a fray in her rug, and my eyes zeroed in on that like it was my lifeline out of this mess. I wanted to tug on it, pull it to see if the entire pink and cream rug would unravel in my hands. If it would feel anything like how I felt on the inside.

"You need to pack your things." My eyes shut as my brain registered her words. "You're done here, Emma. I hope it was worth it."

The numbness that had set in gradually began to recede, replaced by a raw, burning sensation. My heart pounded in my chest like a frenzied animal, each beat echoing the dreadful realization of what had just transpired. I was fired. And it was all my fault.

"Shea . . ." I began, my voice hoarse, but she held up a hand to stop me.

"Enough, Emma," she stated, her voice cold and devoid of its usual warmth. "You have till the end of the day."

With a nod of understanding, I stood up on shaky legs, my mind still struggling to comprehend the magnitude of what had happened. I walked out of her office in a daze, the murmuring of my colleagues feeling distant and muffled.

Noah was leaning casually against a doorframe, a smirk playing on his lips. His dark eyes met mine, and I felt a chill run down my spine. Something in his gaze told me he had a hand in this. And as much as I wished it were otherwise, I knew I had no one to blame but myself.

My phone buzzed insistently in my pocket as I returned to my desk. I pulled it out to see seven texts and three missed calls, all from Jessie. I skimmed the first text, my heart sinking even further. "Have you seen the magazine? Noah is bringing it to you. Call me!"

A bitter laugh escaped my lips. Noah had brought the magazine, alright. But the consequences were far worse than I could've ever imagined.

TWENTY-EIGHT

I didn't remember packing my desk; there wasn't much there for me to take anyways. I didn't even try to find Jessie on my way out; my legs just carried me straight out the front door and onto the subway.

My breaths were shallow. It felt weird that my body just knew it was supposed to keep moving. Up and down. I stared intently at the rise and fall of my belly as I sat there with the cardboard box in my hands.

The numbness that had overtaken me carried me through the entire journey home. The sounds of the city, usually a comforting backdrop to my day, now seemed distant and inconsequential. I was vaguely aware of the bustling people on the subway, the murmur of conversations, the occasional screeching of the rails as the train changed its course. But it all felt far removed from the empty shell that was me.

My hands rested on the cardboard box in my lap, the edges digging into my thighs. I glanced inside—a few personal items, a favorite pen, my coffee mug, and a small photo of Jessie and me on our first day at Spectra. Trivial items, yet the tangible evidence of the life I'd just lost.

I focused on my breathing, shallow and strained. It was strange how the body, no matter what, knew to keep going. Inhale. Exhale. The mechanical rise and fall of my chest seemed the only proof that I was still alive. Still functioning. Despite the crumbling world inside of me.

As the subway pulled into my stop, I moved mechanically, the world blurring around me. The journey home felt like an out-of-body experience, my feet tracing the familiar path on autopilot, carrying me home as I navigated the sea of feelings within me.

I let myself into my apartment, the silence of the space pressing down on me like a weight. My eyes landed on the small dining table, my sketches and swatches from The Prism Society scattered across it. My heart clenched.

A sob tore its way through me, raw and visceral, the box in my hands falling to the floor. I sank onto my couch, burying my face in my hands. My sobs echoed through the silent apartment, a stark reminder of the hollow echo within me. I cried until I was out of tears, until all that was left was an emptiness, a void that mirrored my current reality.

Eventually, I crawled into my bed, my body aching from the pent-up tension. As I stared up at the ceiling, my thoughts spun around the whirlpool of my emotions, each one a cruel reminder of the day's catastrophic events. The darkness that ensued was both a relief and a torment—a sanctuary from the world but a prison for my thoughts. And in its confines, I was left to face the harsh reality of what had just happened.

I heard the front door unlock and swing open, the distinctive creak sounding louder in the silence of the apartment.

Jessie. I turned away, burying myself deeper into the bed, and pulling the comforter over my head. I just wanted to disappear.

She knocked softly on the bedroom door. "Em?" she called out gently. When I didn't respond, I heard her sigh and enter the room. She sat down on the edge of the bed, her hand reaching out to give my shoulder a squeeze. "Hey," she said, her voice cracking slightly, "I heard about what happened. I'm so sorry, Em."

"I didn't know . . . I didn't realize . . ." She trailed off, sighing deeply. Her hand rubbed my back in slow, comforting circles.

"I was invited to a senior design review meeting," Jessie started explaining, her voice shaky. "You know, the one we've been wanting to attend since we started at Spectra. I was in such a rush that when Noah said he was headed over to your desk anyway, I asked him to bring the magazine. I thought he'd just hand it to you."

She paused, her hand stilling on my back. "I saw the article before I gave it to him," she admitted, her voice barely a whisper. "But I didn't think he'd look through it. I should've known better. I should've warned you, Em. I'm so sorry."

Her voice cracked on my name, and I could hear the guilt lacing her words. She was blaming herself for this. But it wasn't her fault. This was on me, and Noah.

I remained silent, the suffocating weight of my reality pressing down on me, even as the sound of Jessie's voice wavered with concern. My phone buzzed continuously on the nightstand, each vibration a sharp reminder of the outside world I was desperately trying to ignore.

"Em, Liam's been calling you." Jessie's voice was now filled with worry. I turned away, pressing my face into the pillow, my silence persisting. "Have you called him?"

Ignoring her words, I stayed cocooned within my blanket fortress, my thoughts spiraling in the darkness. The loss of my job at Spectra wasn't just about losing a job. It was about losing a piece of me, a piece of my identity that I'd worked so hard to build. And now that it was gone, I felt like I was left with nothing.

I wasn't the only one who had made sacrifices for my dream at Spectra to become a reality. When I had set my sights on the New York School of Interior Design, Mom and I had made a game plan. The nights she sat up with a calculator in one hand and a pencil in the other only became more frequent as she squirreled away money to help pay for school.

And when I was accepted into the program, she had beamed with pride. I had an opportunity to pursue a career path that could open up endless possibilities—but now, it seemed like it would all come to nothing.

My lack of focus and dedication at Spectra had been my own undoing. I knew better than anyone else that their rules were strict for a reason; I was a fool to think that I could live the double life and not get caught. The world of acceptance and support that The Prism Society made me believe that I was living in wasn't reality. It wasn't how the real world worked.

The feeling of regret settled in the pit of my stomach like a stone, an overwhelming guilt that felt almost impossible to ignore. I had let myself get carried away in the glamour and the promise of a more colorful world. I had let my friends convince me to take a leap without considering the gravity of the possible consequences. And now I was paying the price.

Anger flared within me, too, hot and fierce. Anger at Liam

and Dominic for their naïveté, for not catching the feature of me in their launch campaign. Anger at the reporter for not doing their due diligence in confirming whether I was allowed to be featured. But mostly, the anger was directed at myself. I knew I should've been more cautious; I should have distanced myself from that project long ago.

As the guilt and anger warred within me, a deep, raw shame started to creep up, making my face burn even as I lay alone in the darkness. It wasn't just the loss of the job that hurt; it was the embarrassment of having to face everyone after this. Who would want to hire me now that I had been fired from the best firm in this industry?

With each ticking second, my mind continued to circle back to the same questions: How had I been so convinced that I wouldn't get caught? Had I allowed the promise of The Prism Society or the promise of Liam to convince me of my career immortality?

I felt my heart shatter in my chest as the harsh reality started to sink in. I had jeopardized my career, my mother's sacrifices, and my dreams for the allure of an underground club. How had I let myself stray so far from the path I had so meticulously crafted for myself? This was why I always followed the plan. To avoid catastrophic failures just like this one.

Tears welled up in my eyes, spilling onto the pillow beneath me. The cold realization was like a cruel slap in the face—I was the architect of my own ruin.

I wasn't ready to face the outside world, so I continued to refuse Jessie's offers of wine, snacks, a night out to distract me. I let my phone buzz gently on my side table, ignoring it. I hadn't even heard the knock on the door or the creaks in the floor as he had walked in, but I felt the weight of the bed sink down when he sat.

His presence was both comforting and a stark reminder of my reality. I didn't have to look up to know that it was Liam. I could tell by the heavy pause in the air, the weight of the silence that wrapped around us. I squeezed my eyes shut, willing myself to stay put, to not turn around and face him.

"Em," his voice broke through the silence, his tone soft and filled with concern. I didn't respond, didn't acknowledge him. I didn't trust myself not to break down the second I opened my mouth. So I stayed silent, my back to him, my breaths the only sound filling the room.

I heard him let out a sigh and felt the bed shift as he moved closer. His hand found mine beneath the covers, his fingers gently interlacing with mine. Even through the fabric of the blanket, his touch felt warm, a stark contrast to the cold dread that had settled within me.

"I'm sorry, Emma," he whispered, his voice barely audible. "I didn't know that you would end up in the feature."

I didn't respond. His words were just a reminder of what I had lost, of my own foolishness. The silence stretched on, the tension in the room heavy. I felt his thumb gently brush over my knuckles in an attempt to comfort me, but it didn't work. The pain was still there; the regret was still there.

The room went quiet again, the only sound being the gentle hum of the city outside. I felt Liam shift once more, his weight lifting off the bed. "I'm here, Emma," he said quietly, "when you're ready to talk."

And with that, he left the room, leaving me alone once more with my thoughts and regrets. The silence seemed even more deafening now, and the weight of my situation bore down on me even harder. But for now, I was okay with being alone, okay with letting myself drown in my sorrow. Tomorrow, I would have to face reality. But for tonight, I was okay with wallowing in the guilt of losing the one dream I'd been working toward for as long as I could remember.

The morning sun shining through my window was a reminder that life was still moving on, with or without me. My phone lay dead on my side table, never having been plugged in, my shoes sat in a heap on the floor at the end of the bed, and my pants wrinkled from sleeping in them. I opened my door quietly, hoping to sneak a cup of coffee and go back to holing myself up in my self-induced solitude.

The living room was dim; the curtains had been drawn last night, so I almost didn't see him there. But on our too-small couch was Liam. He had stayed last night waiting for me to be ready to talk. I walked past him toward the kitchen to silently make my coffee.

By the time I was walking back to my room, Liam had woken. He sat up with tussled hair and a sleepy face, pushed himself off the couch, and followed me into my room.

I didn't turn around as Liam entered my room, instead, I took a sip of my coffee and stood in front of the window. The view of the city below used to inspire me, but now it only reminded me of my failures. Liam stood behind me, his breath warm on the back of my neck.

"Good morning," he said softly, his eyes searching mine as he sat on the edge of my bed. "How are you feeling?"

I took a sip of my coffee, letting the warmth wash down my throat. "I don't know," I replied honestly. "I'm still processing everything."

"I spoke with the reporter," he spoke softly like he was

afraid to spook me, "She thought we'd changed our minds about adding you to the feature when she saw the photo the photographer took of you included in her materials."

I laughed hollowly, "Of course, it would be something so fucking simple, wouldn't it?"

Liam winced at the bitterness coating my tongue, "Em, I know this isn't ideal, but—"

I turned away from the window and set my glare on him, "Isn't *ideal*?" I sat my coffee cup on the table, afraid of where it might land if I kept a hold of it. "Spectra was *it* for me, Liam. It was *the* dream, and I *had* it, and now—" Tears spilled down my cheeks.

Liam reached for me, but I didn't take his hand, "I know, Em, I get it. I—"

"You don't get it," I spat. "This was everything to me. Everything Mom and I had worked for. I *deserved* to be there." I turned back toward the window. "And then I let myself get distracted, and I lost it."

"I don't get it?" Liam stood. "You don't think I've ever worked for a dream? Made sacrifices? Been ridiculed? Almost *everyone* has, Emma; that's part of what it means to fight for your dream."

"Look," he continued, "you did deserve to be there. But maybe you should think about how the fact that if your dream could be crushed so easily by someone else's rules, then maybe you need a different dream."

"How dare you," my voice quivered as all the emotions bubbled up to the surface, and I set to strike; I wanted, no, *needed* someone else to feel this pain I was feeling, "tell me my dreams aren't good enough.

"You just live in your own little world," I continued, heat

building in my chest, "where you think you can just live how you want, do what you want, break all the rules, and get away with it." I could see the hurt on his face, but I couldn't stop. "And you're delusional for it. And believing you, getting sucked into your made-up world, cost me *everything*."

I watched as his throat bobbed when he swallowed, and his eyes darted across my face as if searching for the version of me he used to know.

"Well," he cleared his throat and continued, "I'll leave you to it then." He headed toward my door, "I hope you take the time figuring out what it is you actually want."

My chest heaved from my emotional outburst, and my head felt dizzy. I watched as he turned the knob on my door and walked out. Seconds later, I heard the front door click shut.

TWENTY-NINE

The sharp smell of saltwater hit me the moment I stepped off the plane. California. It had been years since I'd last visited. But now, it felt like the only place I could go. My hometown, a small bay-area town, was a world away from the hustle and bustle of New York City, from Spectra, from The Prism Society, and from Liam.

I didn't tell anyone I was leaving. I couldn't. Not after the way I'd blown up at Liam. I just left a hastily written note for Jessie on the kitchen counter, grabbed my suitcase, and hailed a cab to JFK. It was a cowardly move, running away like that. But at that moment, I couldn't bear to face the people I'd let down. I couldn't bear to face myself.

As the taxi weaved through the familiar streets of my hometown, I couldn't help but feel a pang of nostalgia. The painted clapboard houses, the narrow streets, the small-town diner where mom and I used to have Sunday breakfast—it all felt so familiar, yet so distant. The success, the failure, the shame—none of it belonged here. This was a place of innocence and simplicity. Of bike rides and picnics and of dreams I used to have as a little girl. It was a stark contrast to the life I'd been leading.

Arriving at my childhood home, I took a deep breath before knocking on the front door. Seeing my mom after so long felt like a balm on my wounds. Her eyes, so like my own, filled with worry as she looked me over. She said nothing, just opened her arms wide, and it was all I needed. The sudden wave of emotion was almost too much to bear. I allowed myself to fall into her embrace and breathed in deeply, reveling in the familiar scent of safety she always provided.

She guided me inside despite my protests, swaddled me in blankets on the couch, and bustled around the kitchen preparing tea for us both. When she settled down next to me, I felt a sudden wave of shame for all I'd done. All the hard work she had sacrificed so that I could have a better life all gone in an instant because of my foolish mistakes.

My voice was just a whisper as I recounted my story, but each word hung heavy in the air. I spoke about Liam, about how he had suddenly re-entered my life and brought a semblance of home into the chaos that was New York. I tried my best to explain The Prism Society, sparing her the harsher realities but wanting her to understand the significance of my involvement in it.

Pictures flashed on my phone screen, showcasing the work that I had done with Prism, a painful reminder of what could have been but was now lost. I told her about my friends, Jessie and Dominic, and their unwavering support. I exposed the raw truth about Liam's relationship with his parents, his sacrifices, and the hardships he endured. My voice cracked as I recalled the meeting with Shea, the moment my world collapsed around me.

And when I was done, when I had nothing more to say, she

wrapped her arm around me, pulling me close. "Emma," she said softly, "sometimes, we have to stumble to learn to walk again. You're allowed to make mistakes," she said softly in my ear, but it felt like no amount of comfort could keep away the crushing feeling of displacement that overwhelmed me every time I thought about leaving Spectra and starting over again. "You're allowed to fall," she continued. "And you're allowed to pick yourself up and start over."

I pressed my cheek to her neck, feeling the warmth of her skin and inhaling her familiar combination of floral perfume and sweet shampoo mixed with the crispness of her detergent. "I feel like I lost part of my identity when I walked out of Spectra. I—" I sniffled, my voice shaky. "I don't know where to go from here."

Mom rubbed her hand against my back and spoke into my hair, "Em, a job, a firm, a *person*, none of those things are what hold our dreams for us. The dream is in *you*. It will remain with you wherever you go, whatever you do, whoever you are with. It is your dream, and you have the power to shape it the way you want." Her words weren't a solution, but they were a start, a spark of hope in the darkness I felt.

Throughout the next few days, I took solace in the comfort of my childhood home, allowing myself to experience the small joys that sprung from each corner. I journeyed back in time, immersing myself in the remnants of my past that had been packed away in boxes and shoved into corners of my old room.

I discovered old journals, their pages filled with countless sketches, doodles, and the naive thoughts of a younger me. I traced the outlines of heart doodles surrounding the names of long-forgotten crushes. I grimaced at old drawings and blueprint sketches, remembering how proud I was of them back then.

Throughout the time travel of childhood souvenirs, one thing was constant. I wanted to create, I wanted to design, and I wanted to make people *feel* things in the spaces I created. I believed, even back then, that design could change lives. I could do that even out from the umbrella of connections that Spectra could have offered me.

Amidst the poignant nostalgia, my phone pinged, breaking the silence in my room. A new email notification, its preview visible on the lock screen. It was from Shea. I unlocked my phone, apprehension knotting in my stomach.

The email was clinical, detached. In it, Shea confirmed that Spectra wouldn't be coming after me for the rights to my design work for The Prism Society. The reason was as clear as it was hurtful—it was because the project was explicit, far from the high-profile, prestigious projects that Spectra typically engaged in. I was to consider myself lucky.

But the last few lines of the email were what hit the hardest. Shea had added, almost as an afterthought, that the incident would leave a mark on my professional reputation. I was, in effect, blacklisted from working in the design industry. I should have been prepared for it, but seeing the words in cold print stung.

I put down my phone, feeling a hollow emptiness. It was like I'd been adrift in the ocean, and now, my lifeboat had just sprung a leak.

But there were no tears left in me, just a deep sense of despair. It seemed impossible to bounce back from such a setback. My heart ached, not just for the loss of my career, but for the loss of everything that had taken up my every moment the last four years.

Outside, the sun was setting, casting a soft glow into my room. The nostalgia around me felt like a stark contrast to the harsh reality of my situation. But then, I remembered my mom's words:

"The dream is in you. It will remain with you wherever you go, whatever you do, whoever you are with. It is your dream, and you have the power to shape it the way you want."

I looked at the old drawings and sketches around me, tangible pieces of the dream that was still alive within me. Despite the setback, despite the fear, I knew one thing for certain: This was not the end. I would pick myself up and start over. I would make my dream a reality.

After all, I was Emma. The girl who dreamed of designing spaces that could change lives. The girl who believed, even amidst the odds, that she could make a difference. And no setback, no mistake, no blacklist could take that away from me.

An idea tickled the edge of my reality, and I headed out to get the one thing I always needed when a design idea started to come to life—a new notebook. Luckily, Mom was familiar with the manic energy that came when I needed to get an idea down on paper.

Amidst the fervor of creation, I found myself in a state of euphoria that only true passion can ignite. Time seemed to dissolve, replaced by the rhythmic scratching of my pencil against the pages of the notebook. Inside the edges of that notebook, the traces of my imagination came alive, serving as a strong reminder of the journey I started years ago.

Mom's familiar encouragement echoed in the background, a

soothing cadence against the harmony of my thoughts. She didn't try to coax me out of my fervor, understanding that this was part of my process. Instead, she ensured I was nourished, caffeinated, and took occasional breaks. The space she gave me was a subtle reminder that love and understanding could be expressed in myriad ways.

As I dove deeper into my design ideas, a sense of conviction grew within me. Some part of my intuition kept encouraging me to keep going. The girl that had been lost in the labyrinth of Spectra was now redesigning her path, harnessing the freedom to create without the constraints of corporate aesthetics and approval.

From an outsider's perspective, it would have seemed chaotic—colored pencils, sketchbooks, sticky notes, and crumpled pieces of paper strewn across the dining table. But to me, it was a chaotic symphony, each piece singing its part in my creation.

I found comfort in the organized disarray, seeing the physical representation of my thought process laid out in front of me. Every scribble, every note, every sketch held a fragment of the idea that was slowly taking shape, molding itself into something tangible.

I turned to my old sketchbooks, seeing them not as childish doodles but as pieces of my journey that I could draw inspiration from now. In their simplicity, new ideas took life.

In the midst of my creative storm, I took a step back and looked around. I saw my mom busy in her garden, her face illuminated by the warm sunlight. I saw my old room, the keeper of my past, and the dining table, a canvas of my present. I gazed down at my hands, smeared with hues of ambition, clutching the pencil that was charting my path forward. This scene of creation was a world away from the intimidating glass and steel structures of Spectra, but it was a mirror reflecting my authentic self.

All that passed through those few days taught me more than I could have ever anticipated: I didn't need Spectra or anyone else's approval to realize my dreams. It was all right here —my past, passion, artistry, and those closest to me who encouraged me toward success.

I was left with a notebook full of ideas for the future ahead —one not designed by another but conceived entirely by myself. As I closed the book, I smiled at this newfound knowledge that I could design a life that suited me. And so began a new journey.

THIRTY

The plane rattled and hummed like a time capsule, transporting me back to the city that had witnessed my rise and fall. As we descended closer to New York, the twinkling lights grew larger, more vibrant. I felt a mix of apprehension and excitement as I thought about the metamorphosis ahead of me.

Stepping into my apartment was both disorienting and comforting. The familiar scent of lavender from my candles filled the air. My sketches were still pinned to the wall, each one a piece of my soul captured on paper. Past and present collided in my mind, jostling for space as I settled into the couch with a newfound resolution.

The first few days were difficult. Each morning, I'd watch as Jessie would dress up and leave for Spectra, a pang of jealousy piercing me each time. I'd imagine the Spectra office—the hum of conversations, the smell of freshly brewed coffee, the flurry of creativity—and my heart would clench in longing and regret. I would curl up in my bed, pull the blanket over my head, and let the emptiness wash over me.

But then, the blueprint of my new dream would flash across my mind, and I would get up, determined to sketch my path to redemption. As days rolled into weeks, I set up a little design studio in my room, my pencils and papers scattered all around me as I worked tirelessly on my new project. My design notebook was my constant companion, capturing each idea that sprouted in my head.

The idea that had sprung to life back in California had only grown since then, spurred by the vibrant energy of New York. My designs weren't just about aesthetics anymore; they were about creating safe spaces, spaces that resonated with warmth and acceptance. My work for The Prism Society showed what I was capable of, and The Oasis and clubs like it were the perfect canvas for my future vision.

A flood of memories from my time with Liam invaded my senses, and it was difficult for me to hold back the tears. Every club I had stepped into with him had been a wake-up call, a reminder that I could be more than what society expected of me. As much as I wanted to deny it, he had been the catalyst for this new journey. He had been the one to introduce me to these clubs, to show me that there was a world beyond the corporate offices of Spectra. It was only fitting that I chose to channel my designs into these spaces that had ignited a passion within me.

With a mixture of nervousness and anticipation, I reached out to Zara, the owner of The Oasis. I remembered the ideas she had been brainstorming about adding to their club, and I knew I could help make them happen, especially now that I was out on my own.

I typed out a careful email explaining my ideas and my vision for The Oasis. I let her know that I was starting my own design firm, an independent agency, and while I had a team of one for now, she could trust me with this project. It was a leap of faith, but it was one I had to take.

Pressing the send button felt like opening a new chapter in my life. As I stared at the confirmation message on the screen, I couldn't help but feel a sense of liberation. I was not the Emma who had stepped into Spectra with trembling hands and starry eyes. I was Emma, who dared to dream differently, who was brave enough to let go of the past and look forward to a future that was truly my own.

Zara's response arrived quicker than I expected, prompting me to tackle the remaining items on my to-do list to finalize my plan. I found, quite ironically, that designing a physical space was more my forte than a digital one. With furrowed brows and my face just inches from my laptop screen, I struggled to maneuver elements around while creating my website.

By the time I'd scrapped together a few pages, I was ready to ask for help. I creaked open the door to my bedroom one Saturday, feeling like I hadn't seen the light of the rest of our apartment in weeks. I spotted Jessie buzzing around the apartment, headphones on, quietly singing to herself. I carried my laptop and a stack of empty coffee mugs to the kitchen.

"Well, look who decided to join the land of the living!" Jessie yelled a little too loudly, headphones still covering her ears. I grinned and walked over to her, bringing her into a tight hug.

"I'm sorry I've been such a turd," I said as I lifted a headphone off her ear; she squeezed me tightly back.

She slid the headphones down around her neck and smiled at me. "I've missed you."

"I've missed you too," I said. "I kind of decided to do something crazy." I spun my laptop around for Jessie to see the homepage of the new business I'd decided to open.

My own design firm. Just me, myself, and I (for now). It was simple, but I was hoping it was good enough to land my first few clients. I wanted to help other clubs bring life to their ideas, to help them create the security that The Prism Society had given me.

Jessie's eyes lit up as she scanned my webpage, her finger tracing along the screen as she read through the lines of text. "Haven Designs," Jessie read from my homepage, "crafting spaces that ignite the senses." She looked at me, eyes wide. "Em, this is incredible."

The uncertainty bubbling within me eased at her words. "You really think so? I thought 'Haven' would let my clients know that I care about the safety of their space. I know it's a wild niche to pick, but these places deserve beautiful design too."

I offered a hopeful smile. "I figured I could start with The Oasis and then just go club to club to see how else I can help."

"You know, Dominic mentioned the other night about this club in Seattle . . . 'Midnight Mirage' or something. The owners visited The Prism Society recently, loved what they saw, and are looking for a complete redesign." Her eyes lit up for me.

The mere prospect of expanding my horizons to other clubs, of further spreading my ideas and concepts, was both thrilling and terrifying. It felt like the start of something new, a step forward from the shadow of Spectra and towards carving out my path.

My mind, however, couldn't ignore the ties that linked me back to The Prism Society, to Liam. A knot of worry formed in my stomach. It had been weeks since we'd last spoken, but it felt like a lifetime. I'd finally crawled out of my pit of despair and found that everyone else was still somehow functioning.

"Jess," I ventured, my voice soft, "have you . . . have you heard anything from Liam?"

Jessie's smile faded slightly, replaced by a look of concern. She pulled her headphones off entirely and turned to face me.

"He's been . . . busy," she began slowly, choosing her words carefully. "Thrown himself into getting more members for The Prism Society. Traveling, networking, you know. He's doing what he does best."

A pang of guilt washed over me, leaving a bitter taste in my mouth. I'd treated him no different than the parents he moved across the country to get away from. I'd let him believe that I was ashamed of my work for The Prism Society—all because I was scared to try and figure out what I wanted outside of the confines of Spectra.

Jessie placed a comforting hand on my arm. "Em, you should reach out to him. He misses . . ."

I shook my head, cutting her off. "He wouldn't want to hear from me. Not after . . . I hurt him, Jess. I said some really awful things."

We sat in silence, the hum of the city echoing around us as Jessie offered a nod of understanding. She didn't press the issue, simply offering a comforting squeeze to my hand before standing up and pulling me into another hug. I clung to her, finding solace in the familiarity of our friendship.

After all, as much as I was eager to move forward with my new venture, I couldn't ignore the remnants of the past that lingered within me. Each day was a battle between moving forward and looking back, between the guilt of hurting Liam and the desire to make things right.

But for now, I had a new venture to pour my heart into. Haven Designs was a testament to my resilience, my creativity, and my passion. It was a promise of a new beginning, a venture built from the ashes of my past mistakes. And I was ready to dive into this new chapter of my life headfirst.

Navigating the bureaucracy of starting your own business, I soon found out, was nothing like designing a nightclub. As it turned out, filing for an LLC did not bring the same sense of euphoria as seeing my designs come to life. The long lines at the bank to open my business checking account did not thrill me in the same way that the first sketch of a new project did.

I spent what felt like years on the phone with customer service agents, trying to set up a professional email for Haven Designs. Who knew there could be so many steps to getting a freaking *email* up and running? On the fourth day of battling with tech support, I swore I heard the same representative stifle a laugh as he walked me through resetting my password for the umpteenth time.

"Alright, Ms. Sinclair," he'd said in his calm, customer-service voice, "I'm sending you another password reset link now."

"Great," I'd responded, more than a hint of frustration creeping into my voice. "Let's hope it's the charm."

By day, I toggled between phone calls and paperwork and stared at my screen as I pieced together client materials. By night, I dove headfirst into design, sketching and tweaking and adjusting until my eyes were gritty with exhaustion. I was overwhelmed, running on a concoction of adrenaline and caffeine, but I was excited.

Despite the bumps and mishaps, I became increasingly committed to Haven Designs. I was no longer just Emma

Sinclair, ex-Spectra designer. I was Emma Sinclair, founder of Haven Designs, a company built on my vision. I was terrified of the unknown but ready to face whatever came next. And so, I embraced the chaotic whirlwind that was starting a business, chuckling at my mistakes along the way, and steadily stitching together the pieces of my new identity.

THIRTY-ONE

Listening to yet another podcast, I stood in the busy airport terminal, ready to catch my flight to Chicago. I had found a treasure trove of business advice, motivational stories, and helpful hints tucked away within my podcast app, and I was quickly working my way through the most popular ones.

Zara and Kai had invited me out to The Oasis so they could walk me through their ideas, I could take measurements and sketch up some initial concepts for their space. Every minute of this journey felt like a teeter-totter. One moment I was wildly convinced that I was on the right path, totally unstoppable and capable. The next, I'd get hung up on something stupid, and the doubt would creep in, demanding me to explain who I thought I was.

Embarking on this entrepreneurial journey, I mused, was an endeavor meant for the audaciously optimistic. It was designed for disillusioned fools. It demanded a potent cocktail of blind faith and tenacity to forge ahead in a world where the only rule was that there were no rules. The playbook was nonexistent; instead, I was the author, sketching the rules as I went along.

And the urgency to carve this path was becoming more necessary with every passing day. This project with The Oasis wasn't just about kickstarting Haven Designs, it was also about sustaining me. My savings account, once a comforting cushion, had been depleted considerably, going towards rent, my necessary caffeine infusions, and the various expenses of starting a business.

But I was inspired. I felt a connection to Zara, a kindred spirit in our shared creativity. Her plans for The Oasis were electric, each idea sparking a wave of potential designs in my mind. I knew I could give her ideas the body and form they deserved. All I needed now was to convince her to place her faith in me, to entrust me with shaping the future of The Oasis.

As I finally boarded the plane, the buzz of excitement hummed along with the revving engines. This was it. I was on my way to prove myself, to show the world what Haven Designs was truly capable of.

The Oasis was exactly how I remembered it, an intimate haven of secrets and desires. The moment I crossed the threshold, a wave of memories washed over me—moments of laughter, whispered confessions, and stolen glances. The reminder of Liam was pervasive; his absence echoed in every corner, every hushed conversation, every soft smile.

As Zara and Kai greeted me warmly, their friendliness felt like a balm to the raw wound of missing Liam. Zara, with her infectious enthusiasm, and Kai, with his calm strength, gave me a sense of reassurance that I had made the right choice. Yet, even amidst their warm reception, there was a void that couldn't be filled.

Despite the bustling activity and the exciting potential of the project ahead, my heart ached with the phantom pain of Liam's absence. Jessie had told me he was out at an investor event, weaving magic into the minds of potential donors and raising funds to fuel our shared dream of education within The Prism Society. He was talking to educators from other clubs, building a framework for the shared knowledge he had always dreamed of fostering.

As I moved through the space, every corner whispered his name. The thought of him, so deeply ingrained into the fibers of The Oasis, felt like a vice squeezing my heart. I yearned to reach out to him, to share my ideas, my fears, and my aspirations. But instead, I clamped down on the emotion, forcing it back into the hidden corners of my heart.

The reality was we had been here before, in the terrain of missed opportunities and unspoken feelings. We'd become experts in skirting around the edges of our emotions, masters of vanishing acts. And now, history seemed to be repeating itself: we were ghosts in each other's lives, invisible yet deeply felt.

I took a deep breath, letting the nostalgia wash over me. Then, with a slight shake of my head, I dismissed the melancholy thoughts. This was a fresh start. A chance to carve a path that was wholly mine. We had tried, Liam and I, but perhaps we were always destined to diverge. And as painful as it was to admit, maybe our parting was for the best. As I focused my attention back on Zara and Kai, I knew I had to do this for myself. This was the beginning of my journey—alone, but not unprepared.

Zara led me away from the familiar lounge and bar area down a dimly lit corridor that branched out into multiple rooms. The gentle hum of conversation faded into the background as we ventured deeper into the less-trodden parts of The Oasis.

"These are the rooms we're hoping to convert," Zara explained, gesturing to a cluster of unfinished spaces. They were starkly bare, with dusty drywall and wires snaking along the floors. Still, in their raw state, they were ripe with potential.

Zara had a grand vision for these untouched spaces. One room, she explained, she wanted to convert into a silk room—a soothing, sensual oasis filled with billowing drapes of silk in rich, warm colors. Soft, cushioned flooring and scattered plush seating would provide a comfortable space for guests to relax or explore their senses.

The next room was planned to be a sensory room, filled with tactile surfaces—soft, smooth, rough, ridged, hot, and cold —arranged in an appealingly artistic way. The room would allow guests to explore and heighten their sensory perceptions in a safe, open environment. Here, the lighting was to be adjustable, changing the atmosphere from brightly exposed to soft and mysterious at a moment's notice.

For the final room, Zara envisioned a water room. Inspired by the tranquility of Japanese hot springs, this space was meant to house a large, shallow pool encircled by comfortable seating. Soft ambient music, mingled with the gentle trickling sound of water, would fill the room, and soft lights would dance across the rippling water surface, creating a soothing, immersive environment.

As Zara spoke, I could see her vision begin to form before my eyes, her words giving life to the potential of the rooms. I could feel her passion and dedication to creating spaces that were not just about physical satisfaction but the exploration and celebration of sensuality in all its forms.

"I need your magic, Emma," Zara said, her eyes meeting mine in earnest. "You've seen what we do here, and you understand it. You have the sensitivity and the creativity to bring these rooms to life. To make them safe, inviting, and exciting all at the same time."

I felt a surge of excitement, not just at the challenge ahead but also at the faith Zara had in me. I was ready, eager even, to rise to the occasion, to pour my heart and soul into these spaces, making them a testament to sensual self-expression.

Zara left me alone to get better acquainted with the space. I stood at the center of the first room—the future silk room. Closing my eyes, I took a moment to visualize it, picturing cascades of fabric in hues of burnt orange, deep burgundy, and gold, creating an enticing, cocoon-like feel.

Pulling out my sketchbook and a pencil, I moved around the room, the echo of my footsteps bouncing off the exposed brick walls. I began to sketch, my hand moving swiftly across the page, translating my vision into a rough blueprint. Occasionally, I'd pause to write notes on texture, color, and lighting. The pencil felt warm in my hand, the friction against the paper a familiar comfort, a whisper of my past self guiding my present.

Next was the sensory room. I traced my fingers over the bare walls, imagining them adorned with diverse textures. The room felt alive, eager for the transformation to begin. I envisioned an array of textures—the cool smoothness of polished stone, the delicate prickle of a bristle brush, and the rich softness of faux fur. I scratched out preliminary ideas, my sketchpad quickly filling with various designs.

Finally, I stepped into the future water room. The air felt different here, thicker somehow. It was hot, the lack of air conditioning apparent as a bead of sweat traced a path down my spine. I felt a pang of nervous excitement as I began to take measurements, mentally positioning the shallow pool and imagining the soft rippling of water against its edges.

There was an exhilarating energy in the air, an anticipation for what would come. I could feel the undercurrents of change swirling around me. Each room was a blank canvas, waiting for color and life to be breathed into it.

As I surveyed my sketches and notes, the intensity of the task ahead hit me. Yet, the challenge did not overwhelm me. Instead, it filled me with a sense of purpose and determination. This was my chance to show what I was capable of, to put my mark on these rooms and transform them into something beautiful, something meaningful. I was ready to dive in and bring these spaces to life.

I snapped a few shots to send to Jessie, excitedly explaining my ideas over text. I documented a few "before" photos, hoping to get to use them in my portfolio as the project came together.

As I hit send on my last text to Jessie, I leaned back against the cool brick wall. A smile tugged at my lips as I considered the task ahead. The thrill of the design was a rush, but now came the hard part, the logistics, the organization. I had the vision, but I needed a team to help me bring it to life.

I had a long to-do list, but I didn't let it daunt me. I was excited about the challenge, and eager to put my skills to the test. As I looked around the rooms one last time before leaving, I felt a sense of anticipation. There was a lot of work to do, but I was ready for it. After all, this was what Haven Designs was all about—creating spaces that ignited the senses. And I was just getting started.

THIRTY-TWO

By the end of the week, I had decided it was time to take the plunge, time to confront the past and move toward a future that seemed to be beckoning me with more force each day. With the prospect of The Oasis project hanging in the balance, I decided to take Dominic to lunch. In part, it was a business decision—Dominic, after all, was well-connected and could potentially help me get my foot in the door with a team that could make my designs a reality. But it was also easier, emotionally speaking, to reach out to him than it was to reach out to Liam.

The memories of Liam were still too fresh, too raw, and the thought of reaching out to him brought an onslaught of emotions that I wasn't sure I was ready to handle. Dominic, however, was a comfortable piece of my past that didn't stir up the torrent of feelings that the mere mention of Liam did.

I chose a quiet bistro in the heart of SoHo, a place that felt intimate without being too personal. The clinking of cutlery against porcelain and the soft hum of conversation provided a comforting backdrop as I waited for Dominic.

Dominic arrived, his usual stoic and elusive aura enveloping him like a cloak. His intimidating demeanor seemed to fall away for a moment as he greeted me, a rare small smile gracing his lips. It was these fleeting moments of warmth that reminded me of the deep empathy that Dominic was capable of, despite his often brooding exterior.

As we placed our orders and eased into the familiar rhythm of our friendship, I took a moment to gather my thoughts. My heart pounded in my chest like a wild drum, echoing the importance of the conversation that was about to unfold. I wasn't just seeking Dominic's help, his connections, and his wisdom, but also preparing to venture into unexplored territories, crossing boundaries that could irrevocably change the course of my life.

Dominic's enigmatic silence was both comforting and unnerving as I braced myself to unfold my plans. Beneath the towering edifice of his quiet strength, I was about to lay bare my dreams and ambitions and ask for his assistance to make them a reality.

Dominic's question echoed in the air: "You're doing this on your own? Without Liam?" I felt a wave of apprehension. It seemed like he was ready to take away his support, showing loyalty to Liam.

I paused, my gaze fixed on the tabletop, my fingers nervously fiddling with the edge of the napkin. "Yes," I finally murmured. Taking a deep breath, I looked up at him, tears threatening to overflow from eyes filled with remorsefulness and determination. "I . . . I hurt him, Dom. It's impossible for me to take back what I did. And I don't want to keep causing him pain. The best thing would be if I . . . let him go."

Dominic looked at me thoughtfully, his dark pupils

conveying a deep understanding. He reclined in his chair, and I could tell he was processing something. His voice became gentler as he said, "Emma, it's not just about you being hurtful. You lashed out because of the pain you feel inside."

He continued, "What you don't understand is that you've been a source of power for him, just like he has been for you. Both of you are strong-willed and set on your own paths. You couldn't see that he was trying to reach out to help you, trying to open up a world where he thought you would thrive. And what have you done? You've pushed him to dream bigger and made him recognize his worth. You've held faith in him when he needed it most."

His words hung heavy in the air between us, a poignant reminder of the complex bond Liam and I had formed. I looked away, swallowing the lump in my throat, touched by Dominic's candidness.

"I'm happy to connect you with a team. You can use them for whatever projects you need." Dominic's gaze became more intense. "But I encourage you to really think about how you're shutting Liam out. I know that, together, you two could do incredible things."

Dominic tapped his fingers on the table before scooting his chair back and standing, "I just happen to know that whatever is being left unsaid between the two of you is eating him up." And with that, Dom walked away, leaving the check paid, and my brain more muddled than it had been in a while.

Dominic's abrupt exit left me in contemplative solitude, my fingers unconsciously coiling around the chilled surface of my water glass. A flurry of thoughts stormed through my mind, each echoing the provocative suggestion Dominic had proposed. Was there a possibility for Liam and I to . . . mend bridges? The last image of Liam, where the light in his eyes dimmed, had been playing on a loop in my mind. I was certain then that we had crossed a point of no return.

Could we ever resurface from the murky abyss I had propelled us into? And if we did, would we be strong enough to endure the inevitable tempests that lay ahead together? Or were we destined to scatter at the slightest ripple, just as we had before? We were venturing into unfamiliar territory, neither of us having the benefit of a positive relationship model from our families.

Just as we had at The Prism Society, we had a lot to learn about ourselves, about each other, and about the dynamics of a bond that had been twisted and stretched in more ways than one. And similar to the way we were introduced to the unexplored realms of our sensuality at the club, we would need to navigate our way through the labyrinth of feelings that was our relationship.

We would need to pave our own path, devoid of prior templates or guidance. Just as we had learned to delve into the uncharted depths of our desires and fantasies, we would need to learn how to approach a relationship, to build and nurture it on our own terms.

This was a daunting prospect, fraught with the risk of hurting each other further, of reopening old wounds. But the alternative, leaving those wounds unattended to fester in silence, was even more unsettling. The thought of reaching out to Liam stirred up a whirlpool of emotions that tugged at my heartstrings, hinting at the deep-seated feelings I still held for him.

It was scary and overwhelming, yet tantalizingly compelling.

As I sat there, amidst the clutter of empty plates and half-filled glasses, I found myself seriously contemplating the idea of reaching out to Liam, of confronting our past, our fears, our hopes, and maybe, just maybe, finding a way to rebuild the beautiful connection we once shared.

THIRTY-THREE

Liam had been traveling relentlessly for the past weeks, visiting various other clubs, and gathering support for The Prism Society. His hectic schedule had provided the perfect smokescreen for my secret project, allowing me to orchestrate this event right under his nose. With the way I had left things, I was sure he figured I wanted nothing to do with The Prism Society and would be staying far away. Little did he know that I was so fully immersed in this world that there was no turning back for me now.

To ensure the night would be as magical as I envisioned, Dominic had been a massive help, pulling strings to bring together some of the most prestigious vendors in the city. I had managed to secure incredible artists from around the city to not only showcase their work but put it up for auction.

Some of these pieces were provocative, pushing the boundaries of conventional aesthetic norms, while others were deeply intimate, capturing moments of vulnerability and tenderness. Each one was a statement, a testament to the diversity and depth of human sexuality.

Tonight, The Prism Society was not just a haven for New York's sexually adventurous, but a beacon of advocacy for sexual liberty. And with every last-minute preparation falling into place, I couldn't help but feel a burgeoning sense of pride. This was my statement, my pledge to this community that had embraced me, and I was ready to do it justice.

Now all I had to do was wait for Liam to walk through those doors and hope he saw my commitment for what it was: a demonstration that I was not just a passing participant in his world, but a partner ready to face whatever came next, alongside him.

The usually understated chic of The Prism Society was replaced tonight by an unabashed flair. Under the banner of "Bodies Unbound: An Evening of Liberation," the club was ready to host a charity event like no other. High ceilings dripped with intricate gossamer drapery that refracted the soft lighting into warm, dappled hues, creating a space that felt both intimate and boundless.

The lobby had been transformed into a dynamic fusion of art and experiences. Along the walls were striking large-format photographs capturing diverse, bold, and authentic expressions of human sensuality. Mingling with the crowd were performers —living art pieces—each embodying different facets of sexual empowerment and identity. Their vibrant costumes and theatrical poses invited the incoming guests to contemplate, engage, and celebrate sexuality in all its diversity.

As the architect of this grand event, I moved through the spaces, putting the final touches on everything. I was adjusting a sign here, testing a sound system there, and working with a team of efficient volunteers to ensure every element was in place. Despite the bustling energy around me, my heart fluttered with anticipation.

This night was about more than just a charity event; it was my proclamation, my vow to align myself with Liam's mission publicly. It was a spectacle designed not only to raise awareness and funds but also to demonstrate to those whose pockets ran deep that The Prism Society was worth investing in. With this event, I was stepping into the limelight beside Liam, showing him, and the world, that I was no longer afraid to stand by him and our shared passion for this cause.

Wiping my palms on the sides of my black jumpsuit, I surveyed the scene once more, the pulsing energy of anticipation filling the room. I glanced at my watch—it was almost time. All I needed now was Liam.

Weeks earlier, I had sent Dominic a message with a request. He was to bring Liam along for what I had billed as a casual club meeting. I asked him to keep Liam away all day today, keeping my surprise a secret until the moment of unveiling. Dominic, an unknown participant in my mastermind of plans, had agreed without questioning my motives, replying with a succinct, "We'll be there."

As the clock struck the hour, a sudden surge of activity signaled the commencement of the event. The once empty space filled quickly, the hum of conversation and laughter echoing through the downstairs lobby. Figures in rich attire filed in, like a river of glitter and silk flowing into the space, casting a magical, shimmering glow. Strangers and club regulars alike, their faces lit with curiosity and excitement, congregated, ready for a night to remember.

With every fresh face that entered the club, a wave of gratitude washed over me. I was moved by the turnout, a testament to the power of our community and their willingness to support our cause. The room buzzed with intrigue, its occupants a mix of longtime members, first-time attendees, and influencers from the local scene. Each one of them was here because they believed in the message we were sharing tonight. Their presence filled the room with an electrifying energy.

Through the sea of attendees, I caught glimpses of familiar faces—club regulars who were active in the community and had supported us from the start. Their familiar smiles were comforting, grounding me amidst the whirlwind of excitement.

Each new face, and each familiar smile sent a jolt of thrill through me. They were here! The people were really here, supporting us, eager to contribute to the cause. The sight of their enthusiasm sparked a newfound energy within me. I was filled with pride and swept up in a tide of emotion, my heart overflowing with anticipation. This moment marked the dawn of something extraordinary.

Tucked away by the refreshments table, my fingers nervously straightening out a stubborn tablecloth wrinkle, I felt a familiar energy cut through the noise. A soft gasp escaped my lips as my eyes found him across the room. Liam.

He looked effortlessly captivating in a charcoal suit that flattered his broad shoulders and toned physique. His dark hair was styled perfectly, and the light from the chandelier above cast a soft, glowing aura around him. I'd seen him dressed up before, but tonight there was a certain vulnerability about him, an uncertainty that tugged at my heartstrings.

His ocean-blue eyes scanned the room, widening in surprise and awe as he took in the bustling crowd, the decorations, the energy pulsating in the room. But it was the moment he saw me that real spark ignited. A flicker of confusion, surprise, and . . . relief?

I couldn't read his expression; it was too far away, and the room too full of people. But what I could see, as he stood there frozen, staring at me, was that he was as shocked as I hoped he would be.

As my eyes held Liam's, I felt a surge of adrenaline coursing through me. It was powerful and almost overwhelming, like a tidal wave cresting within me. Yet, instead of heading toward him, I took a step in the opposite direction, my heels clicking on the marble floor. Every nerve ending was on fire as I navigated through the crowded room toward the small makeshift stage.

The cacophony of conversations, the clinking of glasses, the soft hum of music—all of it melded into a distant blur as I ascended the three wooden steps onto the stage. A single microphone stood there, a beacon summoning me towards it. My heart pounded in my chest like a tribal drum, its rhythm filling my ears as I neared the microphone.

My palms were clammy, my fingers trembling as I adjusted the microphone. I took a deep breath, drawing in the energy of the room, allowing it to fill my lungs and steady my shaking hands. This was it. The moment of truth. The moment when my private world would merge with my public one, and everyone—including Liam—would see the whole me.

As the noise in the room started to fade, all eyes began to settle on me, curiosity and excitement painted on their faces. I drew another breath, filling my lungs with courage, with hope, and with a fervor that only came from diving headfirst into the unknown.

I locked eyes with Liam one more time before I began. He stared at me, an intense mix of emotions swimming in his eyes. I gave him a small nod, a silent promise. I was all in, ready to reveal my heart, to share our dreams with everyone in this room. It was terrifying, exhilarating, and absolutely necessary.

"Good evening, everyone," I began, my voice amplified by the microphone, resonating through the room, capturing everyone's attention.

"Tonight is a special night. And not just because of the cause we are here to support, which is very close to my heart. It is special because tonight, I stand before you as myself—as Emma. For some, I am a familiar face; for others, a new one. But regardless, tonight, I am more than a shadow lurking in the corners of the club. Tonight, I am one of you."

I paused, sweeping my gaze across the room, seeing the eyes widened in surprise and the encouraging smiles. "Yes, I am the one behind the design of the club rooms, the one who has been quietly orchestrating the creation of spaces that hopefully speak to your desires, your dreams, your pleasures."

Applause filled the room. I took a moment to catch my breath, to steady my shaking hands. "But tonight, we are here for more than just me. We are here because we believe in the freedom of self-expression, the beauty of our desires, the power of our dreams. And we are here to help others feel the same way."

I looked at Liam again, our eyes meeting in a powerful gaze. "We are here to break down the walls that society has built around the natural expression of love, pleasure, and connection. We are here to make a difference.

"In honor of this cause, I am happy to announce that we will be launching a series of workshops and classes here at The Prism Society. Classes that will provide education and awareness about sexual health, that will promote open discussions, that will help people understand and embrace who they are. Because no one should ever feel ashamed for who they are, for what they desire, for who they love."

The room burst into applause, a sea of nodding heads and clapping hands. My heart swelled with pride, a smile tugging at my lips. This was it. This was what I had been working towards. I took a final glance at Liam, his face a canvas of shock, surprise, and something else . . . something that looked like hope.

As the applause slowly died down, I stepped off the small stage, feeling lighter than I had in weeks. My eyes scanned the room for Liam, but he was nowhere in sight. Turning around, I was pulled into a whirlwind of congratulations, praise, and shared excitement from the crowd.

I was in the middle of a conversation with Zara, who was practically jumping with joy when I felt a familiar touch on my arm. I turned to see Liam standing there, his expression unreadable. Zara seemed to understand that this was a moment meant for just the two of us, and with a wink, she disappeared back into the crowd.

Liam's hand was warm on my arm, his fingers squeezing gently. He pulled me aside, leading me away from the crowd and into a quieter corner. He was silent for a moment, and I watched him, waiting for him to say something, anything.

Suddenly, he closed the space between us, his hands cradling my face as he leaned in, whispering, "I love you."

His words struck me like a thunderbolt. My heart pounded in my chest, my breath hitched in my throat, and for a moment, the world around us seemed to fade away. I stared at him, my eyes wide and my lips parted slightly. He was looking at me with so much intensity, so much sincerity, that it was impossible to doubt him.

As the noise of the crowd returned, as the reality of what just happened began to settle in, I realized something. I had been yearning for this, for him, for us. I wasn't afraid anymore. And as I wrapped my arms around him, pulling him closer, I whispered back, "I love you too."

"Oh, thank fuck," Liam said as he peppered kisses along my neck and up my throat.

"I'm so sorry I said those things," I said into his neck as he pressed his body into me, moving us down the hall. "I was an asshole; I was confusing—"

"Tell me later." Liam's voice deepened as he grabbed my arm and pulled me into the elevator. His hands began tugging at the fabric of my jumpsuit. "This thing has too many buttons."

The elevator doors dinged open, and I had to hold the front of the fabric to my chest so I didn't flash Sierra waiting behind the check-in desk. She smiled at both of us, shook her head, and said, "All rooms are open now; take your pick."

Liam growled into my ear as he led us down the hallway, breaking away just enough to punch in the code on one of the locked doors. I let the front of my top fall away when the door clicked shut behind us.

He was on me in an instant, hands palming my breasts and tugging the material down to expose my skin to the cool air. Liam backed me up against the door we'd just come through and pulled the rest of my outfit down to my ankles. His nose tickled my inner thighs as he leaned in and started placing kisses on my most sensitive areas.

I arched back and grabbed a fistful of his hair, my need for him to be closer matching his frenzied movements between my legs. I released a hiss as his tongue found my wet middle, his fingers holding back the seam of my underwear.

My heels allowed me to tower over him as he kneeled below; my legs were spread wide on either side of his shoulders. I bucked into his mouth as his tongue explored deeper and he used his hands to spread me wide for him. He sucked hard on my clit, and my whole body became covered in goosebumps.

My legs became weak, and I leaned forward, unable to hold myself up, but Liam's hand came up and spread wide to press against my chest as his other hand started to sneak its way down between my legs. I was left panting against the wall, teeth gritted together as he slid two fingers slowly inside me, taking his time to make sure I was ready.

But I was already so unbelievably wet for him, the culmination of all my hard work for this event and finally getting to mutter those precious words to each other coming together in a release that made me buck off the wall as my orgasm rocked through me.

Liam slid my heels off as my body threatened to slide all the way down the wall and onto the floor. But his arms were there beneath me, lifting me over to the bed and placing me on the soft duvet. He let me catch my breath as he slid his fingers that had been inside me past his lips and sucked them clean.

"Oh, fuck me," I had meant to keep the thought to myself, but Liam responded.

"I plan to." His grin was promising as he unbuttoned his shirt and walked to a cabinet against the wall. The doors squeaked open, and I heard the rustling of plastic before he was back over to me, shirtless.

I gasped as hard, vibrating silicone pressed against my sensitive core. I spread my knees open as an invitation, and Liam ran his hands over my knees and tightly gripped the thick skin of my thighs. I heard the clink of his belt and the rush of his zipper as he pulled himself out of his pants, hard and throbbing in his hand.

The hand holding the small vibrator in place never faltered as he tapped at my entrance with the head of him, hot and slick. He made little effort to slide all the way inside me but instead slid himself in just past my entrance and pressed harder into my clit. I was breathing heavily, barely able to hold on.

"Come on me, Emma. I want to watch your pussy as you explode for me." Liam's voice was quiet but firm. His voice was my command, and I did as I was told. "Good girl, that's my good girl."

He'd barely finished his praise, something I didn't realize I was very much into, before he finally filled me, pushing himself up against the back of my thighs. His hands gripped my thighs, bringing my hips up as he rocked himself into me, rubbing against my core.

All I could hear were the sounds of our breathing as he slowed his thrusts and held himself deep inside me. His eyes locked onto mine, creating an intimate bubble amidst the thrumming energy of the room. As our breaths began to synchronize, all I could see within the depth of his gaze was pure, unadulterated love.

He began moving again, this time slower, with more intention. His hands roamed my body, trying to touch everywhere sweat glistened on my skin. Soon his body tensed up, and I watched his face as he found his release, spilling himself inside me.

The feeling of his skin against mine still lingered as we slowly began to redress. His touch was soft, a tender caress as he gently helped adjust the straps of my jumpsuit, his fingers tracing a light path across my skin that left goosebumps in their wake. Our eyes met, and we shared a soft, satiated smile, a shared understanding of the connection we had just reaffirmed. The room was filled with our shared warmth, the echoes of our love.

As he offered me his hand, I slipped mine into it, his grip warm and reassuring. We made our way towards the door, ready to rejoin the ongoing event, both wearing the invisible glow of the love we had just shared. As the door clicked shut behind us, I knew this was just the beginning of a new chapter—one where we faced the world hand in hand, unafraid and undeniably on the same team.

EPILOGUE

SOMETIME IN THE FUTURE

The soft, warm glow of The Prism Society's lounge area hummed with anticipation as the moment of its grand opening approached. The aroma of the fresh flowers that littered the tabletops mingled with the heady scent of exotic spices from the nearby bar, creating a luxurious and comforting atmosphere. The space was alive with a sense of celebration, a testament to the hard work and dedication that had brought us to this moment.

In the middle of this beautiful chaos, Liam, Jessie, Dominic, and I were gathered—a little island of calm before the storm of the launch party. I looked around at my friends—now my chosen family—and couldn't help but marvel at how much we'd accomplished.

I turned to gaze at Liam, who was sprawled out on the plush lounge chair. His eyes were on me, twinkling with a mixture of pride and love that caused my heart to flutter. It's a feeling I've become accustomed to ever since we decided to live together.

Sharing a living space had changed our relationship in ways

I never imagined. It had amplified our connection, deepening our understanding of each other. Every shared morning coffee, and every late-night conversation, all contributed to strengthening our bond. We were in this now, fighting for the same team, working toward our passions together.

Liam caught my gaze and winked at me, a small yet powerful gesture. His silent way of saying, "I'm here, I support you, and I love you." A reassurance that never failed to make me feel cherished.

The conversation turned to Haven Designs, my interior design business. It was blossoming, a dream coming to life. The Oasis project was scheduled to kickstart in the spring, a thrilling new challenge that I was ready to tackle. The Midnight Mirage was waiting in the wings. Dominic had connected me to them, and I was making sure I had the team in place before tackling their entire redesign.

Jessie, ever the voice of enthusiasm, grinned and nudged me. "You're on fire, Em! With all these projects coming your way, you're going to need a bigger team soon."

I laughed, a gentle warmth spreading through my chest. This was my life now. Full of challenges, growth, and love. I felt a swell of gratitude for all the trials and tribulations that had led me here to this moment of success and contentment.

Then Jessie threw a curveball. "Who knows, maybe I'll jump ship from Spectra and join Haven Designs," she teased, her eyes sparkling with mischief. A wave of silence fell upon us, each exchanging glances. She winked at me, leaving the rest of us in stunned silence.

And with that comment, we were left hanging on the precipice of change once again, a new adventure just around the corner.

The Mirage Guild

COMING EARLY 2024

GABI SALAS

ISABELLA

Isabella had two problems: one, the neon pink cocktail umbrella stashed in her weathered brown leather tote bag, a relic from her last tequila sunrise on the beach, was laughably insufficient for the torrential downpour brewing outside; two, she was undeniably, unquestionably, late for her introductory meeting with her new boss. The boss of the job she'd flown six thousand three hundred and thirty-seven miles for.

The drizzle of New York City seemed a world away from the sun-drenched days of Bora Bora. Now it was time to put the crystal blue lagoon waters, endless papaya, and island hopping behind her. According to her mother, she needed to "grow up" and "start her real life."

With a stamped passport thicker than her resumé at thirty-one, Isabella had to beg her baby brother for a job. Apparently, racking up more miles than Phileas Fogg didn't count for shit, and world travel alone wasn't enough to impress potential employers. Luckily, Dominic hadn't hesitated when he offered her the waitressing position at the club he cofounded with his best friend, Liam.

And, no, she would not dwell on the fact that her own *brother* got her a job at a sex club. Nope, she preferred to consider it more *Liam's* business. She rolled her eyes at the thought of her quiet, elusive brother—the sibling who always seemed to have it together, going off to UCLA and coming back with a best friend and a business idea. Dominic, whose new business was taking off like hotcakes, at least had direction.

The black town car pulled up, thank you, rich mom and dad, and Isabella scurried out from underneath the awning of her parents' building, in Gramercy Park, making a beeline for the passenger door. The storm clouds hung around her like a foul smell (or was that just New York?); they wanted to engulf her, to snatch her up and remind her of how little progress she'd made in life. Isabella told them no.

The sounds of the city, and her depressing thoughts, were cut off as she settled into the soft black leather seat and shook off the rain that had pelted her skin. She shivered as the cool breeze from the air-conditioned car hit her, and she tilted the vents away. Her dress already had dark spots of rain staining it, the tight material stretching over her skin. She wasn't made for depressing weather like this.

Isabella, or Izzy, as her friends called her, thrived in the sun. Her favorite temperature was "hot car." You know, the suffocating heat you feel when you first slide into a car after it's been trapped in the sun all day? The kind that takes your breath away and cooks you from the inside out. The kind of temperature they warn you about not leaving puppies or babies inside cars for too long. Yeah, that one.

Izzy's high school graduation gown had barely hit the

ground before she enrolled in online college classes, pulled her passport out of her parents' safe, stuffed some clothes into a suitcase, and booked the first flight out of JFK. Her first stop had been Amsterdam, then Barcelona, then she popped over to Athens. She made a little money submitting her writing to travel magazines, but the bulk of her income came from the inheritance she uncorked when she'd turned twenty-three.

But Izzy had never needed a lot. She could find the most luxurious hotels, which somehow stayed hidden from the tourist crowds and cost nearly nothing. She could tell the street vendors apart by their bright food stalls with red umbrellas that would give her the most delicious meal of her life and their yellow-clad competitors, who would treat her like a rich American foreigner and force her to skip the line at the outdoor toilet outside the Eiffel Tower with her hands covering her butt. But as her friends got picked off one by one (no, they weren't murdered, just engaged), Izzy caved to her mom's plea, for the billionth time, that she move back home.

She longed for days lying on pristine beaches and exploring ancient cities. But now, back in the Big Apple, she swapped flip-flops for heels, beachy waves for sleek ponytails, and wanderlust for the Prism Society's 5 p.m. to 3 a.m. hustle. It was an *adult* club, after all.

The fact that it was an adult club was only a fraction of the reason for the nerves in her belly. Honestly, the nude beaches in France had numbed her. Seeing naked bodies no longer brought out giggles or made her face flush. No, the main cause for the nerves in her belly was that Izzy knew, without a doubt, that she would be the *grandma* of the Prism Society. The rest of the staff were all around her brother's age, except for the one receptionist, Maureen, and that five-year age difference between her and Dominic felt more significant than the Trans-Siberian Railway.

Still, she had no regrets for the magical years of travel with the fleeting romances from Amsterdam to Australia. She wore the callouses earned on cobblestone paths and her newfound culinary snobbery, thanks to countless hole-in-the-wall discoveries, with pride.

New York was the real world and why she'd avoided it for so long, but now that she returned, she had to get serious. The town car stopped in Brooklyn outside a three-story brick building with large arched windows on both sides. She was surprised, if not slightly disappointed, that the Prism Society didn't have a flashy neon light hanging off the corner. From the outside, it looked like it could be an event space for weddings or birthday parties for wealthy people.

As the car splashed to the curb, Izzy's phone buzzed with an incoming message. Glancing down, she found a picture from Natalia, her friend who was still (annoyingly) basking in the sunny bliss of Bora Bora. In the selfie, Natalia grinned widely, the blinding sunlight causing a halo around her golden curls. Beside her was a bronzed Adonis whose name Nat most likely didn't remember.

It was a few minutes after eleven in the morning where Nat was, and she already had the glassy-eyed look of too many Aperol Spritzes. Izzy rolled her eyes at the picture, the contrast between Natalia's beachy nirvana and her own rain-soaked reality made her homesick for a place she wasn't even from.

"Beach bum," Izzy muttered, her thumbs flying over the screen as she sent back an eye roll emoji and a middle finger one. But then, feeling guilty, she typed back, *Nice tits.* With that, she swiftly slid her phone back into her bag and steeled herself for the task at hand. She was in the real world now, no more beachside frolics or carefree flirtations. Izzy scooped up her bag, took a deep breath, and stepped back outside into the rain that hadn't stopped.

With a rhythmic drumming of her heart that seemed to echo the downpour around her, Izzy reached for the roughcast iron handles affixed to the imposing wooden doors of the Prism Society. Adorned with intricate scrollwork, the cold iron clashed with the warmth of the building's aged brick. Despite their ornate appearance, they remained stubbornly immobile under her insistent tugs.

Her dress, a tight cream number more suited for a beachside bar than the dreary NYC weather, grew clingier with every passing second. The rainwater snaked its way down the fabric, staining it a darker shade of taupe and making her shiver from its icy touch. A stubborn stream of water raced down her back, slipping under the material and tracing a cold line along her spine.

As she gave another frustrated tug at the door, she looked up and was promptly drenched by a gush of water cascading from an overflowing copper gutter lodged above the door. The deluge doused her, matting her hair to her face and eliciting a startled squeal as the cold water seeped into her dress, running rivulets down her skin.

With a screech, she pushed herself into the doors, and they finally gave way. *Push, not pull.* The doors could've used a sign. The glimmering skyline of New York City and the towering structures, now hidden behind heavy, ink black clouds, disappeared behind the curtain of rain and the thick door as it slammed shut. Izzy took a deep breath, held her arms out from her body in a hopeless attempt to keep herself dry, and pushed through thick velvet curtains into the club.

As Izzy stumbled into the Prism Society, she could hardly see through the droplets clinging to her eyelashes. She stood there for a moment in the grand entrance, water dripping from her hair and down her face, mixing with the salty tears of frustration that had welled up in her eyes.

With a deep, steadying breath, Izzy wiped the rain off her face with a drenched palm—not exactly a towel, but it would do. She blinked and squinted her eyes trying to adjust to the club's softer, moodier lighting. Her nose picked up an odd cocktail of leather, musk, and a hint of pine. The latter made her smile; leave it to her brother to keep a high-end sex club smelling like a forest.

As sophisticated as it was seductive, the Prism Society felt like a burlesque Narnia with its wallpapered nooks, cozy chairs, and winding staircases. Izzy pictured Dominic, her practical, numbers-oriented younger brother, poring over lighting options and discussing the merits of satin versus silk. She bit her lip to keep from laughing at the ridiculous mental image.

In the middle of the entrance to the Prism Society, Izzy stood like a drowned rat (an on-brand welcome for New York, to be honest). She wanted nothing more than to crawl back to the screened-in porch she and Nat had fallen asleep on four nights ago. Instead, she held her head high, and made her way through the dimly lit lounge, her wet feet sliding in her Chloé wedge heels.

She grabbed a handful of cocktail napkins off a small table to soak up as much rainwater as she could. The paper napkins dissolved into a wet ball in her hands. She took a deep breath, mentally restarted her morning, parted another set of velvet curtains, and headed toward the bar that spanned the back of the lounge.

Her fresh resolve cracked as Izzy gaped at the sight in front of her. A man, no scratch that, a *gorgeous man*, stood shirtless on a wooden ladder that leaned against the shelves high above the bar like a goddamn smutty Beauty and the Beast. Hozier played quietly from the bar speakers as he reached to pull down a fresh bottle of red wine.

His back muscles flexed, who has *back muscles* anyway, as he plucked bottles from the shelf, added them to a box, and began his descent. Izzy shook her head clear, swallowed, and masked her face with indifference as he turned to face her.

The guy, who could definitely moonlight as a romance book cover model, took notice of Izzy as he turned to heave the box on the bar top. Maybe he'd take pity on her and crack open the seal of one of those expensive-looking tequila bottles and pour her a shot. His eyes flared with something Izzy didn't understand as he scanned her from head to toe and back again, his lips parted in surprise.

Izzy could feel the sharp peaks of her nipples push against the rough fabric of her dress. She knew she was soaked, and it was *freezing* in here. She only had to put two and two together (well, that and the blush that crept up on his face) to know that she was showing off way more than she intended to.

Izzy had had enough. "Are you gonna help a girl out or just keep staring at my tits?"

ACKNOWLEDGMENTS

Holy shit, y'all, we did it. And I say 'we' because there were truly so many humans (and espresso makers) who helped make this thing come to life. The journey of writing, believing in yourself, hating what you write, putting yourself out there, and then falling back in love with what you write is a NEVER ENDING cycle that I'm doomed to repeat forever. I CANNOT believe I get to hold my real-life book in my hands!

To the most incredible 'book team' ever in the whole wide world - I love you. To my editor Caroline - you were the first person I ever hired and worked with in this journey, and I owe so much to you. Your words of wisdom, clever ideas, and support (even in my panic texting late at night) truly helped this thing actually happen. Please never leave me!

To Jen, my designer, Molly, my copy editor, Tonia, my formatter - you all are my rock stars. Each and every one of you took my nit-picky vision for what this could be and made it 100x better. I will forever be grateful for your guidance and willingness to answer all my dumbass questions about this whole process - what is a book anyways?!

My dear Beta Readers, Debbie, Heather, Desiree, Julia...I fucking love you. Thank you for saying yes to read this book even on the tight deadline I gave you ;) Debbie - you probably regret telling me you live in the same town as me because I see many coffee shop brainstorming sessions in our future.

To everyone who signed up to be an ARC reader - you have NO CLUE the amazing impact you have on this new author. Thank you for diving in with me. To all my Insta crew - y'all have been around through many creative seasons and it never ceases to amaze me how you guys SHOW UP every single time. I'm obsessed with each and every one of you (well, not the bots.)

To everyone at the downtown OP Parisi coffee shop - this book was CONCEIVED in the far corner seat with a honey oat milk latte. I hope you're proud :) Extra special thanks to Annie Austen, Chelsea, and Liz - the way that you guys just say 'yes' to all my crazy ideas and open up your connections, businesses, and time to support me is wild.

To the best friend group a girl could ever ask for - Amanda, Maddy, Jess, Amy, Taylor, Kearsha, Mary...your check-ins, support, coffee gift cards, and undeniable faith that this thing WOULD happen gave me exactly what I needed when this shit got hard. Thank you for wine-filled nights on your patios, for listening to my tearful Marcos, for buying my book, for letting me use your librarian resources (ahem, Amy), for letting me brainstorm in the hot tub, and for being the best ever hype queens ever. I LOVE YOU.

And I saved the big mushy words for last because I very well might start sobbing at Parisi as I write this.

To my parents...I always say that your overconfidence in me has been the biggest thread of support all these years. I think we all knew that I'd write a book one day, but we probs didn't guess it would be smut (sorry, dad). Thank you for always allowing me to live out my wild and crazy dreams, no matter what.

And finally, to B. Sometimes I worry that you're the one person I've tricked the most into believing that I'm capable of big things. Your undeniable - no questions asked - don't even think about it support of *me* and my dreams is so great, it's silly. Getting this book out there came at one of the most clusterfuck times of our lives and you STILL made room every day for me to explore this. I am so thankful for every time you shoved me out of the house to go write or brought me coffee in bed and kept P out of our room so I could focus. For some reason, you keep saying 'yes' to my big, audacious ideas. I love you bunches and bunches.

Okay, if you're still reading, I have one final person to thank. And that's YOU. No matter the incredible team above, the supportive friends, and the community...none of this would matter without you, dear reader. Thank you for trusting me; I hope I made it worth it.

ABOUT THE AUTHOR

Gabi Salas, the mastermind behind sizzling contemporary romances, believes reading smut is feminist AF. She's the author of the debut series "The Prism Society," a solid one-handed read *wink*. Gabi resides in Kansas City with her husband, hilarious daughter, and a ridiculously cuddly cat named Pepper. When not crafting stories, she's drowning in honey oat milk lattes, binging smutty novels, or dark and twisty murder podcasts. Connect at gabisalas.com

BONUS EPILOGUE

HUSHED HALLWAYS, HIDDEN DESIRES: A PRISM SOCIETY EXCLUSIVE

Get your FREE copy of The Prism Society
bonus epilogue...

Emma's proudest night at The Prism Society becomes an exploration of more than just professional accomplishment. Delve deeper as she and Liam navigate the thrills of her budding exhibitionism kink. But the evening's mysteries don't stop there.

With surprise guests slipping from private rooms and questions that hang heavy in the atmosphere, this chapter promises a blend of intrigue and passion. Uncover what's hidden behind closed doors. A chapter truly not to be missed.